PRAISE FOR *ASSASSINS OF HISTORY: TRANSFERENCE*

"Vernon Dutton has provided an amazing piece of historical fiction in this story. Vernon provides, in vivid detail, a great description of daily life in the nineteenth century during the American Civil War in the year 1862 of this alternate history. The story keeps you on the edge of your seat waiting to see what might happen next."

Josh Williams
Historian/Curator

"Vernon Dutton takes us on a journey back to the Civil War, where the past is not the past as we know it to be. If you ever thought about going back in time to the Civil War, read Vernon Dutton's book, and be careful what you wish for!"

Patrick Falci
Actor/Historian

To Linda
a fellow Civil
War Buff.
Best Wishes
Vernon Dutton

ASSASSINS OF HISTORY: TRANSFERENCE

Vernon L. Dutton

ISBN 978-0-9857444-2-7

Cover Design: Donelle DeWitt
First Printing: May, 2017

ACKNOWLEDGMENTS

I would like to thank my Virtual Assistants, Lisa and Tim Petree, who have stood by me during the transition from retiree to author, coach, and motivational speaker. They have been there to listen to and hone my weird ideas for years. I couldn't have written this book without their support.

I want to thank Lisa Beavers for her excellent copy editing. Her observations as to weak points that needed more clarification were greatly appreciated.

I also want to thank Donelle DeWitt for her wonderful content editing. Also, her exterior and interior design of the book are awesome. Her fantastic front cover caught the essence of the novel's story.

Lastly, I want to express my love, thanks and devotion to my wife, Nancy. Her gracious love, understanding and belief in me have carried me through our 49 years together. Not only is she a great corrector of my manuscripts, but she pushes me to strive for my best.

Nancy, I love you.

TABLE OF CONTENTS

Chapter 1

The young woman standing in the small private room at the bank in Little Rock, Arkansas, pulled the faded manuscript from the safety deposit box. She turned to the first page. It began:

"If you are reading this, I must be dead and you have found this journal in my safety deposit box. You are going to think that the following descriptions are the ravings of an unbalanced mind, but what I'm about to divulge is true. I promise. All I ask is that you please read and digest this journal with an open mind."

I am going to start my account with a rhetorical question.

Have you ever thought you would like to go back into history and live like our forefathers?

Well, believe you me, you better wish, hope and pray you never get the chance, especially when your life hangs in the balance. Besides there is a lot to be said for 21st Century conveniences such as: running water, air conditioning, flush toilets, fast food restaurants and showers.

My name is Shelton Owen Woods. I lived in Little Rock, Arkansas. I will have to warn you that I do not have the acumen of a PhD in Physics. I won't be able to explain what happened in scientific terms. So, you will have to settle for my rather unscientific mundane explanations. Also, you are going to question how I obtained portions of the encounter that I will impart. This will be revealed at the specific time it occurs in the account.

Initially you will need a little of my personal background to understand my fate. I promise not to go back too far, but a small amount of my personal information is needed.

I have always been a Civil War buff. I was raised in the South and all the Confederate Generals were my heroes. Robert E. Lee and Nathan Bedford Forrest were the first, with John Brown Gordon, John Bell Hood and Stonewall Jackson joining the pantheon later in life.

I hadn't been very actively reading Civil War books for years until Ken Burns made his epic Civil War documentary for public television. Then the bug bit me again and I went on a Civil War bender. I fixated on the Battle of Antietam. For some reason it stood out from all the battles mentioned in the Burns documentary. I read all I could about the battle, including the officers, the units, description of the battle site and the deployment of the armies. I thought I had become a Civil War resource of some repute. I could rattle off regiments, brigades, divisions and corps utilized in this battle at a moment's notice.

As I got more into the background of how both armies ended up in western Maryland during 1862, I was forced to go back in my research to June 1862, which was when Robert E. Lee took over the Confederate Army near Richmond and named it the Army of Northern Virginia. This opened up for me the whole idea of Southern strategy employed during the war and I was again reveling in a cloud of Civil War history. So, I read more Civil War history books and I visited the Antietam Battlefield at least once a year, which led to what happened to me.

The incredible events started in September 2012, when I had planned to travel by car to western Maryland to celebrate the 150th Anniversary of the Battle of Antietam. I had scheduled vacation days for the whole week of September 10th through the 14nd plus the following three work days Monday-Wednesday, September 17th through September 19th. I would be leaving the weekend before the 10th and returning on September 18th and 19th.

My wife couldn't go because she had to help take care of her family in Little Rock, but she gladly acquiesced to me being out of the house for about 12 days.

My co-workers were ecstatic to see me go. I had made it quite clear where I was going for my vacation and had about driven them crazy each day with historical facts about what had been happening 150 years ago during the Maryland Campaign. Needless to say, they were sick and tired of hearing about it. They were looking forward to not having to listen to me and thought that maybe, when I returned, I would be so tired after the trip of 2000 miles that I would at least give it a rest when I got back from my foray.

I began my pilgrimage after work on Friday night the 7th of September. Over Friday night and the next two days, while listening to Bobby Horton CDs of Civil War Songs of the South, I motored 1000 miles toward Shepherdstown, West Virginia, which is located just across the Potomac River from the Antietam Battlefield near Sharpsburg, Maryland. Each night I would call my wife and we would exchange the news of our days' events.

During the drive, I began reminiscing about one summer's visit to Virginia. I remembered that my wife and I motored to every Civil War historical marker in the Shenandoah

Valley and had our picture made next to each marker. It took us two and a half days. Years later I read in the book "Confederates in the Attic" that this type of journey is called a Wargasm. Our trek would definitely have qualified.

Anyway, I made it to Shepherdstown on Sunday afternoon, September 9th, and took a drive down the main street, which is called German Street. I love to look at the old store fronts and see what businesses are still there and if any new businesses have sprung up. Getting back on the main highway, I crossed the Potomac River into Washington County, Maryland and two miles later entered Sharpsburg.

Proceeding through town, I turned north on Highway 65 and went to the Antietam National Battlefield Park. As I drove this last mile to my Sacred Ground, I looked off to the east to view all the terrain over which the fighting in the central part of the battlefield took place. Further on, I looked back to the west and saw the position of the 3rd Arkansas Infantry during the battle, which was on a small ridgeline overlooking the highway. Just past this point I turned into the driveway to the Antietam National Battlefield Visitor Center. I parked and, as I went up to the front doors, looked at the cannon situated in front of the building just to the right of the entrance. My mentor and battlefield guide, James Smith, had passed away due to a heart attack, while standing in front of "that" cannon just before he was to give a lecture about the battle. I gave a nod to James' spirit as I entered the center.

The Visitor Center has made a few changes to the history room over the years, but overall it is the same as when I first visited it in 1994.

However, the Antietam National Battlefield Park itself has doubled in size due to acquisitions by the National Park Service and property donated by various non-profit entities over the past 20 years.

I went up to the overlook deck on the second floor and looked out from the glass-encased viewing room at the landscape. You can see all the way from "Bloody Lane" in the south to "The Cornfield" in the north. You can even see the Pry House property in the distance where Union General McClellan spent most of his time during the battle.

Just taking in all this scenery brings a euphoria that I have the privilege to stand on Hallowed Ground, where my heroes walked, fought, were wounded and some died.

After a few minutes of revelry, I went down stairs, paid my five dollars for a park pass and visited the bookstore. The bookstore has a wealth of books not only on Antietam but the whole Civil War. They also have some T-shirts and sweaters so I bought a new T-shirt and vacated the building.

I drove north to the North Woods, which is the northern boundary of the battlefield. This was where the main battle started between 5:00 a.m. and 5:30 a.m. on Wednesday morning, September 17, 1862, when the Union 1st Corps started their advance south from this point with the Iron Brigade in the vanguard.

I got out of the car, faced south and surveyed all points of the battlefield. I deliberated on how the soldiers must have felt on what became the Bloodiest Day in American History.

I have been all over the Antietam Battlefield. I have trespassed, I mean, traversed historic landscapes that were on private property and battlefield property that I wasn't supposed to enter. For example, I walked all the way from the Piper House Bed and Breakfast east following the old Piper's Lane until it crossed the lower part of the Sunken Road. Part of the Lane was privately owned. Also, I have jumped a fence in the very northern part of the battlefield and traversed some woods to a clearing just before a small incline called Hauser's Ridge, which was where the Confederate Artillery deployed to bombard the Union advance during the late morning hours of the battle. In both instances, I didn't get caught.

Due to my previous nefarious visitations, I had gotten this wild idea of having a spiritual encounter with an earthbound spirit of a soldier in a portion of the battlefield called the East Woods. Thus, before I left on my pilgrimage, I proposed to enter the park from the east after dark by way of the old Smoketown Road and sneak onto battlefield property for such a séance.

So, during my initial touring of the battlefield, I decided to implement my stealthy illicit spiritual reconnaissance of the East Woods the next night.

With this venture determined, I left the park and checked into a motel near Shepherdstown. I was beat. After a beer and hamburger at the motel grill, I retired to my room, called my wife with a daily event summary and fell fast asleep with pictures of Civil War soldiers in my head.

The next morning, I awoke with a growling stomach demanding food. After showering and dressing, I bounded down the stairs to the motel's continental breakfast bar and gorged on eggs, biscuits and coffee. Once substantially full, I journeyed back to the battlefield and spent the day touring.

I walked about five miles surveying many historical points in the northern part of the battlefield. Then I drove to the southern part of the battlefield and walked another five miles scrutinizing the historical ground over which many charges and countercharges raged during the afternoon of the battle.

I even studied the area where Confederate General Lawrence O'Brien Branch was killed and where Confederate General A.P. Hill's division hit the Union Army in the flank and saved the Army of Northern Virginia from annihilation.

By this time, it was well past my lunch time, so I went into Sharpsburg and ate a turkey sandwich at the local convenience store and then went to the local ice cream parlor for dessert. To say the least I was stuffed after partaking of the blue-collar gourmet fare.

After lunch, I went back to the Visitor Center and watched their film about the Battle, took a run through the bookstore, went across the street to the Dunker Church and visited the Maryland Monument, which lists all Maryland units from both North and South that fought during the Civil War.

Finally, it was getting dark and the park was shutting down. The park rangers were closing the few existing gates onto the park. However, there isn't a gate closing off the park's eastern entrance from the Smoketown Road.

So, I motored the six miles east to Boonsboro, Maryland and had a snack at a local hamburger joint while waiting for the park rangers to finish their last rounds and vacate the park.

CS

The Dark Mage's Log: Axeylon 5: Galaxy Date: 16312

Lord Dendaras, Ruler of The Eastern Third of the Fourth Galaxy, looked down on his two Watchers with benevolence.

The information that scrolled on the screen of his contact lens indicated Jarbree was experienced and had participated in many transferences. The other, Jarreal, was new to this type of assignment and this would be his first transference. Lord Dendaras didn't take the time to read the additional descriptive information on each of the two Watchers provided by the Eternal Oracle.

"Brethren, may Tantas watch over you and your mission," uttered Lord Dendaras. They bowed, clicked their heels, about faced in unison and

proceeded to their different departure points.

☙

I waited until about 9:00 p.m. before risking my stealthy invasion. It was quite dark and I had arrived the weekend before all the crowds would descend on the site. But still, I wanted to make sure there wouldn't be any tourists or park rangers in the park.

As I was coming back from Boonsboro toward Sharpsburg, I encountered a multitude of blue lights whirling from three state police cars ahead of me. As I approached the scene of what appeared to be a car accident, there was a police car blocking my lane. In front of the police car I could just barely see a wrecked vehicle. A State Trooper was signaling me to go around his car and the wreck. Following his directions, I pulled out in the left lane and proceeded. A quick glance out of the corner of my eye to the right disclosed that two cars had collided almost head on with one ending up in the right lane and the other upside down in the ditch to the right side of the road. The front end of the car resting in the right lane was so completely smashed that the hood was only about one foot long. As I made my way past the wrecked car, another quick glance yielded the sight of a medical crew pushing a gurney apparently containing a body covered with a bloody sheet toward an ambulance. I had chills run up and down my spine. I quickly looked back at the road. I didn't want to imagine what the body under the sheet looked like, but in another sense, I did. Back in high school I attended a safety driving course.

At the end of the course, we were shown a film of the aftermath of car wrecks. I still get the heebie-jeebies remembering all the dead bodies from the film.

As I got back into my lane and headed toward Sharpsburg, another State Trooper had about four cars stopped in the oncoming lane and he was moving his flashlight for me to continue. I complied and, as most people who view a bad wreck, I was just thankful it wasn't me in either of the cars. Then I felt guilty as most people do and hoped no one else was badly hurt. After just observing one of the worst ways for a person to die, I had second thoughts about my little infiltration operation tonight. But I reasoned, if I don't do it tonight, I won't have another time to do it. There will be a lot of crowds during the next few days that will preclude me from my adventure. So, I talked myself into proceeding with my idiotic idea.

In the old days, the road I was traveling left Boonsboro and went west through Keedysville, Maryland. Just past Keedysville, the road split with the left branch continuing to Sharpsburg and the right branch winding in a northwesterly direction ultimately crossing the Hagerstown Pike and continuing to Williamsport, Maryland, where in 1863 part of Lee's army crossed the Potomac after Gettysburg. If you take the Williamsport branch of the road, you will cross over the "Upper Bridge", which is one of the original bridges over Antietam Creek that portions of the Union 1st Corps, 2nd Corps and 12th Corps used on September 16th and 17th, 1862.

Once you cross this bridge and travel another two miles, you will see a gravel road that leads off to the left toward the battlefield. This is the old Smoketown Road. It still retains much of its 19th century character. The wooded terrain and fields on either side of the road appear much as they did during the Civil War. When previously accessing Antietam Battlefield on my annual visits, I always entered the park utilizing this scenic route to get into a 19th century mindset. The Smoketown Road proceeds to and through the East Woods, ultimately dead-ending at the Hagerstown Pike in front of the Dunker Church. During the battle the East Woods was the scene of horrific fighting in the late afternoon of September 16, 1862 and during the morning of September 17, 1862.

This night I traveled the familiar Smoketown Road with my headlights on, but, as I approached the actual boundary of the Park, I switched them off and parked my car at the bottom of a hill just east of the junction of the Smoketown Road and a paved road that turns to the right and skirts the eastern side of the East Woods. This park road continues north to the North Woods. There is a private residence to the west of this aforementioned junction and I didn't want anyone seeing a reflection of my car headlights and get park security involved.

I got out of the car and locked it. Then, I walked up the hill and turned right on the paved park road that goes to the North Woods.

☙

The Dark Mage's Log: 'Earth 9' Date: 20120910

Jarbree observed the slayer's car approach and park near the departure point. The hooded Watcher continued to watch from the depths of the woods as the slayer walked forward. He observed him approach and skirt the east side and then the north side of the woods. "He is moving stealthily," thought Jarbree. "That is good."

Finally, the slayer headed into the woods from the west as he had been told to do.

☙

There is a portion of the East Woods that has been replanted, but the new growth doesn't encompass the complete area that the East Woods originally covered. I walked down the park road to where a remnant of the woods has flourished.

There is a five-foot high, post and rail fence on the side of the road that acts as a barrier between the road traffic and the eastern face of the woods.

Walking further down the road to where the East Woods ends, I hopped the park fence and began marching along the western face of the East Woods. I wanted to enter the woods from the west, which was the way the various Confederate regiments did during the battle.

As I walked south along the western edge of the woods, I thought about the affinity I had for the East Woods. I had been drawn to this place more than any other portion of the battlefield. On one of my previous visits, I had closed my eyes and walked along a park road that is now in the middle of the original East Woods trying to envision in my mind's eye what it must have looked like back in 1862. It didn't really work, but I did scare up a mother bird that must have thought I was going to raid her nest because she practiced strafing runs on my head until I left the area.

Anyway, I finally reached the spot that I thought would be the best place to enter the East Woods. I stood there for a moment and thought of the fighting that had taken place under these trees, of the artillery shells that burst in the tree tops raining down deadly branches and metal shards on the soldiers and the numerous dead and wounded that lay in the woods after the battle.

I took a deep breath and penetrated the gloomy copse of trees. It was really hard to see in the darkness. I had already deemed it unwise to carry a flashlight because the beam would be seen and probably reported to the park security.

I picked my way from tree to tree. I stumbled and almost went down once, but I was able to keep from falling by catching the trunk of a small sapling. My plan was to traverse the woods from west to east, jump the fence, walk to my car and go back to my motel for a good night's sleep, having paid homage to my heroes. In the interim, if I were to encounter a spirit of a Civil War Soldier, so much the better.

As I arrived at the center of the woods, something seemed amiss.

The air had a special tingle to it. I would say it was electrified. It was like standing in meditation and feeling the energy flow between the palms of your hands. But, in this case it felt as if the air was energized and a current flowed through everything in the woods.

I looked around but saw nothing. I knew the park service wouldn't allow an electric fence to be put on the property due to a possible injury to a visitor. So, the source of the energy couldn't be explained.

I continued moving forward and then it happened.

In so many science fiction movies, a machine creates a wormhole with a blinding flash of light or the power from an electrical storm is harnessed or a near death experience is utilized to transport the time traveler. Plus, in these movies the transferee wants to take this fateful trip. All I can say is that their imaginary voyages are just great on the movie screen, when the participants know it is going to happen and welcome the journey, but it isn't fun when you get shanghaied and sent on a trip through time and space against your will.

There was no lightning storm. There was no near death experience. However, there was a chilling, alien phantasm that without warning flashed into existence ten feet in front of me. I could feel in every molecule of my body that this specter had been producing the energy surge I had been feeling.

It was a glowing perfect circle of light with a diameter of about seven feet and it was floating about a foot off the floor of the woods. Silently it drifted toward me.

I was scared out of my wits. My heart was suddenly in my throat. All I could think about was 'alien abduction'. I turned to run and tripped over something, probably a tree root, and fell to the ground with a thud. Twelve years of Aikido training and learning how to fall without hurting myself went out the window. I fell on my face, but I was lucky. I had landed on soft dirt and not a rock or a root.

I staggered to my feet and turned toward the circle. In one of those moments when you are terrified, but perceive weird little things, I noticed the circle's glow didn't light up the whole woods. It was as if the light from the circle was self-contained. The light didn't project outward. It was drawn back into the circle.

The shock of seeing the apparition and hitting the ground like a ton of bricks had robbed me of my breath. I was bent over with my hands on my knees looking at the incomprehensible ball of light.

I finally gasped in a full breath of oxygen, exhaled it and straightened to face the circle. I know that the hairs on the nape of my neck were standing straight up. I let out an audible whine and raised my hands as if I could ward it off.

But it advanced quickly and was abruptly right in front of me.

I know that my eyes were as wide as saucers, no pun intended. I was like a deer frozen in the middle of the road caught in the headlights of an onrushing car. But the circle just paused there in front of me. I was trembling and yet fascinated.

As I focused on the specter, I realized the circle wasn't really a circle at all. It was an orb or a sphere. And the sphere had a metal ring about ten inches wide attached at the top and bottom that rotated around the sphere. It was like one of those old globes of the earth on a stand with a ring around the globe that allowed you to spin the globe while the ring was stationary, except in this case the sphere was stationary and the ring rotated.

The sphere just stood there waiting. I let out a breath that I didn't know I had been holding and looked closer. The right side of the sphere, when the rotating ring reached a point where it was at the 90-degree/270-degree position, showed an opening. The ring's movement was about one full rotation every five seconds.

As the ring's rotation began to reach the above-mentioned position, the sphere moved toward me. I backed up, but the sphere pulled me in through the opening with a sort of sucking sound like a vacuum cleaner.

As I entered the sphere, I saw movement to my left. My eyes focused on a figure. I perceived it to be a human and I yelled, "WHO ARE YOU?" The individual was dressed in a long black coat, black trousers, white shirt and a black wide-brimmed hat. I immediately thought, "Amish male." He looked at me and grinned. He had a three-inch scar on his left check from his check-bone to the edge of his mouth. And even though I was already terrified, the malevolence produced by his leer sent chills up my spine. I could sense this person was the epitome of evil. I didn't have time for more contemplation because the foul creature was suddenly whisked away on the left side of the sphere in the opposite direction and I was gently pushed through the right side of the sphere through an opening.

☙

The Dark Mage's Log: 'Earth 9' Date: 20120910

Suddenly the Orb appeared, exactly on time, but its illumination revealed a different individual than the designated person for the transcendence. Jarbree cursed and moved toward the Orb, but the transfer occurred as quickly as programmed.

Jarbree thought, "I should contact Lord Dendaras immediately. But, hopefully, Jarreal will see the human is the wrong individual and kill him. That is what I will do. I will contact Jarreal to kill the transferee."

☙

I landed roughly on the ground and glanced around. It seemed I had been cast into a gloomy environment because it was cold and dark. The sphere had inexplicably disappeared. I just lay there for a long moment and realized that whatever was supposed to have happened had apparently occurred because I was alone. There was no more inexplicable sphere and no more Amish male. As my breath went from a ragged wheeze to a normal intake of oxygen, I sat up and focused on my surroundings. It was hard to perceive anything. I felt like Alice lost in the rabbit hole without one foot-candle of power.

Unfortunately, I was starting to feel my body again and there were aches and pains in my right leg and right shoulder from the falls I had taken. My night vision finally began to kick in and I began to make out tall shapes around me. I was in a stand of timber just like I had been in when the sphere had appeared, but there were differences.

These woods didn't have any underbrush at all and the woods seemed to have more depth. Whereas before there had been about fifty yards from one side of the woods to the other, now I couldn't see where the woods began and ended. However, just as my eyes were becoming accustomed to the murkiness of the woods, the moon came out from behind a cloud and I could see a fence in the distance. Next to me on the ground, I saw a broken limb about four feet long so I procured it to use as a walking stick. Suddenly the moon was hidden again by a cloud and my night vision went kaput. I felt like one of the blind mice of fable.

Afraid of stumbling and experiencing another fall, I cautiously let my night vision accumulate again until I could make out the trees around me. Since I was facing the ethereal fence line, I got to my feet utilizing the stick as a support to begin a trek forward. However, my head began to spin and I had to kneel down on one knee and close my eyes. Abruptly, I noticed another difference. The air was cooler and I was chilled being clothed in only jeans, a thin T-shirt and running shoes.

I waited a few hours, make that a few minutes, for my head to clear and gingerly stood up again. I felt wobbly but was able to keep my balance with the help of the thick branch. Putting one hand in front of me, I staggered forward using the limb for support and groping at trees to keep from falling. I made it to the edge of the woods and saw the fence line ahead. Again, there was a difference. Even in the gloom this fence was taller than the fence I had vaulted previously and I detected another difference.

Squinting profusely, I could make out that the fence was constructed of very roughhewn wood and not the smooth rails of which the battlefield's fences were fabricated. My mouth went dry when I looked beyond the fence. There was no paved road, only a small wagon trail about ten feet wide. And across the trail there were more woods. This was totally different from the Antietam National Battlefield landscape.

Suddenly a dark figure stepped out from behind one of the last trees in front of the fence and faced me. "Hope you had an entertaining trip," he said. I screamed in fear and instinctively swung the thick limb I had been using as a crutch. It caught the figure on the left side of his head and he went down like a ton of bricks and didn't move.

Chapter 2

The Dark Mage's Log: 'Earth 9' Date: 20120910

When Jarreal wouldn't answer his summons, Jarbree thought, "Surely Jarreal has run his diagnostic check and killed the imposter by now. I will call him later. I must attend to this newly arrived Slayer, who is my responsibility."

☙

I know I was in shock and disoriented from the ordeal with the sphere, seeing the leering man, finding myself in unfamiliar terrain and then this confrontation with a specter out of the dark. These eerie circumstances brought on a moment of sheer panic.

I said, "What have I done?"

I dropped the tree limb and bent down to look at the figure. He was clothed in a hooded robe. I pushed the hood back to look at him, but couldn't see anything clearly in the darkness. I put my hand on his head and I felt something sticky. I brought my hand to my nose and took a whiff. It had a metallic and salty smell. It had to be blood.

As I broke out in a cold sweat, bile rose in the back of my throat, which further heightened my dismay. I just wanted to get out of here. If I left quickly, no one would know I had been here and I wouldn't be prosecuted for hurting this guy. I stumbled to the fence and clumsily climbed over it. Then turning to my right, I began to stagger south toward the Smoketown Road. I progressed about thirty yards, thankfully without falling, and came to where the trail dead-ended into a dirt road. I stopped. Looking to the left, I could barely see where the road went over a little hill. Looking to the right, I could see that the road continued further into the woods, which were so dark that it was impossible to see further than ten yards.

I turned left on the dirt road with the hope of finding my car at the bottom of the hill. I was panting with shock and fear as I tripped and fell to my knees due to two five-inch deep ruts in the road spaced about six feet apart. I staggered to my feet, and lurching between the ruts to the top of the small hill, looked down into the gloom for my car. However, it was so dark that I couldn't see a thing, but I reasoned that my car was down there and I needed to find it and get out of here.

I cautiously shuffled down the hill into the enveloping gloom. Once I felt that I had reached the bottom due to sensing the flatness of the terrain, I hesitantly hobbled to the right side of the road moving my hands out in front of me like a blind man feeling for obstacles. Continuing forward every few feet, I would stop and frantically swing my arms back and forth trying to touch my car, but it wasn't there!

I stopped moving, dropped my arms and bowed my head. I prayed, "Please God. What is going on? I don't understand. What is happening?"

My heart was beating like a rabbit caught in a trap. It brought up burning acid in my throat. I coughed it back down, hugged myself again and muttered out loud, "Where's my car? I wanna get out of here."

I put my hands out in front of me again and wobbled further off the right side of the road until I touched a big tree. I was abruptly fatigued. The adrenalin had worn off. I turned and put my back against the tree, hugged myself and slid down into a sitting position. I asked out loud, "Why isn't my car here? Has it been stolen or was is discovered by park security and been impounded?"

I was so tired and distraught that I went into a daze. I huddled down putting my arms between my legs, my head on my knees and just shook for about five minutes.

As my body came back to some semblance of normalcy, I was able to get a little warmer. I was still somewhat chilled, but I was no longer shaking.

I knew I had to get out of here and fast. I hoped that guy I hit was okay, but I wasn't about to go back and see.

As rational thought seeped into my brain, I came to the conclusion that I had to find out where my car was. But I wondered why some of the landmarks around here had changed. However, that was the least of my worries.

I had to get out of here. I took stock of my options.

One, I could continue following this road, which was the Smoketown Road, to the northeast where it would dead-end into the Keedysville Road. Then I could walk to Keedysville and get a ride to my motel, but that is too long a walk. So that possibility is out.

Two, I could trudge back up the hill I just came down to where the farm trail dead-ends into this road. If I turn right and head north on the farm trail, I would go past the Joseph Poffenberger farm and end up on the Hagerstown Pike. Then I could walk to Sharpsburg and get a ride to my motel. But again, I would be taking the long way home. Scratch that choice.

Okay. Last but not least, I could go back over the hill I had just came down and follow the road into the gloomy woods and continue on, what I hope is the Smoketown Road, to where it dead-ends into the Hagerstown Pike in front of the Dunker church. Then I could turn south, go to Sharpsburg, Maryland and get a ride to my motel. This sounded like the better idea.

So, I picked Curtain Number Three. I figured the mileage to cover was less. Therefore, it would take less time to get to a recognizable city plus I would be less likely to be attacked by dogs, which usually inhabit these rural farms.

Then I got one of those insane thoughts that you don't want to consider, but makes it past all the mind-blocking mechanisms you install in your brain. "What if I am where I started out when the Sphere abducted me, but I am in a different time?" In my mind I responded, "Shut up. You don't know what you are talking about." So, I put that insidious thought in the trash bin of my mind and took action.

I gathered my strength and abruptly stood up, which apparently wasn't the right thing to do. I felt light-headed and had to put my hand against my sheltering tree to keep my balance. My vision was blurred which produced nausea. I had to swallow a number of times to keep from being sick. I stood in this awkward position for several minutes until my equilibrium reached some semblance of normalcy and the nausea abated. Telling myself to take it easy, I hobbled back the way I had come.

I made it to the top of the hill without stumbling over the ruts in the road and saw the farm trail off to my right from which I had emerged a few moments ago. I stopped for a moment to catch my breath from climbing the hill. The moon suddenly came out again and I could see a little more of the road leading off into the ominous woods. I took a deep breath and trudged forward on the Smoketown Road.

The road's construction was hard to see in the gloom, but it definitely didn't feel like a paved road, which the Smoketown Road should have been at this juncture. As I progressed through the woods, a small dirt lane branched off to the left from the main thoroughfare. I remembered that there was a paved road at Antietam Battlefield about where this path was located. I angrily thought, "Well, if this road is dirt and that lane is dirt, maybe the Park Service is trying to make it look like it did back in 1862." I stopped and said out loud to no one in particular, "You never told us you were gonna change things up for the 150th anniversary." I suddenly felt like a fool and reasoned, "You aren't gonna get where you want to go by asking stupid questions. Start walking." So, I sullenly began trekking my chosen path.

The aftereffects of a probable panic attack were wearing off. Also, this part of the road was in better condition, so I was able to pick up my pace a smidgen. Looking to either side of me, I couldn't make out the depth of the timber. All I could see was the road in front of me in the intermittent moonlight. I had another fact that hit me, "These woods are another anomaly. They shouldn't be here." I irritably answered, "Shut up and leave me alone. I don't want to hear it."

After a few more moments of forward progress, I could see an increase of light ahead. I was finally coming to the end of the woods. This caused me to hasten my pace. Once I broke out of the dismal timbered tunnel, I felt as if a demon of fear had been banished from my mind. I felt ecstatic. I stopped and took a few deep breaths. I viewed the landscape.

The road turned about forty-five degrees to the right and a plowed field appeared on the left side of the dirt track. At this location, another abnormality presented itself. There was no white house located at this turn in the road. Plus, there were woods along the right side of the road for about fifty more yards. Again, some of the landmarks were consistent with Antietam Battlefield, such as the forty-five degree turn of the road. But some were not, such as the absence of the house and the wooded area to my right. I reasoned, "The Park Service had to have made the changes." So, I just threw up my hands in frustration and ambled onward.

I quickly covered the ground to the point where the woods on the right of the road abruptly stopped and opened into a grassy field. Even though my mind was in a maddening state, my stamina and strength were returning. My body felt much better.

I trudged another 40 yards and came to a dirt lane bordered by fences on my left that dead-ended into the road I was traveling. My heart began to hammer in my chest. On the right side of the road there should be about four historical markers, but they weren't there. I looked down at the road I had been traveling. It was a dirt road and was rutted. I kicked at the dirt trying to find the underlayment of pavement that was the foundation for the dirt the Park Service had distributed for the 150th anniversary, but I couldn't dig down far enough to hit asphalt. I finally decided that the Park Service had done a great job of making the park visitors think they were back in the 1860's.

I turned and looked at the familiar lane to my left and walked to the top of a small rise. I looked down on a farm house. There was the familiar "Mumma Farm House." However, it didn't look like it did the last time I was here. The house and outbuildings were not the whitewashed color that they were supposed to be. They were drab and weathered. Also, there were overgrown weeds along the lane to the house instead of the finely manicured grass that I normally witnessed. Plus, there were lights on in the house. There shouldn't be anyone there this time of night.

Unfortunately, I didn't have time to ponder the array of anomalies because suddenly I heard the howls of rural canines and became fearful of being mauled by semi-feral farm dogs. This induced me to quickly turn around and hurriedly retrace my steps toward the Smoketown Road. I turned left and began to do a limping jog in the direction that I had been preceding. Thank heavens the mangy curs were content with just barking and didn't follow me.

I plodded along for a few minutes, ran out of breath and then began hobbling again. Every few steps I would wipe the tears from my eyes. I abruptly felt lost in mind and spirit.

To keep my mind occupied I took stock of my surroundings. There was a tall post and rail fence on the left side of the road and a snake rail fence on the right side of the road. As I reached a point where the land on the left side of the road dipped down to where I could see the manmade landmarks to the south. I stopped and turned to view the massive New York Monument, the gazebo-shaped Maryland Monument with a list of all the Maryland units that fought for the Union and Confederacy and the Visitor Center, but they weren't there. I rubbed my eyes and looked again for the familiar reminders of the Antietam Battle. All that was visible was a large field.

My heart was beating like a drum, while my mind kept asking, "Where is everything? The Park Service couldn't have taken down all the monuments, could they? This is very, very wrong."

Finally, I looked toward the only landmark in the distance that was where it should be and thought, "I have to get to that building. I'll get my questions answered once I get there." I shuffled forward, eradicating all useless questions that screamed for my attention by muttering a mantra, "Shut up. The answer is ahead. Just wait. You'll see."

After what seemed like an eternity, I came to where the road on which I was traveling dead-ended into a wider dirt thoroughfare. There, highlighted in the moonlight off to my left, was "The Dunker Church." I staggered to the post and rail fence on my left and leaned against it.

For several minutes, I just stood there despondently staring at the edifice and swallowing back bile that threatened to lacerate my throat.

This building was not the same Dunker Church that I was used to seeing. It was not the bright white-washed building I remembered from prior visitations. It was white alright, but a muted white. Plus, the junction of the Smoketown Road, which I had been traveling, and the Hagerstown Pike, which ran in front of the church, was in such a rustic condition that the Park Service couldn't have created this antiquated landscape. Also, buildings and monuments that should have been present were not here. Lastly, the road in front of the church hadn't been graded to create a level roadbed. The road followed the undulating lay of the land. The landscape in which I found myself was not in the 21st century.

Finally, I was forced to accept that I was no longer in control of my life. I had no car, no motel room, no job, and no family. But worst of all, I had no plausible way to respond to my present situation. This realization hit me with such force that like a fatalistic Samurai warrior accepting his inevitable doom, I simply gave up. My mind, body and spirit, which during the night had run the gamut of terror, offensive onslaught, a panic attack, and existence in an implausible reality, suddenly shut down. Hugging my upper torso, I sat down and leaned back against the post and rail fence. I was so drained of emotion I couldn't even rant, rave or cry. After a few moments, I drifted off into an exhausted coma.

I didn't know how long I was out, but I woke feeling calm. I didn't feel the tremendous fear that had created the psychological panic, which had brought on my mind and body shut down. I guess acceptance of my worst fears had been the catalyst that brought back a sort of tranquility. I do know that my mind began to function again. I was able to not succumb to trying to answer a lot of unanswerable questions that could lead to another panic attack. I reasoned that there were some initial actions that needed to be taken and not worry about anything else for the time being. However, I was going to make one assumption. I believe this was the 19th century.

One of the first things I needed to do was to get warm. The night air was chilly. I knew I had to keep moving to stay warm. For some reason the following thoughts popped into my mind, "Since the building across the road is the Dunker Church, I am definitely near Sharpsburg, Maryland, but when exactly? Maybe I can find an answer to this question in town."

So, I tentatively stood up, which gratefully didn't affect my balance. I looked south down the road toward Sharpsburg and decided ultimately to find out what, in the name of all that was holy, was going on. However, I would accomplish this task logically. I had enough of being put in the dark, both literally and figuratively. I stepped off with sheer determination.

To take my mind off the chill of the night air, I got to thinking, "The sphere had to have been some kind of weird time travel mechanism. And who was the dark figure I hit with the tree limb? I don't know how badly I hurt him. Should I go back? No, I just need to put as much distance between me and the East Woods as possible. But that machine was so advanced that it had to be alien made because our government didn't have anything like it. The only good thing about the sphere was that it didn't cause pain getting me here. There wasn't a bunch of blue viscous material that I had to walk through. It didn't cause a lightning storm when I arrived. I was just swept into it and I was here. But the rapidity of travel didn't make sense. And what about my car? Who's got it?" For a while I mulled over the possible answers as I walked. When the questions got too pressing, I would just take a few deep breaths to realign my mind into a more peaceful state.

After a few tranquil steps, I got to thinking about the leering man who passed me on the other side of the sphere. "Who was he and where was he going?" I contemplated this question until I finally asked the big question, "Can I go back?" "No", suddenly appeared in my mind as if it was written across the sky. So, finally, I gave up the self-interrogation and concentrated on the road, which made me realize again how chilled I was. So, I decided to think about additional actions to take and get my mind off my body.

First, I had to find out the date. Speaking of date, I decided to look at my wristwatch to check out the time. However, due to the night's gloom, I couldn't see the face of the watch. I waited for the moon to appear from the captivating clouds, and when it did, I observed that the watch had stopped.

I decided to take an inventory of my possessions. I felt for my wedding ring and it was still on my finger. I reached in the left front pocket of my jeans for the money I normally carry and it was there. I pulled out the bills. In the moonlight, I could see the numbers on the bills were the same, which were ten $20 dollar bills, one $5 dollar bill and five $1 dollar bills. In the dim lighting, the writing on the bills looked different. I couldn't make out the writing so I put the bills back in my pocket.

Wearily, I put my cold hands in my pockets, hunched my shoulders and looked at "The Dunker Church" as I passed it on my right. During the Battle of Antietam, this small religious structure had been a prize for the Union Army to capture. Its position at the junction stood out like a beacon of hope for the Sharpsburg community. I decided to acknowledge it as good portent for me.

Thankfully, no wind was blowing as I continued trudging south.

☙

Dark Mage's Log: Axeylon 5: Galaxy Date: 16312

Jarbree finally called, Axeylon 5, the Mother Ship occupied by Lord Dendaras and reported that a wrong slayer had been processed to Jarreal. Lord Dendaras said he would contact Jarreal and have the human exterminated immediately.

Suddenly communication was closed down. Jarbree reasoned, "This has never happened in the thousand years since the first transferees. They can't blame

me for the mix up. I didn't recruit this slayer imposter."

ଓ

The one good thing was my leg wasn't hurting as much as it had been. It was still tight, but I wasn't hobbling anymore. I would have loved for dawn to break and bring with it some blessed warming sunshine, but, if the local population saw me in my clothes, would I be made to answer a lot of questions? I believed Sharpsburg was between one to two miles down the road. As a final affirmation, if I passed "The Piper Farm" on my left in about a quarter of a mile, it would confirm the knowledge that this was western Maryland.

The dirt road I was walking on was rutted and crude. It was so different from the paved road over which I drove year after year from Sharpsburg to the Battlefield.

With "The Dunker Church" on my right and behind me, I reached the bottom of a small hill south of the church and looked to my right. In the moonlight, I could barely make out the hill that the 3rd Arkansas and 27th North Carolina had occupied on September 17, 1862. It certainly looked differently now. There was a cornfield on the knoll and there was fencing along the edge of the corn. Anyway, it was from that position that the two regiments had charged across the road I was on and advanced off to my left for about 300 yards. It had helped stymy the Union breakthrough of the Confederate line in the Sunken Road, later given the name "Bloody Lane." And speaking of

"Bloody Lane", I viewed the western entrance to the lane on my left.

Up until now the road had been bordered on both sides with a post and rail fence. At the entrance to Bloody Lane, the left side of the road was bordered by a stone fence about two feet high while the post and rail fence continued on my right.

I just hoped there were no dogs on the route.

I was enthralled by the countryside that was beginning to flatten out and be more illuminated by the moonlight.

I came to "The Piper House Lane" on the left and stopped. I looked toward the barn and house. The lane was totally different. Rather than a nice white gravel road, it was just a rutty dirt path. I could barely make out the house in the foggy distance. My wife and I had spent many a night in that old house, which was a bed & breakfast.

The whole area no longer consisted of the manicured fields, modern-day fences and 21st Century houses that I was accustomed to seeing. Instead, it was a very primitive and rugged landscape. Weeds and high grass lined the fences along the road and the fields, from what little I could see in the moonlight, displayed very uneven cuts of grain, probably wheat, indicating that the harvesting had been performed manually by either a scythe or some crude harvesting machine.

I also was amazed by the fact that the houses that would normally have lined the right side of the road were gone. Only plowed or grass fields occupied the area now. The fields were sectioned by fences into individual parcels.

I had made good time, and before I knew it, I arrived at a curve in the road that went down a small hill into Sharpsburg. As I descended, I looked to my left. It was here that a convenience store normally stood, but now it was a cornfield.

Then it hit me. What was I going to do about my clothes? I was dressed in a T-shirt, jeans and running shoes, and I might add, I was still cold.

If I had guessed right and this was the 19th century, then the normal attire consisted of brogans or boots for footwear, a pair of wool or cotton trousers with bracers (suspenders), a long sleeve shirt, a vest to cover the shirt and bracers (It was considered very rude to show your bracers to the opposite sex.), a coat and a hat. I certainly didn't have any of these accoutrements.

I considered a few options to keep from drawing attention to myself. One, I could see if any clothes were hung out on clothesline in the town to dry and steal them. However, the stolen clothes would no doubt be recognized and I would be arrested as a thief. Not the best way to start an initial visit to a town.

Two, I could see if there was a clothier in Sharpsburg and attempt to buy clothing. This presented two tangential problems. What if my money wasn't accepted? I took out the money and tried to focus on it again, but in the moonlight, I still couldn't make out the writing or even the person's picture on the bills. I reluctantly returned the money to my pocket. I continued my train of thought. If I did walk into the clothier dressed as I am now, it would cause quite a stir and no telling what would happen.

Three, I could proceed to the Potomac River crossing at Boteler's Ford and go over the river into Shepherdstown, West Virginia. Oops, let me correct myself, Shepherdstown, Virginia. If this is the 19th century and before 1863, West Virginia hadn't seceded from Virginia yet. Anyway, in Shepherdstown I could take my chances. However, it would probably just postpone the inevitable, which would be trying to explain the unexplainable clothing I was wearing.

I decided that it would be better to delay what was going to be a difficult situation and to cross the Potomac River near Shepherdstown. Maybe something would turn up and I would be delivered from having to tell an awkward tale.

Meanwhile, I had stopped in the middle of the road while contemplating all the ramifications of my possible actions. Having made a decision about what to do next, I continued down the hill with the idea of entering the first street I saw to my right and traversing it west through town. Once through town, I could turn south and proceed until I picked up the road that proceeds west from town to Boteler's Ford and the Potomac River. Then it would be a straight shot to Shepherdstown.

I heard a growl come from a house located on the right of the road as I came down the hill toward the edge of town. All of a sudden, a dog came charging out from under the front porch of the house barking loud enough to wake the dead.

I must have jumped about three feet in the air. The dog caught me completely by surprise.

ꟹ

The Dark Mage's Log: Axeylon 5: Galaxy Date: 16312

Lord Dendaras commanded the Mission Officer to contact Jarreal. When no answer was received, Lord Dendaras conferred with his Director of Order. He told the Director that a human had been transferred to 'Earth 3' and required immediate eradication. The Director asked for the extermination code. Lord Dendaras gave the Director the requested codes. However, moments later the Director communicated to Dendaras that upon implementing the code the instruments indicated that the Slayer had already been dead for one Earth day. Lord Dendaras shouted, "That is impossible." The Director stated, "The elimination instructions were correctly transmitted and the return information of the death date is accurate. The Lord quickly cut the line of communication with the Director. Lord Dendaras thought, "What is going on? Who was transferred? How can someone make

transference and not be implanted with an eradication module?" Lord Dendaras tried to further analyze the situation and couldn't. He reluctantly thought, "This has never happened before. What will be the historical consequences?"

Lord Dendaras called for the Security Officer.

I was so scared that I didn't have enough time to even yell. I just backed up, came up on the balls of my feet (as I had been taught in Aikido) and extended my arms out in front of me in preparation for the attack.

In the moonlight, I estimated the dog to be of medium build, about thirty-five to forty pounds, long-haired and not scared of me at all. He went directly to the attack. I put my left arm out for him to bite on. When he did, I plunged the fingers of my right hand toward his eyes. I must have made contact with one of his eyes because he yelped, let go of my left forearm and ran squealing back under the house porch from whence he came, shaking his head from side to side.

With that blasted dog howling to high heavens, it was bound to wake the household and create a search to see what had caused the dog's yelping. I had no time to lose. I began running toward the street that I envisioned would be there and, thank the Lord, it was. I entered it and began a steady pace to get to the western edge of town as quickly as possible. My adrenalin was definitely pumping and my leg was holding up. I ran four blocks before I started to give out. I heard a few dogs bark, but none came after me. I didn't realize that there was a hill that I had to climb at the end of the road, which caused me to stop running.

Nevertheless, breathing heavily, I kept up a fast walk. I reached the top of the hill. The road dead-ended into a farm road running north to south. I turned left on the southern branch and hoped to hit the main road going to Shepherdstown.

The moon had gone behind a cloud and it was so dark that I almost missed the road I wanted. The only thing that saved me was stumbling in a rut on the main road. I turned right and headed west to Boteler's Ford.

I tried to keep up a fast-paced walk, but, after what seemed like an hour, which was probably only a few minutes, I knew I had to stop and rest or I wouldn't make it to my destination. I found a tree next to the road, sat down, and leaned back against it. I felt something trickling down my arm. I was bleeding. This was just what I needed: a dog bite in the supposed 19th century without any antiseptic available.

I took off my T-shirt, tore off an arm of the cloth, wrapped it around the place on my arm that hurt the most and tied it off. Then I put the shirt back on and leaned back against the tree. I hugged my upper body with my arms to generate some warmth and dozed off.

I woke with a start not knowing how long I was out. I was shaking and knew I had to get a move on to keep from getting hypothermia. So, I reluctantly got to my feet and, feeling light headed but not nauseous, I staggered onward following ruts in the main road leading westward.

I wanted to get to the Potomac River before sunrise and it seemed like it was taking forever to get there. At one point just outside of Sharpsburg, the moon came out and I could see "The Grove Planation" off to my left. This is where President Lincoln and General McClellan had met after the Battle of Antietam in 1862. I continued westward on the dirt road but saw few houses on the way.

At one point in my journey, I could see a house off to my right and heard two dogs barking. I continued on my way, but I sensed the dogs' barking was getting closer as they ran down the farm lane toward the main road. I stopped in the middle of the road. I couldn't out distance the canine posse trailing me. The coming confrontation could signify the abrupt end of my existence. My wife or anyone I knew would never know what happened to me and no one here would know who I was.

But suddenly, I didn't care. Anger welled up in me from deep in my psyche. I was mad as a hornet and I was sick of yelping dogs attacking me in the night. I didn't care if these mongrels were as big as Saint Bernards. I was looking forward to this battle.

I looked down at the road bed. With the aid of the moonlight I selected two large rocks. Catching the scent of my bloody arm, my canine adversaries' blood lust must have been aroused because their barks turned to baying as they broke out of their farm lane and raced toward me. I had just enough time to distinguish they were just curs and each ogre only weighed about forty pounds.

This raised my spirits. At least I would not be facing indomitable hounds from hell. I allowed the reptilian portion of my brain full sway. I raised a primeval banshee squall and threw one rock with all the force I could muster at the face of the lead dog. It hit the beast a glancing blow on the right side of its head and it went down like a poled ox. The second mongrel, seeing the leader of the pack get its just desserts, thought retreat the better part of valor. It veered off the road to the right into a tree line. As most cowardly dogs, once they have been successfully accosted, they reverted from their hound-from-hell persona to the loud barking of mangy mutts. Even though savoring the victory, I didn't wait around to see what might happen next. I couldn't run any more. I was too tuckered out. I turned and continued tottering west at a somewhat steady pace as the dog's barking faded into the distance.

After what seemed like an eternity, I came to where the main road went straight down what seemed to be a steep hill. It was hard to make out what was at the bottom of the hill.

I thought for a moment, but couldn't remember where this road might have led in olden days. I said out loud, "I sure hope this is where I think it is." Looking to the right in the very early morning light I could barely make out a very large house, possibly two or three stories tall. I suddenly remembered that this must be Ferry Hill, where Henry Kyd Douglas, Stonewall Jackson's aide, lived.

Scanning to the left again and looking down where the road made its steep descent, I remembered this was the road that led to Boteler's Ford. So, I turned into its entrance and began the downward plunge.

Just then, I heard some singing in the distance, probably near the bottom of the hill.

Chapter 3

The Dark Mage's Log: Axeylon 5: Galaxy Date: 16313

Agent 714, Jarlene, the security officer stood before Lord Dendaras in the throne room as he gave her orders in person. "Make a full investigation. Find Jarreal! If the infiltrator is still there, kill him. If he isn't there, find him and kill him. I have an Astral Conveyance Vehicle waiting for you. You have only two 'Earth 3' hours until their dawn. Now go!"

"Yes, my liege," she responded, bowed, clicked her heels, about faced and marched out of the throne room.

Once Jarlene left, Lord Dendaras thought, "Unfortunately, we can't go back in time and rectify the situation. Apparently, we don't have control of the infiltrator. He has no tracking device and

no extermination code. Time is of the essence."

ꕤ

I skirted the road to the left, entered a tree line and crept down the hill paralleling the road.

Soon I heard some slurred words in an off-key warbling voice coming closer. Eventually, I made out a figure on either a mule or a horse singing an indecipherable ditty at the top of his lungs. As the gloom of the night was slowing giving way to the early morning light, I saw it was a bearded man on a mule. He didn't have a saddle, but just a horse or in this case a mule blanket that he had used for a barrier between him and his animal. He had his left arm wrapped around a jug, which must have contained some kind of whiskey due to his readily definable inebriated state. He had the mule's bridle reins in his right hand.

He stopped the mule in the middle of the very steep road and positioned the jug to take a swig. He placed both hands on the jug and started to bring it to his lips. He tilted his head way back, probably due to the container being almost empty. This realignment caused him to lose his balance. In almost slow motion, he flayed his arms, dropped the jug, made an attempt to catch the jug, hit the ground with a thud and didn't move. The jug broke and what little amount of liquid that hadn't been previously dispatched was quickly absorbed by the dirt road. His noble steed didn't move other than to look back to see why the load he had been carrying had suddenly gotten lighter.

I moved out of the tree line and approached the man. The mule must have been older than Methuselah because it didn't even move a muscle when I approached the scene of the unfortunate loss of his load. The reek of whiskey permeated the air and it wasn't just from the broken jug. It was also from the drunken heap of humanity lying in the middle of the road.

I put my hand on the man's chest to see if he was still breathing. He was. The mule just looked back at me with a sort of quizzical gaze, if you can attribute human facial features to an animal.

I decided to drag the fallen imbiber off the road to examine him further and tie the mule to one of the trees in the tree line. A plan was starting to form in my mind.

I grabbed the back-country example of a boozehound by his arms and, after many stops and starts, dragged him through the tree line to a small field beyond.

I kept looking at the mule, but it just stood in the middle of the road with most of its weight on its front legs and the hoof of its left back leg planted next to its right back leg in a jocular sort of way. It made no attempt to leave the scene. The mule seemed to be waiting on someone to tell it what to do. It observed my machinations with the sot, but did little else.

Once I got the man off the road, I went back for the mule. I picked up its reins and pulled it toward the tree line, but it wouldn't budge. I next grabbed the bridle next to its jaw and tried to pull it again, but to no avail. It was like one person trying to move a heavy stalled car by himself. I wanted to hide this animal as best I could because I didn't know how many people were familiar with its owner and would recognize the mule if it was found riderless in the vicinity. This could lead to a search for the sot and probably me being incarcerated.

I finally left the mule in the road and walked through the tree line to the field, which I hadn't paid any attention to before. The field was full of head high corn. Each stalk abounded with young roasting ears, as we refer to them in Arkansas. I picked a few and started shucking them as I walked back to the mule.

As I approached the mule, I believe it could smell the corn. Its ears shot up as it turned to look straight at me and it moved its back leg to a stance with its weight equally distributed on all four legs. I held out the three small savory ears of sweet corn and the resuscitated animal moved toward me. I backed up and it continued to follow me through the tree line. Once I got to the field on the other side of the tree line, I turned around and held out my hand with the corn. The mule came to me and I expertly fed the roasting ears to the lop-eared beast by putting the corn in my palm with the fingers of my hand beneath its chin. I had been taught this as a young city boy while visiting my friends to ride horses on their farms after Sunday church. The mule crunched on the corn to its heart's content. I got its reins and tied the contented jackass to a tree. I put some more roasting ears on the ground in front of it and made sure the additional treats could be easily reached. Hopefully this would keep the munching hybrid occupied enough to prevent it from braying.

The first part of my plan was accomplished. Now, I implemented the second part.

I wanted to see what this guy was carrying on his person. I unbuttoned his coat and laid it open. The stench of his body odor that immediately hit me was sickening. However, I forced myself to rummage through his coat pocket (He only had one.). I found a few coins amounting to about $2 dollars. I had never seen this type of money so I took a few seconds to study the coinage.

Next, I turned his trouser pockets inside out and found a folding knife, some twine, and a large key. On closer inspection, I found a longer knife that had a blade of about four inches in a homemade leather scabbard stuck in his belt. Taking stock of his valuables, I relieved him of his folding knife, which seemed to be pretty generic cutlery. His long knife looked as if it could be recognized so I discarded it along with his coins, twine and key.

This part of my plan included confiscation of the sotted soul's apparel and donning it to fit in with the populace. So, I stripped him of his coat and pulled his bracer straps (suspenders) off his shoulders and down so I could get his trousers off. I unbuttoned his fly buttons and taking his trousers by the cuffs pulled them off his body. His underwear or drawers were filthy. If I thought the body odor was bad before, now it was absolutely revolting. I didn't want to even think about the stains that made up the majority of the seat of his undergarment. I unbuttoned the four buttons on the front of his shirt, which probably hadn't been washed since Noah's flood, and manhandled it off him. Finally, I untied his brogans' (shoe) laces. They had so many knots in them to repair breaks that I wondered whether they could really be laced up. I pulled the brogans off his feet. His socks had holes in the heels and toes on both feet. The toes that stuck through the holes had some sort of red rash on them. Needless to say, I left the socks on their master's feet. My socks would provide a lot better coverage and would be well hidden in the brogans.

During this whole sequence, the drunken man hadn't moved. All the jostling hadn't elicited a groan, a moan or even a sigh.

With the well-oiled mule rider's clothing at my disposal, I began the monumental task of dressing in his paraphernalia. I took off my clothes except for my underwear, socks and T-shirt.

At that moment, the stripped intoxicant snuffled and sat straight up.

I was standing to the man's left side. He looked at me and said, "Who are ya?"

I yelled, "The devil incarnate," and slugged him with a right cross that in his pickled state laid him out colder than a cucumber. A pain suddenly shot through my right hand. I moved my fingers and they were mobile, but they hurt like the dickens.

The Dark Mage's Log: 'Earth 3' Date: 18620911

Agent Jarlene arrived on the scene and immediately found Jarreal. He was alive, but still unconscious and suffering from

a severe head trauma. Jarlene placed the injured Jarreal in the Astral Conveyance Vehicle (ACV), entered the coordinates for Axeylon 5 in the computer, and returned with the comatose Watcher.

ᴄᴙ

For some unapparent reason, I looked down at the wrapped wound in my left arm. The makeshift bandage was held in place by some coagulated blood. I would worry about that later. One crisis at a time!

The sky was starting to really lighten up and I wanted to get across the Potomac River before dawn if possible. So, I began to put on what looked like 19th century trappings.

First, I put on the shirt. With my T-shirt as a buffer the shirt's grime only accosted my arms. Next, I slipped on the trousers. The prior owner probably outweighed me a good 50 pounds, but was shorter. Once I pulled the bracer straps up on my shoulders, the trousers hung loosely on me, but they didn't drag the ground.

However, I could feel the dirty coarse wool trouser material rubbing against my legs and knew that it would soon chaff my legs badly if I didn't procure some type of long underwear for a cushion. Lastly, I stuffed my feet in the man's brogans, which were about a size too large. Needless to say, they were uncomfortable and rubbed against my heels even with the socks I was wearing.

I stood up and let out a breath I didn't know I had been holding. Once I inhaled, I bent over and retched. The combination of the time travel, the panic attacks, the dog confrontations, the wounded arm and now my newly purloined and reeking clothes brought on a nausea that suddenly hit me.

I straightened up and got dizzy. I put my hand against a young sapling to keep my balance. Then the thought hit me, "What am I going to do now?" I realized I was in a very precarious situation.

A new thought barged its way into my consciousness, "How can I get back?" I stopped moving for a few seconds and pondered this mental intrusion. Unfortunately, all that came to mind were worst case scenarios.

I knew I had to get control of myself and let go of these thoughts. I closed my eyes and descended into a slightly squatted Wu Ji stance. Next, I completely relaxed my body and took twenty deep slow meditative breaths. I gently straightened up and felt better.

Suddenly the thought hit me, "Keep to your plan."

This thought snapped me back into my strategy. If I was going to make a perfect getaway, I had to do something with my old clothes. So, I confiscated the drunk's long knife and went into the tree line. I dug for a few minutes in the soft ground, which produced a hole deep enough to bury my tennis shoes, jeans and wrist watch. I put my wedding ring in my trouser pocket.

I dropped the drunk's long knife next to his half naked body, turned and hiked down the hill toward the Potomac River.

I walked a few feet before a tree branch slapped me in the head. It suddenly dawned on me that I had forgotten the drunk's hat. I turned around and went back to the disrobing site, but there wasn't a hat to be found. I ventured back to the road from which I had dragged the stoned mule rider and there was the hat in the middle of the road next to the broken jug.

I picked up the hat and put it on my head. It reeked of whiskey and was so large it pushed my ears down so that I must have looked like the village idiot. As an afterthought, I decided to pick up as many pieces of the jug as possible and get them off the road.

Once back at the site of the purloined clothes, I threw the jug pieces into the field. The drunk was still out cold and the mule was contentedly munching on the sweet corn, so I headed down the hill to the river.

I meandered down the steep hill staying in the woods until the foliage abruptly stopped. I halted and looked out on a landscape for which I wasn't prepared. Before me lay about fifty yards of open ground that ended with the C&O Canal (Chesapeake & Ohio Canal). I had forgotten all about this man-made obstacle.

When I had visited this area in my prior life, it was drained of water and there were only a few historical markers. Back then the canal's towpath was used for hiking and bicycle riding. What lay in front of me now was a fully functional lock with a cross bridge over it and about four houses in the general area. Apparently, these houses were occupied by the people who operated the lock.

In the distance, I saw an old rickety bridge across the Potomac River. It would have been an easier conveyance for a crossing. However, no matter what, I had to get over the C&O Canal first before I could do anything.

The canal towpath was between me and the canal. There was no way I was going to be able to wade the canal. I had to take the bridge over the lock to either get down to Boteler's Ford or go to the rickety bridge to cross the Potomac River.

In the early morning light, I could see a boat entering the lock headed north. There was a team of two mules on the towpath that was harnessed to pull the boat through the lock. If I could get across the lock bridge during the interchange unopposed, I would be able to walk down to the river bank and take my pick of ways to cross over to Shepherdstown.

I walked out of the woods and headed toward the lock bridge.

I only had 21st century money and didn't know if there was a fee for crossing the bridge. I now wished I had relieved the drunk of his few coins.

My clothes stank of whiskey so I put a little stagger in my step, which wasn't so hard due to the pungent smell. I was a little inebriated just from whiffing the aroma of my coat. I approached the team of mules that was hitched in a single file harness with a teamster who sat on the first mule. He was urging the team down the towpath. The mules' harness had a large rope that was attached to the boat. They were pulling the boat into the lock. Since the process was both tricky and dangerous, the teamster's attention was on trying to fit the boat in the lock without doing damage to the sides plus stopping the boat without busting the upstream gate.

I walked, make that staggered, past the teamster, who at a quick glance appeared to be a roughhewn youth of about fifteen. He snickered as I stumbled past and then as the whiskey aroma hit his nostrils said, "Got any left?"

I answered, "Nope", and continued to the lock bridge.

There was a man operating the closing mechanism for the lock's upstream gate. The gates, located at each end of the lock, were configured like a draw bridge, except they were placed horizontally at the ends of the lock. The lock bridge was a part of the upstream gate. Since this gate was closing, the bridge's two halves were coming together to provide a platform for crossing over the top of the lock to the Potomac River bank. The boat was finally secured in the lock and the lockkeeper closed both gates. I walked quickly toward the lock bridge.

The person who had closed the lock's upstream gate barred my way. He pulled himself up to his full height. He was a larger version of the teamster. He mouthed off, "Whar ya think yar goin?" He finished his challenge with curled lips that settled into a sneer, which revealed two missing front teeth on his upper row of teeth and three on his lower row. He was stout and two inches taller than me. He must have weighed 150 pounds, but it looked as if it were all muscle.

I pulled down my hat so my face was hard to see. "Ova ta tha ottah side of tha rivah", I replied in my deepest southern accent.

"Ya gonna have ta pay toll for that thar privilege," he spouted with a pleased smirk on his face.

I bent down as if to put my hand in a pants pocket, brought the flat of my palm up toward his face from a couch and said, "Well herah tis." My movement was a complete surprise, and although my palm barely touched his chin, he jerked his head and therefore his upper torso backward so violently that he became airborne. He flailed his arms to gain purchase with Mother Earth to no avail. For a split second, his body was about two feet above and parallel to the bridge. His head and shoulders were the first body parts to greet the wooden floor of the bridge. The rough landing completely obliterated his opposition to my escape plan. I felt for a pulse in his neck just to make sure I hadn't sent him to the Other Side. His heart was still beating.

I figured it was time to vacate the area as quickly as possible. I didn't know how long the lockkeeper would be out or if anyone had seen our little tussle, so I quickly crossed over the bridge and, deciding on the Boteler Ford crossing, walked down to the Potomac's eastern shore. I plummeted south along the bank hoping to discover Boteler's Ford.

I lurched along for about four hundred yards in a stupor with my head down looking for any hindrance to my passage. The sun had come up and a few feet of scattered fog had gathered on the river. For some reason, I stopped and looked across the river. There stood an old mill. From some of the descriptions I had read about the ford and the old mill that used to be on the Virginia side, I knew this was Boteler's Ford.

The river was down, and even though foggy, I could hear water rushing over rocks. I took off my brogans and socks, tied the brogans together with their laces, flung them over my shoulder and walked down into the river. The water acted as an elixir as it came up to my shins. The cool liquid had a calming effect on my body and being.

After several moments of enjoying the refreshing feeling, I began to gingerly walk across the river, testing each step for anything sharp.

About half way across I happened to look up river and saw something black in the water swimming toward me through the morning mist. It was a snake! I had just enough time to yell, really I screamed, and tried to run to the other side. As the snake slithered past my left leg on its way down river, my feet lost their tentative grip on the slick river bottom and went out from under me. I fell backwards with another yell. This time it really was a yell.

Well, I did two out of the three things you are supposed to do in a martial arts fall. I spread my arms out in a 45-degree angle and slapped them downward to break my fall. I also rolled my head toward my chest to keep my head from hitting the river bottom. However, I didn't relax my body and the water wasn't very deep where I fell, so it didn't provide much of a cushion. Subsequently, when my body simultaneously hit the rocky river bottom and I slapped my hands down to break my fall, my body suffered a severe jolt that felt like a surge of electricity from my hands to my shoulders and then down to my back. I almost passed out.

A few minutes later I finally gained some semblance of cognizance and I took an inventory of my body. My palms hurt and tingled, my shoulders were sore, my back ached and my neck was strained from bending it toward my chest and holding it there when I hit the river bottom.

I finally relaxed and really didn't care what that snake did next. I just let the water wash over me. The river water felt good. I looked to my left and my hat had come off, but it was caught on a wooden stake sticking straight up out of the water. I splashed over to it on my hands and knees and plucked it off its binding pole. Then I laid back down in the soothing Potomac. My brogans were on the bottom of the river, but my socks I could see in the distance drifting down stream. I had been holding them in my hand, but must have let them go when I fell.

I could feel the water soak into the homemade bandage I had wrapped around the dog bite. The wound was starting to hurt. I pulled my coat sleeve back to view the bite. It was really on my forearm just above my left wrist. I let the water soak the bandage. Then I gently removed it from my arm and kept the injured arm under the water until it began to sting. After a while, it quit stinging and just ached intermittently.

I stayed in the prone position in the river for a few more moments and let the soothing water flow over me. I finally got up on my knees, picked up my brogans and stood trembling on wobbly legs. As the water began to drip off my clothes into the river, I swear it made a brown dirty stain heading down stream.

The seriousness of my situation fell on me like an avalanche. I had to get to a place where I could sleep. I had to get new clothes. I had to get food. I had to get out of this river. The perils I faced precipitated another panic attack. My whole being took on a fight or flight urgency. I lurched toward the river bank.

About five feet from Old Dominion's shore my body began to go numb and I started to lose consciousness. I fell forward with half of me in the water and half of me on the bank. I looked up and with blurry eyes saw the mill I had spotted from the Maryland side of the river.

And that's when I blacked out.

Chapter 4

The Dark Mage's Log: Axeylon 5: Galaxy Date: 16314

Agent Jarlene stood at attention before Lord Dendaras, who sat on his throne, which was situated on a six-foot dais. "What did you find at the scene, Agent?" He questioned.

"I found Watcher Jarreal in a state of severe trauma." She answered.

"What did you do?" He continued.

"I put Jarreal in the conveyance vehicle and brought him back to home base," she said.

"You did nothing else?" demanded Lord Dendaras.

"No, Sire," she conveyed.

"Why not?" he challenged.

"The Watcher was in a critical state and the dawn was coming soon. I thought it best if I investigated after I had transferred Jarreal."

"That is an unacceptable explanation for your cause of action." Lord Dendaras bellowed. "Undoubtedly the human you were supposed to eradicate has had interchange with 'Earth 3' personnel by now and thus changed our calculations for the future. He needed to be exterminated quickly to salvage the situation. Your bungling of this affair is deplorable. You will present yourself to the Lower Dungeon for sentence."

Agent Jarlene bowed her head and said, "I plead for mercy Sire."

"We will see if that is available after the first round of punishment," he declared.

Agent Jarlene let out a sigh, bowed lower, clicked her heels, about faced, and left the throne room.

Lord Dendaras observed the back of the uniform. There were no stains. There was no fear in her.

☙

I woke to someone shouting, "Ovah herah, Papa. He's bad hurt."

Apparently, someone came to the speaker's summons because a moment later I felt myself being pulled out of the water. Then I blacked out again.

When I woke up, I was in a small bed. I tried, but I couldn't keep my eyes open. I drifted off into a fitful sleep.

Much later, it seemed, I woke to a faint breeze blowing over my face. The one window in the room was open. There wasn't any glass in the window. There were just two large shutters hinged with homemade pieces of leather that opened inward and rested flush with the inside wall. I heard birds singing, insects chirping and the flow of a river as a background melody.

I stirred and sat up. I discovered I was in a bed with a blanket over me. When I moved, the bed made weird sounds. I swung my feet out of bed and put them on the floor. I pulled back the blanket and found I was naked as a jaybird. I kept the blanket pulled around me and took inventory of my situation. My arm felt funny.

I pulled the blanket back to look at my left arm. There was a lump of some unknown substance tied to my left wrist with a long slender cloth.

I untied the cloth with my right hand and my teeth. A piece of green material fell out in my lap. It had been tied to my wrist where the dog had bitten me.

I looked at my wrist. It was still lacerated, but the cuts were starting to close and scab over. I picked up the green glob and examined it. I swear it looked like moss that grows on the north side of trees. I remembered an old John Wayne movie in which the doctor used tree moss to keep a wound from getting infected. The thing I remember most from this type of medicinal cure was not to scratch the wound when it started to heal.

Once I understood my body was on the mend, I began taking inventory of my surroundings.

The room must have measured about twelve feet by twelve feet. There were wooden pegs in the far wall with clothes hung on them. They looked like the pants, bracers and coat I had purloined in Maryland. Brogans were on the floor below the clothes. My modern underwear, hat and mutilated T-shirt were draped over my coat.

In the corner was a small table with a stool under it and a candleholder on top with a half-burnt candle.

I got to my feet and again heard a weird sound from the bed. I felt very unsteady. I was light-headed and had to sit down. Again, the bed made an unaccustomed sound. After a few moments, I stood up and again a funny sound emanated from the bed. Once I felt more stable, I knelt down on my knees and, dropping my head almost to the floor, looked under the bed. I don't know what I expected, but what I saw was a very long rope that started at the head of the bed and looped across the bed, back and forth until it reached the foot of the bed. Suddenly it dawned on me. I had been lying in a rope bed. Instead of slats to keep the mattress in the bed frame, a rope was used. I had slept on one of these types of beds years ago. I fondly remembered the noises that occurred whenever I made a movement of any kind.

I was able to stand without feeling nauseous. I dropped the blanket and stumbled toward the clothes pegs over a squeaky plank floor. I had just reached the pegs when the door opened and a young woman said, "Well, it's 'bout time ya got up."

My mouth dropped open as I looked at her. She looked familiar. She must have been the one who had been yelling for help as she tried to pull me out of the river just before I passed out.

I stood there with my mouth wide open and she started to laugh. I looked down and realized that I had dropped the blanket when I meandered toward the clothes. I was standing before her buck naked.

I beat a hasty retreat to the bed, grabbed the blanket and wrapped it around me. She just continued to laugh. Whether it was my predicament or my manly endowment, I couldn't be sure. She just said, "Food's ready when ya want it. Bettah get dressed afore ya come in tho." She turned and pulled the door to as she left the room snickering.

During my dressing process, I know I turned every shade of red thinking about what had just happened. However, the delicious aromas from the next room negated much of my embarrassment. After fumbling for what seemed like an hour, I finally got my bracers affixed to my trousers. Then I donned my 21st century underwear, slipped on my shirt, put on the trousers and, tucking the shirt in my trousers, buttoned up the trouser fly.

All the clothes that had been so filthy were now clean and sweet smelling.

I slipped the bracers over my shoulders and, as I was buttoning the top button of my shirt, rubbed the back of my hands against my neck. I felt whiskers. I quickly ran my hands over my face. I had a good four days' growth of beard. I needed a shave. So, I filed that information away for future reference.

I saw the hat I had almost lost in the Potomac on one of the pegs. I retrieved it and took a big whiff of the crown portion. I turned up my nose. It still had a gamey reek, but not as bad as it did on the Maryland side of the river. I replaced it on its peg. Lastly, I slipped on my brogans, sans socks, and tied the battered laces gently so as not to require adding another knot to the multitude already in place.

At long last, I opened the door and entered the next room.

This room was larger. It measured probably about fifteen by twenty feet. A large wooden rectangular table was situated in one side of the room with benches along its sides and arm chairs at both ends of the table. In the opposite corner of the room was a fireplace located on an outside wall with three iron rods affixed to the left side of the fireplace at different heights. The rods were on swivels that allowed them to be swung over the fire so that pots, small cans or buckets with bent half-moon metal handles could be hung on them for boiling food. There was also a large grate on the bottom of the fireplace floor that allowed skillets to be placed for cooking.

The young woman was spooning out eggs from a skillet into a metal plate when I entered the room. She looked up, chuckled, and motioned with her head toward the table. I walked over to the table bench closest to the wall, sat down, and leaned back against the wall. I felt rested, but not up to full strength. I watched her as she continued to spoon out victuals on the plate from a skillet, a Dutch oven and one of the cans hanging from a rod. How did I know her?

These thoughts were suddenly chased away by the wonderful aroma of country cooking. I didn't know I was hungry. In fact, I discovered I was ravenous. My stomach let out a deep-seated growl that I camouflaged with a cough.

The young woman walked forward with what I would call a "truck driver's plate" full of food. There were three eggs, sunny side up, two biscuits with what looked like sausage gravy and a thick ham steak.

She put the plate in front of me and said, "tha knives and tines are in tha cabinet," and motioned with her head to a six- foot tall wooden cupboard in the corner at the other side of the room.

I jumped up and walked quickly forward. I instigated an assault of the lower drawers until I found a knife and tine (her word for fork) that suited me. I traipsed to the table in a jiffy and dug into the food.

She brought over two steaming cups of coffee in tin mugs and placed them on the table. She pushed one toward me. Then she sat down on the bench opposite me, drank her coffee and watched me eat.

I literally attacked the food. I ate like a man who hadn't had a decent meal in years. After a while, she said, "Ya shore do use yar knife and tines queerly." I stopped with a fork full of ham about halfway to my mouth. It had caught me completely by surprise. You might say it was a slap in the face. It brought home to me how arrogantly I was treating this woman. She and her family had taken me in, nursed me back to health, and I hadn't even thanked her.

I sheepishly put down the fork full of ham on my plate and, ducking my head in shame, stammered, "I apologize for my crude manners. I must seem like a vagabond to ya. I haven't even thanked ya for saving my life. Please accept my deepest and sincere thanks for all ya done for me. Ma'am, I don't know how I'll ever repay you."

An awkward silence ensued. I was so embarrassed by my selfishness that I couldn't look her in the face. I know I turned red from ear to ear.

She kept her gaze on me and then said, "Apology accepted." Then she added without a judgmental tone to her voice, "Ya might want to know that ya was out about a day. And ya know something else that's different about ya? Ya speech is Southern sounding, but not from this part of tha South. Whar ya from?"

I took a chance and said, "Arkansas." She grinned then and said, "Well that's good. For a while I thought ya might be a Yankee Spy."

I grinned and said, "No how and no way am I a Yank. Nor do I adhere to their political persuasion."

She grinned and then declared without a bit of embarrassment, "Oh, yeah. And that thar underwear of your 'n is tha queerest I's ever witnessed."

I took another chance and responded, "They's a newfangled type from France. Just came up from Nawleans to Arkansas." She grinned again, but I couldn't tell if she believed me. I went back to eating, but at a slower pace and trying to push some of the food onto my knife and then transferring it to my mouth. This seemed to satisfy her. She continued to look at me as I ate. I felt self-conscious and didn't really look her in the eye. She seemed to be considering what I said and appraising me at the same time. I finally finished eating and began to drink my coffee.

I looked up at her and she grinned back at me. I had been leaning forward with my elbows on the table and the coffee cup in front of my face. I suddenly put the cup on the table and jerked upright as if a bolt of lightning had hit me.

In my mind I said, "Oh my Lord!"

☙

The Dark Mage's Log: Axeylon 5: Galaxy Date: 16314

There was a heart rending scream that signified a plea for pity which echoed from the lower regions of the Palace on Axeylon 5. Lord Dendaras looked skyward with closed eyes and a face displaying ecstasy as he savored the scream's fear and terror. Then he looked down on the recalled and trembling Jarbree and proclaimed, "You have disgraced the office of Watcher. How did you let an imposter travel in place of our contracted slayer? Answer me!"

Jarbree stuttered, "S-S-Sire, the slayer approached in his vehicle as instructed. He entered the woods as he had been directed. It was dark. I could only see his form and he had the same body shape as our slayer. Besides, no unauthorized entity has ever been transported before."

"Did you run the diagnostic check via the chip embedded in his arm as was protocol?" queried Lord Dendaras.

Jarbree turned white as a sheet. "I... huh... It was dark. I thought he was alright," he whined. Having thought of a new excuse, Jarbree reasoned, "Besides, Sire, he would have been checked on his arrival on 'Earth 3' by Jarreal."

Lord Dendaras rose from his throne with a horrific look on his face, pointed an accusing finger at the Watcher and bellowed, "You are a dishonor to the Watcher Guild. I will personally deal with you in the Lower Dungeon. Your agony will be prolonged for ages. Your screams will be audible to the populace as both a warning to all Watchers to follow protocol and as punishment for you."

Jarbree fell to his knees and gasped, "No Sire. Please. I promise it will never happen again. Have mercy!" Blood from his back pores was running in rivulets down his backside staining his uniform black.

Lord Dendaras averted his gaze from the almost prostrate figure and turned to his guards. With a sneer of abhorrence, the potentate rendered his verdict, "Take this pitiful excuse for a member of the Recognized Way to the dungeons to await my creative imagination for his punishment. As a precursor give him thirty infestations of scarabs."

"No, no, no," screamed Jarbree as the guards dragged him out of the throne room.

Lord Dendaras watched the exit with a mocking grin on his face, relishing the stained back of the Watcher's uniform.

☙

I realized this woman looked just like my Grandmother when she was a teenage girl in the few pictures I had of her in an old photo album back home.

I asked, "What's your name?"

She replied, "What's your 'n?"

I thought quickly and just pulling a name out of the air said, "James Hager."

Her eyes narrowed to slits as she ogled me closely. "I thought ya said ya weren't no Yankee Spy."

"I ain't", I said, reverting to what I call redneck Southern colloquial speech.

"Tha Hagers been known to be Unionist from up north in Hagerstown. Is that why youse in this area roaming about and getting yaself in such a shape that needed tending to? Did the Rebs get after ya and hurt ya?" she asked.

"No, no, no," I responded. "I don't know nothing 'bout no Hagers from Hagerstown. I came to Baltimore from Arkansas about a year ago and was teaching school." I took a chance on American history and added, "When all tha ruckus about Abe Lincoln's election came to tha fore, I determined to jine tha Confederates and lit out for Virginny. On my jaunt from Baltimore to Virginny I ran into a lot of trouble."

"First, my horse went lame and I had to sell him fur a lot less than what he was worth. Then I ran into Yanks coming up from tha south, probably Washington City, and had to go further north than I wanted to get past 'em. I guess all tha travel and worrying about getting stopped by tha Yanks got me under tha weather and I just broke down. So those're tha reasons, ya found me in such distress. And by tha way, as I remember, ya was a'pulling me out of tha water when I blacked out. Again, I want to thank ya for all tha help, for washing my clothes and for feeding me tha delicious victuals." I hoped my appreciations blunted her reservations about my impromptu story.

She eyed me for a few seconds and said, "It t'weren't nothing. My name's Hattie Gray by tha way."

Again, I nearly choked. That was my grandmother's maiden name. Her grandfather's family lived in Carrollton, Georgia during the Civil War and moved to Alabama after the war, but they definitely weren't from Virginia or from this area of Virginia, which became West Virginia in 1863. Her prior interrogation and her personal information had stopped me from trying to find out a vital piece of intelligence. What was today's date?

However, first I needed to make a proper greeting. I calmed my breathing and dutifully enunciated, "Hattie, I'm pleased to make yar acquaintance."

She smiled. I couldn't help but see she was missing a front tooth in her lower row of teeth.

Then I asked, "I've lost count of days. Could ya tell me which day it is?"

"Why it's tha 12th of September," she said.

"And just to make sure, what year?" I asked.

"Why 'tis 1862," she volunteered in a suspicious voice.

I looked down at the table for a moment and looking up I further probed, "Have therah been a lot of soldiers around herah over tha last few days?"

She eyed me for a long moment and then declared, "Nope." Then she questioned, "Ya sure ya didn't fall on yar head instead of a-getting' sick?"

I just chuckled and took another swig of coffee. I did the math in my head and realized Hattie was alive 38 years before she was supposed to be. My eyes must have glazed over in contemplation because I suddenly came to my senses and looked up. She was eyeballing me quizzically. So, I got hold of myself and asked, "What do I owe ya for taking such good care of me?"

That broke the awkward silence and she responded, "Ya had a good amount of cash on ya, when ya came into our care. It's in your coat on tha clothes peg in tha bedroom. I leave it up to ya."

It surprised me that the money I had kept with me wasn't considered worthless or counterfeit. I thought I would have to trade manual labor for anything I owed her. I replied, "I can't remember tha amount I had. I bettah recount it."

I got up and headed for the bedroom. I pulled my coat off the peg and pulled the money out of the pocket. The cache consisted of ten faded $20 bills, a $5 bill and five $1 bills along with my wedding ring. However, the real kicker was they weren't the kind of U.S. Treasury bills with which I was familiar. They were U.S. Treasury bills that had to be compatible with the currency of the 1860's because Hattie had referred to there being a good amount of cash on me when they found me. The scary factor was that these bills were totally different from the currency I had before I was conveyed here.

I just stood there for a few moments in a quandary as unanswerable questions again invaded my mind, "Why did my money change to the currency of this time period, but not my clothes? Who was orchestrating this whole experience? Can I get back to my time period?"

I walked over and sat down on the edge of the bed and put my head in my hands. I just sat there for a minute trying to figure things out and getting nowhere.

Hattie stuck her head in the door and said, "It's all thar, ain't it?"

I looked up, smiled and said," I had no doubts 'bout that." I had a sudden inspiration and asked, "Do y'all rent out rooms?"

She answered, "Not usually, but that thar room ain't being used at this time and we could stand tha money."

I asked, "Would ya rent it to me for a month, while I get back on my feet?" She answered, "Yeah, I guess we can."

"Would ten dollars for tha month including breakfast and dinner plus fixing my clothes be okay?" I offered.

"Yeah, I reckon that'd do me okay," she said. I handed her the five-dollar bill and five one dollar bills. She thanked me and turned to go.

I had another thought and said, "Ya keep referring to 'we' all tha time. Who's we?"

"Me, Papa, my brothers, A.B. and C.D., plus my sisters, Jewel and Poppie," she declared.

"Are all of ya located in this house?" I asked.

"Nope. Me, Papa and my brothers live in tha other two cabins out back. My sisters are married and scattered around tha area, "she volunteered.

"Where's your Papa and brothers?" I inquired.

"They'd be at tha mill grinding corn for meal. I hope that's all yar questions. I done spent a heap of time yakking with ya. I need to get some chores done. Why don't ya go for a walk and get some of yar strength back. The town's just about a half mile that away." She pointed northwest. "And by tha way, ya mentioned you's a teacher. The old scrawny teacher we had done got run off by some of tha mean boys in his class. So, there might be a job open fur ya."

"Okay, who's tha person I need to talk to about tha teaching job?" I asked.

She volunteered, "T'would be tha bank president, Mr. Throckmorton. He's sort of tha hiring and firing high mucky muck for tha school. He's located in tha town bank. Ya can't miss it. It's on German Street and close to tha edge of town nearest to us."

"Well, I better get fully dressed and see what will transpire," I said. I started to go, but turned back and asked, "Oh yeah, do ya have a razor I could use? If'n I'm gonna interview for a job, I need to look my best," I explained.

She looked at me and replied, "Yep, Papa's gotta straight razor and foaming soap. He and my brothers don't use it much, but yar welcome to it."

I looked at her in shock. I had once again forgotten what time period I was in. Years ago, as a teenager I had tried to shave with a straight razor and nearly cut my face to shreds.

"What's a'matter? Ya look green around tha gills," she diagnosed.

"Nothing," I maintained. "Does he have a razor strop and mirror too?" I asked.

"Yep, I'll get all tha shaving kit together along with some hot water in a pan for ya. Ya can take it out back. There's a stump next to tha barn with a nail in tha barn wall. Ya can loop tha wire on tha back of tha mirror over tha nail to see whatcha doing and put all your shaving gear on tha stump," she answered.

"Thanks Hattie," I replied.

I retreated to my room and contemplated the fate of what was about to happen to my facial features. I was not looking forward to this ghastly procedure.

Hattie yelled, "It's a'ready. Better come and get this done while tha water's hot." I walked into the big dining room/kitchen like a man going to the gallows.

Hattie took one look at me and uttered, "What's wrong wit cha?"

"Nothin'," I retorted. I draped the strop and a small rag over my left arm, picked up the soap dish with the bristle brush in my left hand and the razor in my right hand. Then I tried to pick up the hot water pan while holding all the gear, but couldn't manage all the paraphernalia at once. Hattie had to end up carrying the hot water pan to the stump for me while I carted all the other shaving gear.

When she set down the pan, she looked at me and declared, "Jim Hager, ya are one troublesome gent." Then she left me to my fate.

With a sigh, I slipped my bracers over my shoulders and removed my shirt, which I put on a fence post near the barn. Then, I surveyed the situation and determined that I needed the razor to be ultra-sharp for my four-day beard. So, I fit the hole in the handle of the razor strop over the nail in the barn wall, and holding the end of the strop in my left hand, I began to slide one side of the razor up the strop and then switching sides sliding it down the strop with my right hand. I even got a decent rhythm going. In fact, I got so enmeshed in sliding the razor up and down that I got it too close to my left hand and cut my thumb. It wasn't a bad cut, but it took me awhile and the use of the small rag to stop the bleeding.

Putting some water in the shaving foam dish and jostling the brush around until a good lather was built up, I was ready to try my hand at 19th century shaving. So, I took down the razor strop and laid it over the stump and put the mirror on the nail via the wire. Next, I applied enough lather on the right side of my face from the ear down to my jawline to completely saturate the beard. Remembering the configuration of a razor, which was like a jack knife, with the first four fingers of my right hand, I picked up the weapon on the dull back side of the razor blade and pulled the handle away from the razor with my left hand. I positioned the razor in my right hand with the handle at a ninety-degree angle from the back of the razor with my pinkie holding the handle open so it couldn't close. Looking in the mirror, I gently placed the razor at a forty-five-degree angle to my beard on the right side of my face at ear lobe level and began a downward movement toward the jaw line.

The razor moved like a hot knife going through butter. I couldn't believe it. I was elated. I immersed the razor in the hot water to remove any leftover beard or soap. I again lathered up and performed the same ritual working my way toward my nose. At the last moment, I decided to keep a mustache so I didn't shave my upper lip. I shaved my lower lip down to my chin and only cut myself once in the process. Then came the really hard part, I had to turn to show the left side of my face and work the razor across my body while looking one-eyed into the small mirror. I did okay from the ear to the jaw, but I cut my chin again when I attempted to further remove whiskers from this troublesome facial area.

Thence, I decided I needed the razor to be sharpened again. So, I put the razor strop over the mirror on the nail, performed the sliding up and down of the razor on the strop and disengaged the strop from the nail. Lastly, I applied lather across my neck area and shaved downward from the jawline. I did okay until I came to a small mole that sat above the skin on the right side of my neck. I lacerated it pretty good, and I bled like a stuck hog.

I completely saturated the small rag in blood before I finally staunched the bleeding. I did a survey of the battlefield that was my face and did a quick redo of some facial parts that needed further attention. Finally, I decided that enough was enough.

However, looking in the mirror I saw a different person staring back at me. Who was this thirty-something person? My hair had always been a sort of dishwater blonde color, but it had been invaded by the color white over the years. Now it was back to the color it was when I was a young whippersnapper. The mustache was red, which it had been in my youth. I looked down at the remnants of the beard in the water pan and they were red also. I hadn't even noticed these changes due to my inane fear of shaving. In addition to changes in the hair and beard color, a lot of my facial wrinkles were gone along with the turkey gobbler skin under my chin.

My money had changed physically and so had I during the transfer here. I tried to understand the implications. Questions raced through my mind, "Why had this happened to me? Was it because of Karma? What was that Sphere? Where did it come from? Can I get back to my time?" I was starting to get a headache and decided to just drop my interrogation of the Powers That Be for the moment.

I threw out the water in the pan, put on my shirt, resituated my bracers and walked back to the house. Once in the house, I gave the shaving kit to Hattie. She took one look at the blood soaked rag and glanced at my face. "Your neck's still oozing some blood," she pronounced. "Wait herah," she ordered and fetched another rag from a drawer in the tall dish cabinet. Putting a dab of bacon grease on the rag, she gently applied it to the lacerated mole on my neck. I winced because it burned like fire for a moment and then gratefully settled into a dull ache. "Therah. That ought to do it," she decided.

"Again, I am in yar debt," I declared. She grinned from ear to ear.

I retreated to my room and put on my coat. I walked back to where Hattie was scrubbing breakfast pots and pans and asked, "How do I look?" She looked me up and down. Then she declared, "Ya look adequate."

Disappointedly I asked, "Just adequate?"

She nodded, turned back to her cleaning and said, "Yep, adequate."

I left in a huff leaving my weathered hat behind.

I took my time on the walk to town enjoying the sights and sounds of nature. The day was warming up and the trees were just starting to turn colorful for the fall. The bees were buzzing. The birds were chirping. Butterflies were flittering everywhere. I hadn't felt this good in a long time. The country dirt road led upward from the Potomac to higher ground and turned north. I followed it to town with the idea of getting some clothing that made me look better than just adequate.

I reached town in about forty-five minutes. As I said, I took my time and enjoyed the day. The road I had been traversing contained residential homes. But once I got close to town, the residential area stopped and different types of business shops occupied both sides of the main street. The business area even had wooden sidewalks in front of some of the shops. This had to be German Street, but the pockmarked dirt street was a far cry from the paved road and concrete sidewalks of the 21st Century. I saw the bank Hattie had mentioned on the right side of the main street. In my time the bank had been converted into a restaurant.

However, I didn't stop. I crossed to the left side of the road and began to look in the shops' windows, hoping one of them had some decent clothes for sale.

The street sloped upward for about three blocks to an intersection I could see in the distance. Men and women were walking up and down the thoroughfare utilizing the sidewalks where available. The back and forth street traffic also consisted of a few men on horses kicking up dust from the dry road bed, as well as a few carriages with men and women occupants.

I nodded at a few people on the sidewalk and got a few odd looks, probably because I didn't have a hat. On the second block of my window shopping, I happened to see some hats and work clothes through the window of a hardware shop. So, I entered for a better look.

There was a young clerk behind the counter who ignored me for a while as I milled around looking at the clothes and hats that were piled on a table and a few shelves. I pulled out some black wool trousers and a black coat from a pile on one of the shelves. I put the trousers up next to my waist to see if they possibly fit. They didn't drag the floor so that was good. I tried on the coat and it fit me like a glove. I also found a blue checkered shirt and held it up to my shoulders. It was a little big, but I didn't know if it would shrink with washing, so I kept it. Next, I found a wide brim black felt hat like the ones we wore for Civil War reenacting. This reminded me. Shouldn't there be Union forces coming this way for the Battle of Antietam? I tucked this question away for the time being.

Absentmindedly, while my thoughts had drifted to the Civil War, I had pulled out a twenty dollar bill and handed it to the clerk to pay for the clothes. The clerk's exclamation brought me back to the present.

"I ain't got change for this much money, mister. I'll have to go to tha bank," he complained.

"Take your time young fellow. I'll watch tha store for ya til ya get back," I promised.

He gave me an uncertain look. So, I added, "Don't cha worry, young fellow. I won't steal nothing. I aim to buy these herah clothes. I need to make a good impression for a job interview today."

He sighed and, taking a chance I wasn't a thief, went down to the bank. It didn't take him too long to return with the needed cash for my transaction. It was good to know that my money was good in this part of the country. It cost me two dollars and fifty cents for the coat, two dollars for the trousers, seventy five cents for the shirt and one dollar for the hat. Once I got the change, I asked, "Do ya have a room in tha back that I could change out of my old clothes into tha new ones?"

He looked at me rather strangely, but offered, "There's an empty office on tha second floor ya could use."

I nodded, took my new wardrobe upstairs and hastily changed into the apparel utilizing the bracers off my old trousers. The only problem was my feet were getting chaffed by my brogans, since I didn't have any socks. I really didn't want to get debilitating blisters.

I descended the stairs and viewed myself in a silver plated full length mirror that was in the back of the store. I didn't look half bad, which meant I didn't look but half good either. My clothing really made me look like an Amish man that you would see in a National Geographic magazine. Again, I was amazed at the physical transformation I had experienced. I got close to the mirror and looked at my face again. I still looked like I did in my thirties. Next, I viewed my shoulders and swore they were broader, which they must have been when I was younger. All I could do was shake my head at the anomalies that had occurred.

My feet suddenly called out for some relief. The brogans were rubbing them raw. So, I went looking for some socks on the clothes tables and found three pairs of knitted white socks with red piping around the tops. They were twenty five cents a pair. So, I bought two pair. I pulled off my shoes and slipped on the socks. My feet said, "Thank you."

The last bit of wardrobe that I needed was footwear. I walked around in my socks looking for boots or brogans. The store happened to have a whole shelf stocked with boots. I pulled a pair down and tried them on, but I couldn't get either boot on due to my high instep. I worked my way down the shelf until I found a pair of black boots that I could get on without too much effort. Once I stomped my feet down into the tunnels of leather, I went to look at my selection in the store mirror. For once, they didn't look like clown's shoes on my feet. The price of the bright shiny boots was twenty dollars, which I readily paid.

I continued to look at the various items for sale until I got an urgent call from Mother Nature. So, I quickly sought out the clerk and probed, "Is there a toilet in the area?"

With an exasperated glance out the back of the store he stated, "Thar's an outhouse out tha back, to tha left and down tha alley."

"May I leave my old bundle of clothes herah for a moment?" I begged.

He gave me a curt nod. So, out the back door I went like a cannon shot. I followed the proverbial path to the famed edifice that we all made fun of when I was a kid. Years ago in my youth at deer camp and during a few months in Viet Nam, I had used an outhouse so I wasn't totally grossed out by the smell.

However, I didn't know what I would use as toilet paper, when I entered the odorous abode. I took off my coat and hung it on a peg in the door. The single hole in the wooden plank bench utilized as a toilet seat wasn't as filthy as I imagined it would be. So, I unbuttoned and dropped my trousers and did my business. When looking around for something with which to clean up, I spied an old newspaper someone had left. I reached for it to use as toilet paper. However, the headline of the newspaper caught my attention. "Confederate President Jefferson Davis meets with the Army Leaders in the Confederate Capital in Atlanta."

଼

The Dark Mage's Log: Axeylon 5: Galaxy Date: 16314

Lord Dendaras scowled down in exasperation on two new Watchers. He had religiously studied their background via the Eternal Oracle. They both had presided in over fifty transferences without any problems. Jargunn was to take over the mission for the still comatose Jarreal and Jardean was to take over for Jarbree, whose muffled

soul-wrenching screams could be heard from the depths of the alien ship.

Looking at Jardean, Lord Dendaras ordered, "You will proceed to 'Earth 9' and take over Jarbree's mission. Your slayer has been put in a deep sleep at the coordinates issued until you arrive. Complete the mission and get him back to 'Earth 3'."

Lord Dendaras cocked his head, closed his eyes and listened to the ghastly screams coming from the innards of Axeylon 5. He opened his eyes and smirked, "I don't have to remind you of the consequences for failure, do I?"

Jardean gulped and stammered, "No Sire."

Looking at Jargunn, Lord Dendaras instructed, "You must find the imposter and see the extent of his interchange with the local inhabitants of 'Earth 3'. We must know how much of their history he has infected so we can repair or possibly reconstruct it after his demise. But first we must know about his interchanges with the local inhabitants.

Search for him only at night. You will understand why that is preferable once you are planetside."

"Yes, Sire." Jargunn responded respectfully.

Waving his hand in dismissal, Lord Dendaras commanded, "Go!"

The two Watchers bowed, clicked their heels, about faced in unison and marched out of the throne room.

☙

I gasped as I read the headline and felt a rush of heat start at the top of my head and go to the bottom of my feet. "This is ludicrous. It's impossible. I needed to read this article, but not here," I said to no one in particular.

I quickly utilized the back pages of the paper, which I hoped didn't have continuations of the story on the front page, for cleaning up. I got my wardrobe back on, stuffed the paper in the top of my trousers, covered the paper with my coat and proceeded through the back door of the hardware store.

As I reentered the store, I had another thought. I wondered what time it was and if I had enough time to make it to the bank before it closed. So, I asked the hardware store clerk if he had any pocket watches for sale. He said he didn't, but indicated the Apothecary at the end of the block and cattycornered from the bank might have some. I asked him what time it was and he said he didn't know. He didn't have a watch. I thanked him, picked up my old bundle of clothes and hurried out.

I walked to the end of the block doffing my hat to every lady or couple I met on the way. The men touched the brims of their hats in response. So, I knew I was performing the correct cultural greetings for this century.

I entered the Apothecary and was immediately struck dumb. I had seen so many old pictures of the insides of these establishments, but to be in one for real was amazing. I slowly walked along the glass counters on one side of the room viewing all the remarkable items for sale. There were medicines of every description in small bottles with larger medicine jars on shelves behind the counter. On the far side of the room, there was an elaborate wooden wall of shelving with drawers from the floor to about waist high that were filled with packets of medicines for daily use.

From the waist to almost the ceiling, there was shelving with medicinal products for sale in bulk. At what I will describe as the checkout counter, there were various jars of hard candy, such as peppermint sticks. Making a few covert glances toward the three men behind the counters as I made my cursory inspection of the store, I comprehended I was being sized up as a trophy by the predatory salesmen. They all converged on me like sharks smelling blood in the water when I finally asked, "Do ya have any pocket watches for sale?"

One of the clerks produced a watch from under a counter and declared, "This is tha only one we got left."

I thought, "Either there had been a run on pocket watches, or there wasn't much demand for a time piece in this part of Virginia." I asked, "May I see tha merchandise?" The clerk passed it to me with such care that you would have thought it was a Rolex. I inspected the front and back meticulously and then asked the age old question, "How much?"

Another of the clerks, who seemed to be the head honcho, quickly responded, "That would be three dollars."

Apparently, this bunch thought they had the last pocket watch on earth. "I'm shocked," I reacted and began to leave the store. The head clerk quickly recovered, "But since ya look like a nice gentleman, we could let it go for two dollars."

I turned back, smiled pleadingly and lamented, "I only have budgeted one dollar for such a luxury, but I have just moved into tha area and have plans of residing here so I know I will be a good customer in tha future."

The clerk put his hand up to his chin as if to contemplate what I had promised. He finally looked at the other two clerks and, nodding his head, which they immediately imitated, conceded, "Well, in that case, I guess we can let it go for one dollar."

I quickly whipped out a dollar bill and the transaction was complete. As I took possession of the timepiece, I asked, "What time is it?" The head clerk produced his own watch and I set the time on my new 19th century pocket watch.

Then on a lark I asked to see a bottle of tincture of iodine. The clerks were very solicitous because they wanted to make a more profitable sale than one dollar. I took the pro-offered bottle and read the small print on the bottle quite readily. I didn't need glasses anymore.

Where I came from, I needed glasses with 1.75 magnification lens to read any small print. My body had definitely changed in more ways than one. I thanked the disappointed salesmen and started to leave the apothecary when I spied a toothbrush and what appeared to be a tin can of tooth powder incased in a glass medicine cabinet. I hadn't seen tooth powder since I was a kid back in the early 1950's. I asked, "How much for tha brush and powder?"

The head clerk, allowing no further negotiation, demanded, "One dollar!"

I thought this was a rip off, but I grudgingly paid and added the dental hygienic articles to my burgeoning baggage.

I left the Apothecary and stopped on the sidewalk to inspect the dental objects. The toothbrush was just like the one I had bought for Civil War reenacting. The bristles were quite hard and took up about two inches of the nine-inch instrument. I read the label on the powder tin, but didn't know enough about chemicals to understand what the ingredients were. I wrapped the items in the old clothes and put the roll under my arm.

The day was warm and I had put off reading the disconcerting newspaper article long enough. So, I strode a few blocks toward the Potomac River, which was northeast of German Street, the main thoroughfare of Shepherdstown. In comparison with the 21st century, the streets were lined with homes and not Shepherd University, which occupied this area in my time. I couldn't find a town park that had benches so I meandered back to German Street and roamed it until I found a small café located almost at the main intersection at the top of the hill on the west side of town.

I entered the establishment, sat at a small table, put my bundle of clothes in an adjacent chair and ordered a cup of coffee plus some bread and cheese. Once I received the order, I pulled out the newspaper and opened it to the front page. It was the Richmond Enquirer. Evidently, this was the main newspaper for this region of Virginia.

As per the headline I had previously read, Confederate President Jeff Davis had called a meeting of his Generals. The article said this was supposed to be a secret conference, but somehow the newspaper had found out about it. It listed the Generals that had been seen going into the meeting: General Robert E. Lee, General Joe Johnston, General Thomas Jackson, and General Albert Sidney Johnston. The last name made me utter a gasp and I almost dropped the cup of coffee I was raising to my mouth. I sat the cup down with a bang and spilt coffee on the table.

The lady behind the counter looked up with a start and asked," Is anything wrong?"

"No, I'm sorry. I just had a little mishap with tha coffee saucer," I apologized. She came over immediately and cleaned up the puddle of coffee. I gave her an 'I'm sorry to have caused a mess' look, which drew a chastising stare as she trooped back behind the counter.

I sat there almost reeling. I had vertigo so bad that I had to grip the table with both hands to keep my equilibrium. Albert Sidney Johnston was killed at Shiloh on April 6, 1862. But here it was September 12, 1862 and he had been reported alive on September 7th, which was when this paper was printed. Also, the Confederate capital was in Atlanta, Georgia and not Richmond, Virginia. Lastly, there was no mention of Robert E. Lee being in charge of the Army of Northern Virginia. He was supposed to have taken over the Confederate Army in Virginia in June of 1862, named it the Army of Northern Virginia, run Union General McClellan off the Virginia Peninsula and beat the Union Army at Second Manassas. Also, various portions of his army should be marching north to Hagerstown, Maryland, on the move to attack Harpers Ferry and guarding the South Mountain passes west of here at this very moment. But apparently the historical events hadn't happened that way.

"What is going on?" my inner voice demanded. I was sweating profusely in my new clothes. My heart was pounding. I had to get out of this enclosed space and get some air. I hurriedly asked what I owed, which was five cents. I left the money on the table, put my uneaten bread and cheese in my coat pocket and hurried out the door.

I walked up German Street to the main intersection at the top of the hill. There was nothing much on the other side of the junction, except the west side of town. If I continued west over the crossroad, I would ultimately come to Martinsburg, Virginia. Instead, I turned left and traveled south toward Kearnysville. After a few minutes of stopping and starting, I got my breathing and heart rate under control. Finally, I asked out loud, "What is going on?"

I had progressed on the dirt road to where a small cemetery was located off the beaten path to the right. I stopped and surveyed the tranquility of the graveyard. I was definitely in the mood for peacefulness so I unlatched the iron entrance gate and sauntered through the burial grounds to a big oak tree in the back of the cemetery. I laid my old clothes on a patch of dry green grass and sat down. I put the rest of my paraphernalia on the ground beside me. Then, I put my head in my hands and took stock of all that had happened.

One, I had gotten thrown back in time and not of my own accord.

Two, the general area in which I entered this time frame was the same general area I had been in before the time travel took place.

Three, my wrist watch had stopped.

Four, my money had changed to the money acceptable in this time period.

Five, my grandmother had shown up here in Virginia instead of Alabama. I pegged her age at eighteen in this time frame. She had actually turned eighteen in 1918. Therefore, she had shown up three generations before she should have on this earth and one thousand miles north of Alabaster, Alabama, which was her hometown.

Six, the big problem was the history here was completely different from the 1862 history I had known.

Seven, the only good thing about this exile is that I was younger. I had no idea how much younger, but I was definitely younger.

I kept saying to myself, "How can this be? It doesn't make any sense. Have I lost my mind? Have I been hurt and in a coma dreaming all this? Why did that Orb or Sphere or whatever you want to call it put me in this vulgar parody of the 19th century? For that matter, who in blue blazes operated that Sphere?"

The big question is, "Did I kill that man that appeared out of the gloom when I arrived here? I have never killed anyone in my life. I didn't mean to hit him. However, he shouldn't have jumped out at me like that. Also, what was it that he said?"

Oh, I remember, "Did you have an enjoyable trip? No, that wasn't it. Did you have an entertaining trip? Yes, that was it. He must have been waiting on me. Was this some sort of alien abduction? If they find his body, can they track it to me? I doubt it. The 19th century doesn't have advanced forensics. But wait! If the drunk, whose clothes I stole, finds my buried clothes and learns that I suddenly showed up here in Shepherdstown, he might be able to track me down."

"What have I really, really gotten myself into? It's got to be some kind of a time warp. I don't want to live in another age. I like it in the 21st century. I love my wife. I love my house, car and job. I love my life."

After I had spent some time wallowing in self-pity and asking myself unanswerable questions, I shouted, "Enough," and leaned back against the tree. I wiped the tears from my face and closed my eyes. Utilizing a Taoist embryonic breathing technique, I slowly inhaled and exhaled the clean air for a number of minutes.

Feeling rested, I opened my eyes and looked up at the beautiful yellow and orange leaves above me. Turning to the surrounding terrain, I beheld the beautiful green grass of the cemetery around me. I observed the trees and unique houses on the other side of the road. It was such a serene landscape.

I had passed only two wagons moving toward town, when I set out down his road. There were no vehicles moving in the immediate area now. It was quiet and all you could hear were the calls of birds and buzzing of insects making their presence known. Occasionally a cow would make a sound in the distance.

Then out of the blue it hit me. A long time ago I had seen a science fiction movie starring Bruce Willis with a unique premise. I couldn't quite pull the complete concept out of my memory bank. It was at the edge of my consciousness or you might say on the tip of my tongue. Then it emerged full blown in my mind: Parallel Universes.

I said it out loud, "Parallel Universes."

That had to be it. That was why all the history was different, but the customs were the same. I immediately felt better, but then another load of questions jumped into my mind, "What about the Sphere? How did that figure into the equation? Why was the Sphere moving to a parallel universe?"

Again my mind couldn't comprehend what the Sphere signified and how it operated. Finally, I literally threw up my hands and said out loud, "Getting the answer to one of the big questions is enough for today."

I must have been there for what I estimated to be about thirty minutes. I pulled my watch from my trousers' pocket and saw it was 2:30 p.m. Then I thought, "Besides, I have to see about getting an appointment with the banker who has a big say in hiring a school teacher."

Letting out a groan, I got up from my perch under the big oak and dusted off my britches. I gathered up my bundle of old clothes and started to walk toward the cemetery gates.

I heard a clink and looked down to find that the toothbrush and tooth powder tin had fallen out of my roll of clothes. I stooped and picked up the articles and then thought, "Now is as good a time as any to try them out." I brushed a leaf off the toothbrush and put it in my mouth. I uncapped the powder tin and jiggled the tin until there was a good supply of powder in my palm. I pulled the brush out of my mouth and jabbed the bristles into the powder. A lot of the powder stuck to the bristles due to the wetness of the saliva. I quickly put the brush in my mouth and began the ancient up and down motion we were all taught as children.

The sweet taste of peppermint erupted in my mouth and I gurgled my appreciation. Once I had finished my dental hygiene for the day, I expectorated the excess foam and put the articles back in my clothes roll. Then, I proceeded through cemetery gates and turned left.

As I ambled along, I listened to the sounds of the land. I could hear chickens clucking in some backyard coops. There was a multitude of robins and blue jays flying around making all kinds of calls. The sun was at my back and the warmth felt good, but it was just starting to get a little hot due to my black clothing absorbing the heat.

I made it back to the main intersection that I had encountered just a few minutes ago. I turned right, which was eastward, and walked three blocks to the bank.

It was an imposing two story structure with an outside brick wall sporting beautiful lead inlaid glass doors for an entrance. I entered, went to a teller's window, which was behind a proverbial barred opening, and asked to see the bank president. The teller looked me up and down and, due no doubt to the new clothes and boots, probably thought I might be of some importance.

He asked my name and raised his eyebrows when I said James Hager. Apparently, the name had some clout in the area. He quickly excused himself and went through a door behind the tellers' counter. He continued to the back of the building and entered a room which I determined to be the bank president's office.

He came back in just a few seconds and said, "Mr. Throckmorton will see you now."

I moved to the side of the teller windows to a swinging wood entry gate about waist high that led to the area behind the counter. I took my time and looked at all the elaborate interior woodwork. You definitely don't see this type of workmanship anymore. As I passed through the swinging gate into the Holy of Holy's, I looked for the huge metal vault that I knew must exist in a 19th century bank, and sure enough, there it was at the back of the room. Its two-foot thick door stood wide open showing all the integral and complicated locking mechanisms.

I took off my hat and entered the lair of the archetypical robber baron of the 19th century, the town banker.

Mr. Throckmorton rose from behind his desk and came forward with his hand extended and introduced himself, "Hello, Mr. Hager. I am Elias Throckmorton."

As we shook hands, it was all I could do to keep from laughing. If ever a person was the epitome of what I pictured an old-timey banker would look like, Mr. Throckmorton fit the bill. He was about five foot, three inches tall, weighed about one hundred twenty pounds dripping wet and was dressed in a black linen suit with a white high-collar shirt decorated with a red bow tie. He was bald on top with a three-inch band of hair starting over his left ear and traversing the back of his head to end up over his right ear. Sweat glistened on top of his bald head, which he mopped with a white handkerchief as he moved back to the leather swivel chair behind his desk.

After seating himself and motioning me to a chair before his desk, he inquired, "What may I do for ya this fine day?"

I countered, "I would like to make a deposit of one hundred forty dollars."

He smiled with great delight revealing yellow teeth with enough gaps to remind me of a crocodile getting ready to attack his prey along some African river. He immediately called, "Mr. Eldredge, please come herah for a moment." The teller with whom I had originally spoken entered the office. Mr. Throckmorton gestured toward me and directed, "Please open a new account for Mr. Hager and deposit his cash."

Mr. Eldredge turned to me and I counted out one hundred forty dollars in specie. I looked up and saw the questioning look and raised eyebrows on his face. It was as if he wanted to ask, "How did someone such as you come to possess this amount of money?"

I handed him the money and smiled as if to say, "None of your business."

He frowned and left the room to prepare my bank account book.

I then broached the subject that was foremost on my mind, "Mr. Throckmorton, I have another matter I wish to discuss. I have just taken rooms in tha area and learned that tha local school teacher's job was vacant. I have held similar positions and would like to be considered for tha job." This took him by surprise and he just stared at me for a moment. He was weighing the idea plus the one hundred forty dollars I had just deposited and could withdraw at a moment's notice.

He came to a decision, leaned back in his chair, entwined his fingers across his stomach and asked, "What background do ya have in teaching?"

"I have taught school for five years," I lied.

"Where?" he asked.

"Little Rock, Arkansas and Baltimore, Maryland," I answered.

He smirked at the mention of the first city I named, but perked up at the second. This quickly led to, "How many students were in yar schools?" he cross-examined.

"Ten to fifteen, depending on tha time of tha year," I responded.

"You know some of the children in our school aren't really children. There are two boys in their late teens that get sent to school by their father each year after harvesting and fall planting to learn their letters and some 'rithmatic. He wants 'em to take over his farm and small mercantile operation when he passes away. His boys have been real stubborn and refused to learn what they need to know to carry on tha business. In fact, they've run off tha last two school teachers. Are ya still interested in tha job?" he quizzed.

"I'll have a go at it. What does it pay?" I asked.

"That's up to tha teacher, but tha last teacher charged $2.00 per pupil for six months of schooling," he replied.

"Is therah a list of tha parents with children who attended tha last school term?" I questioned.

"Yes, I can supply you such a list. Do you want tha job?" he inquired with a note of nervousness in his voice.

"Yes, I'll take tha job," I affirmed.

We shook hands and he breathed a sigh of relief. He grinned at me like the Cheshire Cat. I immediately knew something was amiss.

Mr. Throckmorton asked Mr. Eldredge to bring a list of the attendees of the school's last term. Mr. Eldredge readily supplied him a list, which he presented to me. It included the names of the parents that had previously enrolled their children in the Shepherdstown Day School, as it was referred to by Mr. Throckmorton, as well as their names and ages.

I use the word children very loosely. There were 15 names and they were listed as follows:

Janie Mumma-13
Jimmy Poffenberger-12
Jenny Williams-10
Jeremy Sage-16
Jonah Sage-17
Wilfred Throckmorton-11
Paul Piper-14
Peggy Newcomer-17
Deborah Miller-16
Esther Line-14
James Clipp-14
Ruth Pry-16
Maryanne Mercer-17
William Douglas-12
Wayne Coffman-15

After contemplating the names, I questioned," Where can tha families be found?"

He replied, "Don't worry about that right now. All tha children are helping their folks 'bringing in tha sheaves'." He smiled at his effort at levity and I smiled too. "The children won't be available until tha first week of October when harvesting is done," he added.

I remembered the maturing fields of corn along the road on my fateful slog from Maryland to Virginia. I wanted to ask if the young ladies would be out in the fields along with the boys, but thought better than to be facetious with my employer on the first day of the job.

Throckmorton further elucidated, "You can ask anyone in town as to tha locations of tha families, but it would be bettah to wait closer to October to begin contacting them. I will put out tha word that therah is a new experienced teacher for tha Day School and you can count on my son, Wilfred, to be yar first pupil."

I thanked him profusely, shook his sweaty hand, and as I was leaving, stopped at Mr. Eldredge's desk and picked up my account book.

My name was written in perfect calligraphy at the top of the bank book. A one hundred forty-dollar deposit was listed in the transaction space with today's date stamped in the margin. I remembered the first bank book I had received back in the 1950s at the ripe old age of six. This bank book looked exactly like that one.

With a dubious teaching job lined up, I decided to head for my humble dwellings on the river.

If I was going to be a teacher, I needed to know what had happened in the Civil War in this universe. The newspaper article I read had very little information and speculated only that something was afoot. That's when it hit me. Newspaper! I could go to the local newspaper office and hopefully they had back issues that I could read to catch up on the history of this place.

I took my time going back to my room at the mill. Thinking things over, I had accomplished a lot.

First, I had probably deciphered the riddle of where I was: a parallel universe.

Two, I had procured a job, not an easy feat for a stranger in a strange land.

Three, I had a plan in mind for learning about this time period. I definitely felt satisfied about my day's activities.

However, I think I had exceeded the little bit of strength I had built up. By the time I arrived at the mill, I was very fatigued. I went straight to bed without my supper.

Chapter 5

The Dark Mage's Log: 'Earth 3' Date: 18620915

Jargunn landed in the East Woods at midnight on the second night after the imposter had been transferred to this spot. He willed his Astral Conveyance Vehicle (ACV) back into orbit in the stealth mode to await his summons.

Jargunn hated this assignment. It was really beneath his dignity and position in the Watcher's Guild. To add insult to injury, Lord Dendaras had commanded him to search only at night for the imposter.

"Why?" he asked himself. "Probably because it wouldn't be appropriate to have a "Scent Droid" rummaging around the countryside in full view of the populace during the day. That makes sense," he answered. Continuing his thoughts, "But why couldn't I disguise myself and live on 'Earth 3' until I found the imposter? I really don't know the answer to that last question. However, Lord Dendaras did hint at a possible answer to that query."

Before traveling to 'Earth 3', Jargunn had inspected the Sphere that had transported the imposter. It had not been employed in other transferences since then. Jargunn utilized the alien scent module to record the imposter slayer's scent and transferred it to his hand-held tracking unit. This special unit, however, required being positioned no higher than three feet from the ground to successfully track a scent. Another complication was that it wouldn't work if Jargunn was in a cloaking mode.

These were the primary reasons Jargunn was forced to come to 'Earth 3' at night and physically track his prey.

In Jargunn's mind the physical requirements of this assignment were what made it such degradation. He would have to bend over to place the hand-held tracking unit close enough to the ground to detect the imposter's scent. His back would suffer greatly. Looking up at the 'Earth 3' moon, he raised his fist skyward and ranted, "This is a mission that should have been assigned to a novice Watcher!"

Regaining control of his angst, he settled his essence and employed a logical analysis of the one serious problem that needed to be avoided. This was the discovery of his existence by any of the local inhabitants. It could create a historical flux or paradox and too many of these events had occurred during the first thousand years of time transference.

Thus, as a member of the Watcher Guild, he could be put to death for producing such a paradigm.

It took Jargunn about ten minutes of personally scanning the "East Woods" before the alien scent unit picked up the imposter's scent signature. Bending over to hold the tracking device at the required height for a positive read out, Jargunn began his pursuit.

Jargunn's tracking device took him to Sharpsburg.

The cur that had attacked a previous night traveler spied the passage of the Watcher with his one good eye from under his owner's front porch and just growled. It had experienced enough injury from strangers in the night.

Jargunn followed the tracking beam through town and onto the road toward Shepherdstown. After just a few hundred yards, he heard two small four-legged animals making the most primal cries as they ran down toward him from a residence sitting back off the road. Once the animals entered the road, they charged him.

The Watcher threw up a force field that the animals barreled into at full speed. The collision knocked both animals off their feet and silenced their savage howling for blood. They landed in a heap on the dirt road. After a brief time, the subdued ravagers regained consciousness. Emitting wails of pain, they put their tails between their legs

and staggered back to the lair from whence they launched their fiasco.

Jargunn snickered low in his throat. His first inclination was to shred the animals, but there had been enough hijinks for a lifetime on 'Earth 3' already.

The Watcher continued his westward movement adhering to the imposter's scent like a blood hound.

On reaching a steep downward slope of the road, Jargunn came upon a confusing scene that seemed to have been a confrontation. He investigated small shards lying in the road possibly from some broken vessel, which on inspection had housed an awful smelling liquid. Following his tracking device from the road toward a tree line, he unearthed buried clothes in an adjacent field. From this cache of imposter paraphernalia, he deduced that there had been a clothing exchange of some sort. On closer inspection he discovered human footprints descending the slope and human footprints plus a four-legged animal's footprints ascending the slope.

Using the scent device, Jargunn reestablished his tracking of the imposter.

Progressing down the slope, Jargunn approached a small but deep waterway situated next to a large rapidly-flowing body of water. He recalled in some bygone lecture that 'Earth 3' allowed for floating vessel movement up and down waterways in this time period, but he wasn't knowledgeable in how they operated. Yet, since there was no vessel traffic now, Jargunn moved toward the wooden enclosure built into the small waterway.

However, four-legged animals housed in a structure nearby picked up Jargunn's scent and began making awful noises, including kicking the sides of their enclosures. The residents of a few local buildings suddenly exploded out of their dwellings next to the waterway with primitive, but, dangerous weapons. Apparently, they were on high alert for some reason. The rapidity of the response to the noise of the Earth animals disconcerted Jargunn so he

turned on his cloaking protection and retraced his path up the hill.

It was getting close to dawn so he called for his craft to rendezvous at the top of the hill. It landed in its stealth mode without sight or sound. He boarded it and departed for home base. It made no sound on takeoff, but it left a perfectly round ten-foot diameter circle of crushed corn.

During the hyperspace return to Axeylon 5, Jargunn communicated what he had found and the possible implications of a clothing transfer to Lord Dendaras.

"Interesting", responded Lord Dendaras. "At least the imposter has possibly kept his 21st century identity to a minimum."

Jargunn informed Lord Dendaras that he had almost been discovered, but had escaped without being seen by any humans. He also passed along that dawn was now breaking on 'Earth 3' and asked if his orders were still to track the imposter only at night and, once he caught the imposter, to kill him.

Lord Dendaras responded, "I have changed my mind. Don't kill him. We need to interrogate him. Monitor this imposter's travels, but, as always, without disruption to or discovery by the local residents. I want a full report of his activities. We will talk again after your next foray to 'Earth 3'."

"Yes, Sire," Jargunn responded with a grimace. Already tired of this boring job, Jargunn thought, "Lord Dendaras had only said not to kill the human. I would love to have a clandestine meeting with this imposter and give him a few lumps and bruises for all the chaos he has caused. But, I doubt I could get away with it. So, Human, you better show up soon or I might just forget my orders. Unfortunate accidents on Earth Planets have been known to happen."

☙

The next morning a deep sense of melancholy affected my mind and I went into a soul-bleeding stupor. I evaded Hattie's kin folks by feigning fatigue. I stayed in bed until they left for work and got in bed early that night before they came home from work.

During the day I constantly wasted time pondering my situation. I wondered if my wife was desperate since I hadn't contacted her in what seemed like a month, but had to be just a few days. I felt so guilty for not communicating with her even though it was impossible. I longed to go back to my own 21st century. I kept wondering if it was possible to return. I raised the questions, "If I could go back, would I be back in the same place, the Antietam Battlefield Park, and at the same moment I left it? Or, would I have lost the amount of days spent in this parallel universe?" I even envisioned traveling back to my universe in the Sphere. However, I reasoned, "I probably killed one of the beings affiliated with the Sphere so getting a return ride in the Sphere is out. I bet those beings would like to get their hands on me. I wonder why they haven't found me." Each time I thought about possible alien retribution, I broke out in a cold sweat.

For another day I evaded the Gray family and tried to answer a multitude of unanswerable questions that my conscious mind peppered me with, but to no avail. After a few hours of contemplation on the subjects, I would get an ensuing severe headache and have to quit trying to figure a way out of my plight.

Each time at this point of mental exhaustion, I would sit under a tree in what seemed an opiate-induced state and watch the barge traffic on the Potomac. In the afternoon I shuffled south down the road along the river and stared at the late blooms of some of the flowering weeds along the river bank for a few hours.

My moping around had Hattie worried. She had tried to engage me in conversation over the last two days when I meandered in for a late breakfast or an early dinner. I barely answered her. I was feeling so depressed and desperate. The thought of committing suicide even crossed my mind. I knew that wasn't the answer, but I hated being in what was an incomprehensible situation.

Finally, after two days of soul searching I came to the conclusion that, if I was going to find a way back home, it would take time plus I better embed myself deeply in this culture to evade any aliens trying to find me. So, I decided to really enmesh myself in the role of the local school teacher. I had the job already. Why not take advantage of it? Also, I determined for the second time since my arrival, there would be no more moping around and no more pity parties. I would face the consequences come what may.

I ate an early supper for the last time and went to my room. As I lay in bed, one disconcerting thought crept into my consciousness, "If I keep asking people about the progress of the Civil War up to this point, they're ultimately going to get suspicious and it could blow my cover. My background story of how I got here was flimsy at best. I don't need anyone researching the facts of how I arrived in this part of the country."

After a particularly fruitless hour of mentally groping for a plan that would solve my lack of Civil War knowledge in this universe without causing suspicion, a workable idea popped in my head. I could go to the newspaper office in Harpers Ferry to do Civil War research on the pretext of seeing the historic city before school started. There I could familiarize myself with the Civil War information I needed to know both for my own aggrandizement and for teaching at school.

There was just one important point I needed answered before putting this part of my plan into action. In this time period back in my old universe, the Yanks had possession of that city. I needed to find out whether the Rebs or the Yanks were garrisoned there now. If the Rebs occupied it, I shouldn't have any trouble entering and leaving the town.

So with this genesis of a plan imbedded in my mind, I slipped off to a sound sleep for the first time in days. I mean nights.

When I ventured in for breakfast the next day, I was a different person. I could tell that Hattie noticed a change in my behavior. She responded with a happy attitude. We had a lively conversation about what had been occurring in town and at the mill.

Ultimately, I brought the palaver around to the Civil War news. Then pretending my unfamiliarity with the Civil War in the east, I ventured one last ignorance question, "When I was living in Arkansas, I never asked anyone about what had happened to Harpers Ferry during the war. Please tell me, is it occupied by the Yanks?"

She looked at me with that "he's still definitely addled" look and said, "Lord have mercy child. Where ya been? Stuck in a cave? General Jackson done took Harpers Ferry in May of last year. He has an army in the Valley (Shenandoah Valley) and been keeping tha Yanks at bay for nigh on to a year and a half. They's been trying to get at him, but Ole Joe Johnston has been giving 'em fits over near tha coast for about tha same length of time. They traded off helping each other when tha Yanks come out of Washington City and head this way or toward Fredericksburg."

I muttered, "Well, I haven't been keeping up with tha particulars. I just know'd I wanted to be in this here part of tha country and not under Yankee rule." She just sighed and shook her head.

Then I ventured, "How far is it to Harpers Ferry?"

"'Bout eighteen miles and much too far to walk unless ya planned to spend tha night. Ya planning to go down therah?" she responded.

"Since I've heard so much about it, I would like to check out tha town," I answered.

"Ya could rent a horse or a horse and buggy at tha livery stable in town," she suggested with a smile. I could tell she would be glad to get rid of me for a few days.

"Thanks for tha idea, Hattie. I think I'll leave first thing in tha morning." That brought an even bigger smile to her face.

ଓ

The Dark Mage's Log: 'Earth 3' Date: 18620915

Since Jargunn had been given his new assignment on the spur of the moment, he had not been able to properly research and prepare for his mission. He never had been in this time period on

'Earth 3'. Once back at Axeylon 5, he contacted the Eternal Oracle for information concerning the local 'Earth 3' government entities of 1862, detail maps of the area, in which he had been operating, and an in-depth study of the primitive method of navigation up a waterway against a current.

After a short nap, Jargunn learned from the information supplied by the Eternal Oracle that the governmental entities in his area of operations were the states of Virginia and Maryland. Also, in 'Earth 3' a small man-made waterway called a canal, which implemented a lock system, allowed movement of vessels against a waterway's current. The canal in his area of operation was the Cincinnati and Ohio Canal (C&O Canal).

Jargunn also studied the detailed maps of the area he had traversed during the preceding 'Earth 3' night and what was on the other side of the waterway called the Potomac River. He deduced that the imposter had traveled to the river in order to cross from Maryland into Virginia. On further study Jargunn believed the imposter had chosen one of

two possible methods of crossing the river.

Either the imposter had forded the river somewhere near where the primitive lock on the C&O Canal was located or he had crossed the river using a spanning structure called a bridge. Jargunn thought the imposter had chosen to ford the river because there wouldn't be as much traffic.

Once it was fully dark on 'Earth 3', Jargunn returned and landed his ACV near the ford so as to be down river from the lock and thus preclude any Earth animal reaction to his presence. He exited the vehicle and willed it back into orbit.

He had a hunch the imposter had used the ford to cross the river. True to his assumption, his tracker picked up the imposter's scent on the eastern bank of the Potomac River near what his maps called Boteler's Ford.

Jargunn switched on his cloaking device and crossed the Potomac at the ford. There was one thing that was eerie in his crossing. He walked on a dry river bed across the river because there was a dry space between his body and the river's flow. The water never touched him.

Once on the other side of the river, Jargunn switched off the cloaking mode, found the imposter's scent with his tracker again and followed it up the bank to one of three buildings situated on the west bank of the river. He found only one of the buildings to be inhabited. There was a family seated around a rectangular table eating a meal. The scent of the imposter was heavy in this abode. Thus, he must be present at the table.

Jargunn switched off his tracker and implemented his cloaking device. Taking out his recorder, he crept toward an open window to catch any information that might be imparted by the inhabitants.

All of a sudden an earth animal in a nearby structure started making a loud nasal sound just like the animals near the lock. To add to the cacophony it also

began kicking at the walls of its paddock. The sound was very abrasive. So, Jargunn had to retreat from the area or risk being discovered.

Jargunn wondered, "How could these four-legged Earth animals detect me even in a cloaking mode, and why do they react the way they do when I am near to them?"

ଓ

I was up at dawn, rip-roaring and ready to go. At last I had a workable plan and a mission to accomplish. Harpers Ferry, here I come. One of the first things I was going to check at their newspaper office was whether John Brown had attacked the town on October 16, 1859.

Before heading out, I sat down to a hearty breakfast with the whole Gray clan. It was the first time I had a chance to talk with Hattie's brothers and her Papa. I introduced myself to the men and we all shook hands. They all had very strong grips and I wondered how my grip felt to them. I hope it gave the impression of strength. We males always wonder about that when we shake hands. I knew that my non-calloused hand indicated I hadn't had to perform manual labor for a living.

I learned that Hattie's brother, who was dubbed A.B., was formally named Albert Benjamin and her other brother,

C.D., was short for Charles Doss. Both men were of average height, five feet, four inches tall and both weighed about one hundred forty pounds. The muscles in their forearms, which were visible from their rolled-up shirt sleeves, stood out vividly. Also, their neck muscles appeared like ropes from their skulls to their shoulders. There wasn't an ounce of fat on them. They asked some of the same questions about my past that Hattie had rendered and seemed satisfied with my patent answers.

Papa, who must have topped out at five feet, two inches and weighed one hundred ten pounds dripping wet, possessed the commanding force in the room. He sat at the head of the table as any God-ordained potentate and ate without looking at me, but you could tell he was taking in all my answers to the Gray brothers' questions with a critical eye or make that a critical ear.

It took a while to tell my story again, which was beginning to sound a little far-fetched even to me. However, I stuck to the particulars and put a little passion in the telling to hopefully dispel any speculation that I might be a Yankee spy or escaped criminal. I hoped my version of the information would get around to the rest of the town. Having paid Hattie ten dollars didn't hurt either.

At one point in the interrogation Hattie chimed in, "Jim's been given tha job of school teacher by Mr. Throckmorton for tha next session of school."

That brought an affirmative, "Hum", from Papa as he glanced up to look at me more closely. I believe her outburst had allayed any fears that I would not be able to provide the monthly rent. My newest rent subsidy was undoubtedly what had provided the beef steak served at this morning's breakfast.

Eventually, the brothers ran out of questions and we ate the rest of the morning meal in awkward silence. Every once in a while, I looked up and saw one of the brothers taking a surreptitious glance my way then quickly look away. I knew they were very doubtful of the tale I had spun of my sudden appearance in Virginia.

Finally, the meal was finished and the brothers left to do some weeding work and check on their fields of corn. Later they would join Papa, who left to open the mill for business.

I asked Hattie, "Mind if I use Papa's razor again?"

She fetched the heinous weapon, and as she handed it to me, ordered, "Mind what yar doing this time." I nodded in the affirmative. I took the necessaries out to the stump again and only cut myself twice without the previous degree of bloodletting. I also brushed my teeth.

Once I reentered the house, Hattie gave me some bread, cheese and some salted pork, which she put in a poke sack and tied the end with a strip of rawhide. She handed me a full canteen of water and uttered, "Yar gonna need this too."

I had worn my new suit to breakfast. So, I donned my new hat, which I was rather proud of, and stuffed another sack with my handy newspaper, the old shirt I had worn when Hattie found me, a change of socks and my dental paraphernalia.

After tying the ends of the sacks together with Hattie's rawhide strip, I slung the sacks over my left shoulder like saddle bags. I stood before Hattie and told her, "I might be gone for a few days."

She smiled and then confessed, "I's worried 'bout ya for a bit, but I'm glad ya done revived yaself." She smiled that gap-tooth smile that I had come to appreciate and I hugged her goodbye. I guess she felt protective of me, since she had been the rescuer and caregiver for this wandering and unusual person who had abruptly come into her life. My sudden appearance on the bank of the Potomac and almost on her doorstep must have been the beginning of an adventure that was a reprieve from her humdrum life.

I then held her at arm's length, smiled and expressed, "Hattie, thanks for everything. I owe you my life." She looked down with an embarrassed grin and uttered, "Twirtn't nothing." I quickly hugged her again and promised, "I'll take care of myself. Don't worry 'bout me."

"I ain't gonna worry too much, but watch out for bad men on tha road," she added. I nodded that I would and left for the livery stable in town.

I hadn't walked too far when the sun started breaking over the eastern horizon and the partly cloudy sky erupted with streaks of pink fluff that looked like cotton candy. I just stood for a long moment and beheld the magnificent handy work of Mother Nature. Then I quickly focused on the job at hand.

When I arrived in town, I pulled out my watch. It indicated 7:00 a.m. I went to the livery stable and heard someone in the back working in a stall. As I approached the sound, I could see that there were three horses in the stable. One was a black stallion, which fixed me with a fierce stare and laid back his ears. Another was a red and white mare that was contentedly munching hay. The last was a small brown gelding that was just standing in its stall with a dopey-eyed gaze.

I continued my approach to the back stall, steering clear of the stinking refuse in the main thoroughfare. Once I got to the stall from which the sounds of labor were emanating, I stopped and observed the worker.

He was mucking out one of the stalls and the reeking waste that I had deftly maneuvered around was from his previous efforts. He sensed my presence and looked up.

I said, "I'm Jim Hager, the new school teacher. I need to hire a mount for a few days for a trip to Harpers Ferry."

The idea of collecting a rent fee peaked his interest, so he propped his rake on a stall wall, touched his hand to his forehead and introduced himself, "I'm Bill Heintz, tha owner of this herah livery." Getting right down to business he asked, "How long ya planning to be gone?"

I responded. "'Bout three days, I reckon."

Looking back at the stalls of horses, he informed me, "Tha black stallion and tha mare ain't mine to rent. They's just stabled herah by a local family. But I could rent ya tha brown gelding."

"How much would ya charge?" I asked.

"Bout $1.00 a day in advance, but ya gots to promise me that ya'll return Beauregard in good condition," he stipulated.

"That I'll do, Mr. Heintz," I promised. "However, I'll need to wait for tha bank to open to withdraw money for tha trip and to pay for tha rent of yar horse. I will return with tha money as soon as tha bank opens," I advised. I actually had some money in my pocket, but wanted to draw out more money for the journey.

With the dealing done, we shook hands and I left the livery stable.

To kill time, I walked to the cafe I had frequented the day before. I ordered a cup of coffee, sat at an empty table and laid my poke sacks on the floor. A man at another table in a black suit that was almost identical to mine said hello. I smiled and responded with, "Hello, this is a fine day isn't it?"

He was a little taken back by my forwardness, but responded, "Yes, it is a fine day that the Lord hath given us."

I immediately surmised this must be a local minister.

He asked, "May I join you?" I extended my hand to the empty chair at my table. He sat down and offering his hand began, "I'm tha local Methodist Minister, Pastor Jake Chambers."

I responded, "I'm Jim Hager." We both solemnly shook hands.

He peppered me with all the same questions that everyone else had asked, but then he queried, "Where are ya staying?"

I mentioned, "Tha Gray's home."

This caused him to raise his eyebrows in surprise. Then he said, "I understand that ya have been given tha local school teacher's job. Doesn't that give you pause to stay with tha Grays?"

I replied, "I guess word gets around fast about my being appointed to tha new job. But, I don't know why staying with tha Grays would give me pause in my job. Hattie Gray was tha one who suggested I talk with Mr. Throckmorton about tha school teacher vacancy."

He raised his eyebrows again and said, "Really?"

I thought this was odd and added, "Why would ya say that?"

He just shrugged and said, "Oh, nothing. Forget I mentioned it."

I didn't try to pry any additional information, but planned to talk with Hattie about it when I returned.

Pastor Chambers slyly got to the point of bestowing his presence on me. "Since ya will be in tha forefront of tha community, a pillar of tha community, ya might say, which church will ya be attending on Sunday?"

This had never occurred to me as a responsibility that would accompany my new job, but I began to understand that cultural and religious duties were thrust on certain office and job holders in a 19th century town whether they liked it or not. In a very respectful and sincere voice I told the Pastor, "I'm an ecumenical believer."

This baffled him and he gave me a quizzical look.

So I further explained, "I don't attend just one specific church, but visit a different one each Sunday."

This brought forth a most non-ecumenical question, "How can ya adhere to tha tenets of each faith to get into heaven? It would seem to be an impossible task."

"Well, I believe therah are some basic tenets of each faith that if undertaken will allow anyone into God's realm," I rationalized.

He looked at me as if I had grown horns. "Well, we'll have to speak more 'bout this," he said.

I interjected, "Yes, we will." Then I got up, extended my hand, which he reluctantly shook, put a nickel on the table and walked to the bank.

The bank was open when I got there and I got a withdrawal of $40.00. The teller eyed me grudgingly, but didn't question my extraction. I mean withdrawal.

Once I retrieved the money, I returned to the livery stable. Mr. Heintz, true to our deal, had Beauregard saddled and ready to go. I paid him four dollars for four days, mounted the dazed animal, bent down to look Mr. Heintz in the eye, which made him move back a step or two, and asked him pointedly, "What type of tricks has Beauregard played on previous riders?"

"Well, Ole Beau don't like any steam whistles from boats or trains. They make him a bit skittish. If'n he gets real tired, he's liable to just lay down in tha road. If kicked too hard, he's liable to buck ya off. That's about all he does," Mr. Heintz admitted.

In my estimation that was more than enough tricks to contemplate. I looked at the man rather dubiously and uttered, "Uh huh." I saluted him and kicked Ole Beau hard in the flanks, which must have roused him from his perpetual daze, because he trotted out of the stable at a fast clip. I directed him south on the Shepherdstown Pike toward Halltown. I was told this was the better road than the one that skirted the Potomac River. The Halltown road was longer, but not as rugged.

Beau kept trotting so I let him go and just hung on for dear life. He had the worst gait that I had ever experienced. I was bouncing up and down like a rag doll with my vertebrae being jammed with each step of this four-legged threshing machine. After about ten minutes I finally had enough and capitulated by pulling back on the reins and saying whoa. Beau stopped abruptly which pitched me forward but not far enough to have the front part of the saddle do any damage to the tender parts of my anatomy.

Beau just stood there in the middle of the road with his head tucked in and his shoulders scrunched as if he believed he was going to be hit over the head. I reasoned that is what usually happened to the poor dumb animal due to his unusual means of locomotion. I took a moment to appraise the cayuse and map out a plan on how to handle this anomaly of the equestrian species.

I reached down and patted him on the side of the neck and gently touched him with the heels of my brogans. He shambled forward at a walk toward Harpers Ferry and hopefully answers to some of my historical questions.

Ole Beau and I got further acquainted as the day went along. We stopped by a stream after about what seemed like five hours, but was only two. I took Beau down to the stream and he slurped the clear water willingly. I didn't let him have too much. I remembered that from the Saturday morning 'My Friend Flicka' TV shows when I was a kid.

I sat down by the stream, drank liberally from my canteen and ate a portion of the victuals that Hattie prepared. When I had eaten my fill, I refilled my canteen in the cold stream that I hoped wasn't polluted. Since the water was cold, I reasoned it came from a spring and was pure. Then we got back on the road.

We didn't seem to pass a lot of wagons on the road, but there were a few riders that passed us heading north. They weren't in a hurry, so I stopped to talk to one older gentleman. I asked, "Have you heard of a Yankee army being in the area?"

"No", he replied, but added, "I did read in a newspaper that therah is one that's supposed to be coming out of Washington City any day now and move into northern Virginia with a mind to take Fredericksburg. General Johnston will probably maneuver his army to delay tha Yanks without puttin up a fight. But he's gonna have to fight to keep Fredericksburg from falling into enemy hands."

Well, it seems some things never change no matter what universe to which you are assigned. Joe Johnston would rather back up than move forward for an attack in any realm.

I asked about Stonewall Jackson's Army of the Valley. The man just looked at me quizzically and said, "If you mean General Thomas Jackson, he's probably gonna reinforce

Johnston again. They stymied a Yankee move like this back in 1861."

I asked the name of the Commanding Yankee General that was leading the advance and the gentleman said, "Well, it's Hancock, of course." My lower jaw dropped and I must have seemed like a dunce to the traveler. I apologized and explained I had just gotten here from Arkansas and was trying to catch up on all the news. That appeared to satisfy him. We exchanged some further pleasantries then parted ways.

I decided to stay in Halltown for the night. It was just an hour's ride from Harpers Ferry and I had been beat to a frazzle by Beau. Thank heavens that each town, no matter what size, usually had a livery stable. I got Beau bedded down for the night for just fifty cents, which included combing, water, some hay and a sprinkle of oats.

I asked Mr. Johnson, the livery owner," Is therah a hotel in town?" He just laughed and said, "Thar ain't no hotel, but Widow Hawkins takes in boarders for one dollar a night plus breakfast."

I thanked him, and following his directions, walked down the street with my poke sacks thrown over my shoulder for about two blocks, turned right for one block and found the white two-story boarding house of the Widow Hawkins.

Apparently this was a very popular rest stop. There were about five men sitting around the parlor smoking cigars, reading or talking when I entered. I asked for the widow and was directed to the room across the hall. Once I entered the room, I was taken aback by the beautiful woman that sat behind a desk in the middle of the room.

She looked up and smiled. I stuttered, "Do ya have any vacancies?"

She laughed and informed me, "Well, I haven't ever heard it put quite like that, but, yes, I have a vacancy. However, ya will have to share it with a drummer from Richmond."

I remembered that a drummer was like a traveling salesman. I grinned and quipped, "That depends on what he's selling."

She laughed again and informed me, "His wares are men's shirts and trousers."

"That's fine with me. How much for tha night?" I parleyed.

"One dollar and breakfast is included," she negotiated. I nodded my acquiescence, paid the fare, and was given a key to a room on the second floor.

The Widow Hawkins informed me, "Mr. Holstein will be tha other room occupant tonight."

I thanked her and went across the hall to the gentlemen in the parlor and asked the assembly, "Is Mr. Holstein herah?" An older man replied, "Mr. Holstein has gone to tha local saloon to celebrate a rather large sale he made in Harpers Ferry at a local hardware and clothing store."

I thanked the man for the information and left the parlor. I went out on the front porch and sat in a well-used rocking chair to watch the beautiful sunset. I allowed myself to utterly relax my body and mind. Slipping into a sort of daze, I traced the events of the last week and of how far I had progressed mentally and emotionally in those few days. It was amazing to me that I had been able to take on a 19th century persona and was still alive to boot.

I drifted off into a trance of sorts and dozed for a while. Chilly night air carried by a light breeze woke me after the sun had gone down. I decided it was time to go inside. Due to Beau's horrible ride, my sacroiliac felt damaged. I suffered pain in my back as I got up and tottered stiffly into the boarding house.

Men were still reading and smoking cigars in the parlor. I looked across the hall and saw the Widow Hawkins still working at her desk. I doubted she would want my company because I bet a lot of the men that stayed at her establishment tried to hit on her. I mean tried to get in her good graces. I had to stop thinking in my universe's jargon and utilize as much of the 19th century common thought and speech that I knew.

The Widow Hawkins glanced up and saw me looking at her. She smiled and queried, "Is therah something ya wanted to ask?"

I smiled back and in a rather low conspiratorial voice answered, "Therah are a few things I need to know, but in private."

She raised her eyebrows, but I quickly raised my hands and stated "By private, I meant out on tha porch. It has to do with tha local history."

She looked at me for a long moment and agreeably said, "I'll join ya on tha veranda in about ten minutes." I thanked her and once again occupied my previous seated position on the porch.

True to her word she came out on the porch in about ten minutes. I stood up and gave her my chair and leaned against the railing. I stared at her for a few seconds not knowing how to broach the subject about which I wanted to gather information. She looked at me expectantly.

I finally began, "I'm not from around herah. I've been isolated out west without a really good news source. Do ya mind if I get yar ideas about how tha War has progressed herah in tha east?"

She let out a breath that I didn't know she was holding and relaxed. Apparently, she had thought I was going to try some funny business with her. I also noticed that she had taken her hand out of the cloth bag that she had placed in her lap. I fixed my gaze on the bulge in the bag. It was my turn to raise eyebrows when I looked into her eyes. She just said, "A lady can't be too careful these days."

I bet there was some kind of small pistol concealed in the otherwise harmless purse. I remarked, "I guess yar right. Please forgive me for frightening ya. I really just wanted tha war news from yar prospective." I would never underestimate this lady again.

I began our conversation by stating that I hadn't really understood what had initially started the War. Our state, Arkansas, had entered the Confederacy after Lincoln had called for an allotment of troops to put down a rebellion. I was hoping this was true of the present universe's history, which would correspond to my old universe's Civil War's History. She nodded and I breathed a sigh of relief.

Then she began a description of the historical events. In summation they were as follows:

First, there was the firing on Ft. Sumter in early April, 1861.

Second, the Confederacy was formed in Montgomery, Alabama, with South Carolina, Florida, Georgia, Alabama, Mississippi, Louisiana and Texas seceding from the Union.

Third, when Lincoln demanded troops to put down the Confederacy, Arkansas, Tennessee, North Carolina, Virginia and Delaware also seceded.

Fourth, Delaware was quickly brought under the thumb of the Federals, when Union General McDowell's army attacked a small Delaware militia force at Newark, Delaware and defeated them in June of 1861. Delaware was quickly occupied by Federal forces and put under the auspices of the Union military.

Fifth, the Confederacy moved its capital to Atlanta in May of 1861 due to the rail connections and centralized location.

Sixth, in the local region, the Yanks began building up McDowell's army around Washington City, while the Rebs formed an army near Richmond under General Joe Johnston and another small army under Thomas Jackson in the Shenandoah Valley.

Seventh, the Yanks occupied Northern Virginia from the Potomac River near Washington City southwest to Centerville, Virginia. Confederate General Johnston moved his army up to the south bank of the Occoquah River near Manassas Junction.

Eighth, in early August, 1861, the Federal Army moved south to attack General Johnston's Army. Johnston retreated provoking the Yankee army to follow him closely and thus out pace their supply and ammunition trains. He retreated to Warrenton, Virginia, called upon General Jackson to reinforce him, and with their combined forces bestowed a complete defeat on the Yanks, sending them streaming back to their home base at Fairfield, Virginia.

Ninth, Winfield Scott, General-in-Chief of all Federal forces, replaced McDowell with General Hancock, who was made the commander of the forces around Washington City.

Tenth, General Burnside had been put in charge of Union forces in North Carolina that were getting ready to attack the Confederate capital of Atlanta.

It took about an hour for the Widow Hawkins to relate her knowledge of the sequence of the War since 1861 plus her opinions of the various political figures, generals, newspaper owners, journalists, novelists and the abolitionists.

Finally, she asked, "Might we suspend further history lessons for tha night. It has been a long day and I'm rather tired. Also I need to get outta tha night air."

"By all means, Mrs. Hawkins," I responded. "I really appreciate all yar insights. It has helped me immensely."

As I escorted her into the house she added, "I don't cotton much to tha novel "Uncle Tom's Cabin" or tha abolitionists. I believe thar tha cause of tha War."

I nodded my assent. However, before we parted there was one bit of information I wanted to gather. So, I asked, "Was Harpers Ferry tha scene of any action prior to tha war?"

"No, tha Confederate army under Jackson occupied it in 1861 and it has been in tha hands of tha Confederates ever since," she informed me.

I further probed, "Back in Arkansas, where I'm from, we heard that at one time John Brown had targeted Harpers Ferry for a raid. Did that ever occur?"

The Widow quickly responded, "He may have wanted to raid Harpers Ferry, but he never got tha chance. He was killed in southeastern Kansas in 1859 by a band of Missouri militia. I can't remember tha name of tha militia unit leader, but tha eradication of John Brown was a great accomplishment for tha South."

I was jolted by her information and it must have shown on my face because with concern in her voice asked, "Are you ill, Mr. Hager?"

I smiled and returned, "No, it has been a long day for me also. I believe I'll turn in." After a few more pleasantries we parted company and again I profusely thanked her for the historical update, shook her proffered hand and went to my room.

As I trudged up the stairs to my room, I thought, "John Brown's demise in Kansas is another completely different historical event in this universe." When I entered the room, I found that my roommate had not arrived so I undressed and helped myself to the bed, which thank goodness didn't have any bedbugs. I tossed and turned for a while, but finally I slept pretty soundly, which was remarkable due to the strange surroundings and my worrisome thoughts.

ᘓ

The Dark Mage's Log: 'Earth 3' Date: 18620916

Jargunn determined to be better prepared for gathering information during the coming night. He again landed on the Maryland side of the river and traversed the Potomac. This time he brought a directional microphone recorder which would pick up any table conversation during the evening meal through the window from a distance and not alert any Earth animals of his presence.

Hopefully, some information on the imposter's whereabouts would be imparted. Any data recovered could then be transported to Axeylon 5 for Lord Dendaras's listening pleasure.

Jargunn crept within seventy-five yards of the only lighted building and activated his microphone.

One of the men began speaking. "Where's ya school teacher, Hattie?" said a raspy male voice.

"Papa, he ain't MY school teacher. Since ya must know, he's taking a sightseeing trip to Harpers Ferry," was a female's reply.

"Well, I still think he's addled in tha head," retorted the voice of an old man.

Jargunn nodded and said under his breath, "Okay earthling. You have slipped my clutches again, but I shall catch you at this Harpers Ferry."

Jargunn moved a safe distance from the house, contacted the Eternal Oracle for the GPS coordinates for Harpers Ferry, and willed his ACV to land near the west bank of the Potomac. He boarded and piloted his vehicle south in stealth mode to Harpers Ferry.

He navigated over the town called Harpers Ferry and found a favorable spot to land on a flatland near one of the two rivers that bracketed the town. Disembarking he willed the ACV into

orbit and set out to cover the short distance to the 'Earth 3" hamlet.

Once in the town of Harpers Ferry, Jargunn utilized his cloaking device and traversed the whole town undetected by the humans. Even though the locals couldn't see him, Earth 3 animals could detect him. More than once, he had to vacate an area due to their irrational and erratic behavior.

Jargunn waited well into the night for the streets to clear of the populace and their animals. He was able to suspend his cloaking mode and, using his scent tracker, checked the majority of the town for the imposter. However, there was no scent recognition anywhere in the town. It was getting close to dawn when he finally suspended his surveillance and piloted his ACV back to Axeylon 5 to make his report.

☙

I awoke at dawn to a bell being rung, which I instantly surmised was the call to breakfast. I looked around the room and comprehended that my supposed roommate had not made it back from his foray into the licentious side of town.

I quickly poured water into a wash basin and washed my face. I smelled of my shirt and it didn't have too bad a fragrance so I dressed, ran my fingers through my hair and sought the dining room. I was ready for a good breakfast.

Well the good breakfast didn't pan out. It definitely didn't meet the standards of the breakfasts I'd gotten at Hattie's table. The Widow Hawkins provided some kind of sludge they called mush. I got a bowl of it and had to add a lot of honey to get a passable taste and I mean that figuratively and digestively. I also procured two biscuits that were about four-fifths done, which means that the middle parts were still doughy. I added a slug of butter and many spoons of honey to kill the taste of the unsavory items of supposed nutrition.

For a beverage, a pitcher of cool milk graced the breakfast table. It had an unfamiliar taste. However, thinking back to Pine Bluff when I was a teenager, I remembered drinking unpasteurized milk provided for the noon meal by some farm family friends. Their milk was fresh, which is more than I could say for the Widow Hawkins' brew.

With my guts growling due to the alien food I had ingested, I got my poke sacks, went to the livery stable, had Beau saddled up and rode east to Harpers Ferry. Beau was sort of used to me by now and we meandered for only an hour before we reached our destination.

I checked Beau into the Harpers Ferry livery stable, which was on Bolivar Heights. This is a ridge on the southwest part of town that looks directly down on the town proper. Standing on this prominence I viewed a majestic site.

Below and to the east of town, the Potomac River and the Shenandoah River converge into one mighty confluence. The convergence then poured between two jutting elevations: Maryland Heights on the north and Loudoun Heights on the south. It was a breathtaking vision. I stood for twenty minutes looking at the mighty Potomac River, reinforced by the Shenandoah River, as it rushed through the crevice created by two mountains and flowed headlong to empty into the Chesapeake Bay and ultimately the Atlantic Ocean. The beauty of this image devoid of any 21st century encumbrances was awe-inspiring. At long last I was able to tear myself away from this dream of Mother Earth and tend to my information-gathering agenda.

The livery owner had given me directions to the local newspaper office. It entailed that I walk down a road with a steep incline from the top of Bolivar Heights to the bottom of the hill where the road dead-ended into the main thoroughfare of Harpers Ferry. Once at this junction, I was to turn left and walk two blocks to the newspaper office.

I followed the directions and, once I entered the newspaper office, asked to see the owner. A man came forward and said he was Mr. Matthews, the owner.

I introduced myself and asked if he had any back issues of his paper from the previous year up to today's date. He suspiciously asked why I needed to look at them. I stated that I was the new school teacher in Shepherdstown and wanted to have the correct information when I taught current history for my class in the fall.

He seemed to accept my answer and directed me to a back room of the office which had stacks of newspapers by year from 1857 to the present. The newspaper was printed on a weekly basis except for special editions, which dealt with startling national news events.

I dug into the papers beginning with 1860 and only perused the articles that dealt with the presidential election of 1860, the secession of the southern states and the forming of the Confederate States. I concentrated on the war from 1861 to the present. It was most illuminating. Amalgamating the printed information, I was able to construct an outline of events from 1860 to the present.

The election of Lincoln, the secession of the Deep South, Lincoln's call for quotas of troops to put down the secession and the secession of the rest of the slave states, except for Missouri, Kentucky and Maryland, were just about parallel to our universe's history with Delaware's secession being the exception.

However, as I had gleaned from the newspaper in Shepherdstown, the man I had met on the road to Harpers Ferry and the Widow Hawkins in Halltown, 1861's history in this universe differed in some important aspects from my universe. The Harpers Ferry newspaper gave an even clearer picture of what had happened in this 19th century parallel universe than the word of mouth information I previously received. Some of the historical differences described were definitely interesting.

For instance, Union General-in-Chief Winfield Scott had not been replaced by General George McClellan. Also, "The Anaconda Plan", which was a blockade strategy to strangle the Confederacy's maritime trade, was proposed by General Scott and implemented in both universes. The big difference was that Scott got to hold his military position and conduct the course of the war for the Union, including "The Anaconda Plan."

I had never really researched the naval battles or the closing down of the Confederate coastal ports and river ports in my universe other than the taking of New Orleans and Vicksburg. The only significant Union Army advancement made from occupied Confederate ports and Atlantic coastal islands in my universe was the Virginia Peninsula Campaign of 1862. So, the following historical events in this Universe that led to an inland Union invasion were totally different.

In this universe, General Scott organized his "Anaconda" system of blockade into four navy/army coalitions:

The North Atlantic Blockading Squadron;
The South Atlantic Blockading Squadron;
The East Gulf Blockading Squadron; and
The West Gulf Blockading Squadron.

An army of 60,000 soldiers supported by navy flotillas was assigned to occupy the Confederate forts and ports, which were initially to be taken by the Anaconda Blockading Squadrons. For this plan to work, the Union Navy needed a succession of ports for coaling of their steam ships along the Atlantic and Gulf coasts. So, the first order of business was to take Confederate ports that could provide coaling locations and at the same time start to close down Confederate shipping and trade.

Beginning in August, 1861 and continuing until February, 1862, the North and South Atlantic Blockading Squadrons took and occupied enough Confederate coastal ports and forts to open up the Pamlico Sound and Albemarle Sound off the coasts of Virginia and North Carolina to Union gunships. This began the eradication of harbors that could cater to the Confederate blockade runners.

The next big joint Union navy and army expedition in the East was to land an invading Union Force in the heart of the Confederacy. This historical event in my universe was the Virginia Peninsula Campaign of June, 1862, but in this universe it began further south.

Union General George McClellan, in the first week of March, 1862, was assigned the task of landing ten thousand men at Beaufort, North Carolina, marching inland and capturing New Bern, North Carolina, building up his army and moving south toward Atlanta, the Confederate Capital.

It seems that Union General George Brinton McClellan had the same propensity for whining for more reinforcements in both universes. True to form, McClellan landed his troops at Beaufort, North Carolina, but indicated to Lincoln he needed another twenty-five thousand troops before he could march the thirty-five miles necessary to take New Bern, North Carolina. Lincoln and Union Secretary of War Stanton were adamant that McClellan should advance toward New Bern with the forces he already had. After much coaxing and placating with the promise that he would be supplied with a much larger army once New Bern was taken, McClellan advanced on New Bern, which capitulated with hardly a fight.

McClellan then asked for the needed rearmaments, resupplies, and reinforcements needed to begin a campaign to take the Confederate capital at Atlanta.

The wide mouth of the Neuse River at New Bern, North Carolina was a perfect port for the Union buildup so

Lincoln and General Scott complied with the request for more troops and supplies. The buildup lasted through April and May of 1862.

The Confederates quickly learned of McClellan's presence and began a buildup of their own at Goldsboro, North Carolina located seventy-five miles northwest of New Bern. The stage was set for a confrontation that rivaled the Virginia Peninsula Campaign in my old universe.

By the end of May, 1862, Union General McClellan had over ninety thousand troops, three hundred cannon and two thousand cavalry. He named his force the Army of the Atlantic. However, he still stalled and wanted more. Lincoln stated there were no more troops to send without stripping the army protecting Washington City from the twin threats of Confederate Generals Joe Johnston and Thomas Jackson.

The Confederate army commanded by Confederate General Robert E. Lee, who was in charge of the defense of the Confederate Atlantic coast, had advanced to Kinston, North Carolina, which was about thirty miles from New Bern with an army of fifty-five thousand men. Lee had his army dig rifle pits and breastworks on the north bank of the Neuse River.

McClellan took over a week to move his army toward the dug-in Confederate position and, once he had deployed his army south of the Neuse River, began a three-day bombardment of the Confederate positions. The Confederates would simply move out of the range of the Union cannon during the day, reoccupy the positions during the night and make any needed repairs to their breastworks.

Finally, McClellan began crossing the Neuse River on June 18, 1862. As usual, he had not used his cavalry as a scouting force and didn't know the extent of the Confederate positions waiting for him. Confederate artillery cut the advancing Union brigades to pieces. A large Confederate infantry blocking force was in the breastworks to hold the main Union advance at bay, while two Confederate divisions had earlier secretly crossed the Neuse River and attacked each of the Union flanks once the battle had begun. It was a disaster for McClellan. He had two divisions chewed up. To make matters worse, the Confederate Cavalry under Ashby Turner circled the Union army and caused havoc by attacking the Union supply trains in the rear. Then the Confederate blocking force, utilizing prefabricated bridge sections, quickly crossed the river and attacked the front of the Union line. Numerous units of the Union army were routed. However, enough Union regiments gave ground grudgingly to allow the Union army to retreat back to New Bern, North Carolina without being completely annihilated.

By the end of July, 1862, McClellan's Army of the Atlantic had not progressed any further than New Bern since the disastrous defeat outside of Kinston, North Carolina. McClellan refused to move without more reinforcements, horses, mules, rations and equipment. Lincoln and Scott had gotten so sick of his complaints that they relieved him of command and sent General Ambrose Burnside to take his place.

On August 15, Burnside arrived in Beaufort, North Carolina via a naval flotilla along with two corps of reinforcements, which consisted of about twenty-five thousand men, ninety-six cannon, six thousand horses and mules plus much needed supplies and equipment. It was sort of asinine that Lincoln and Scott had not sent the reinforcements and equipment to McClellan but did convey them with his replacement. McClellan no doubt became enraged because he didn't even greet Burnside when he arrived. McClellan simply got on his personal boat and set out for Washington City. He was never heard from again and must have been absorbed into the matrix of the army.

Burnside had apparently been told to meld the additional reinforcements into McClellan's force and attack the Confederates as soon as possible. Needless to say he did not have the organization acumen that McClellan had. However, McClellan had already worked on the reorganization of the Army. So, Burnside didn't have to do too much to bring his Army of the Atlantic up to speed. At the present time, he was in the process of getting all the new equipment issued, the men drilled and the horses and mules distributed.

So what happened out in the west? Of the following nine chronological events and or battles, items one through five plus item nine occurred with the same exact outcomes as they did in my universe. Items six through eight did not.

One: In August 1861, the Confederates won the Battle of Wilson's Creek near Springfield, Missouri.

Two: In November 1861, General Grant captured Belmont, Missouri.

Three: In February 1862, Confederate Fort Henry and Fort Donelson were captured by a Union army and navy joint venture under General Grant and Naval Flag Officer Foote. This caused the Confederates to pull back from north central Tennessee to Corinth, Mississippi, located just south of the Tennessee border.

Four: Nashville, Tennessee fell to Union forces on February 25, 1862.

Five: In March 1862, the Confederates lost the Battle of Pea Ridge in northwest Arkansas, which eradicated the threat of the Confederacy taking Missouri.

Six: The Battle of Shiloh, however, had a totally different outcome in this universe. On April 3, 1862, Confederate General Albert Sidney Johnston surprised a Union Army under General William T. Sherman and General Ulysses Grant at Pittsburg Landing (Shiloh) and defeated it. The Union army retreated north into Savannah, Tennessee, where it held a line of hastily prepared breastworks. During the night of April 4th, the battered Union army was ferried to the east side of the Tennessee River, where it joined Union General Carlos Buell's force on April 6th. Buell had proceeded from northern Tennessee to reinforce Grant, but had arrived too late to be of any help.

Seven: Another very important outcome of the Battle of Shiloh in this universe was Confederate General Albert Sydney Johnson was not killed.

Eight: After its mauling at Shiloh, the Union army in the west pulled back to Camden, Tennessee, which is about seventy miles north of Savannah, Tennessee and seventy-five miles west of Nashville. Camden is on the west bank of the Tennessee River and is a good spot for a supply depot and staging area. The Union Army of the West, now dubbed the Army of Tennessee, had been taken away from General Grant after the debacle at Shiloh and offered to Sherman, who refused it. It was then given to General Rosecrans, who refitted the Union army at Camden and was presently marching his men down the west side of the

Tennessee River toward Savannah, Tennessee, the Confederate stronghold in southwestern Tennessee.

Nine: The last important historical event, which took place in my universe and in this universe, occurred on April 24, 1862. Union Flag Officer David Farragut ran his naval flotilla past Confederate Fort Jackson and Fort St. Philip at the mouth of the Mississippi River and captured New Orleans. The great trade center of The South was now closed to Confederate commerce.

After an all-day reading and note taking, I had finally collected all the vital historical information I needed. So, I thanked Mr. Matthews, the newspaper owner, for access to his files. I also asked if there was a good place to bed down for the night. He recommended the Stephens Hotel on Shenandoah Street, which was a few doors down from the newspaper office. I thanked him again, and throwing my poke sacks over my shoulder, proceeded toward the hotel.

I had spent a lot of time in the newspaper office. It was fully dark when I began walking to the hotel. As I ambled down the wooden sidewalk, I came to an alley between buildings. When I walked down the sidewalk steps to traverse the alleyway opening, a big man stepped in front of me and asked, "Whar ya a-goin' on this beautiful night?"

For some reason, I was immediately drawn to the distinctive coloring in his beard. Then I felt another man slink in behind me. I began to turn around to see who had cutoff my rear escape route, when the man behind me put his left arm around my neck in a choke hold to keep me in place.

Chapter 6

I don't know why I reacted the way I did. It must have been a reflex Aikido move learned years ago. But I turned my head and body 90 degrees to the left and just sat down with all the force I could muster. Moving my body unlocked my chin from the top of my assailant's forearm and allowed my head to slide down between his forearm and chest. He still had hold of the very top of my head, but my neck was no longer in jeopardy of being broken when I sat down.

In fact, my move catapulted the man who had me in the headlock forward over the top of me. He abruptly let go and tried to use his hands to break his fall. However, his head and shoulders crashed into the knees of the man in front of me. It was a perfect linebacker block. Both men went down in a heap. I wasted no time in scrambling to my feet, grabbing my hat and sacks and running toward the hotel less than two doors down.

I entered the small lobby at a run. The clerk behind the desk was startled when I yelled between gasps of breath, "I've just been mugged."

This produced a quizzical expression so I further explained," I been attacked by two men just two doors down."

A man sitting in the lobby who had been reading a newspaper stood up and approached me. "Could ya describe tha men who attacked ya?" he asked.

"Yes, but I really only got a look at tha man who was in front of me. He was about 5 feet 10 inches tall with a black beard. I could smell whiskey on his breath when he spoke. But one feature that stood out was a white streak in tha middle of his beard," I explained.

That last remark made the clerk and the newspaper reader perk up and really take notice. The clerk pulled out a pistol from under his desk and laid it on top of his ledger. The newspaper reader said, "I'll go out tha back door and get tha town marshal."

The responses to my last bit of information sort of spooked me. I asked the clerk, "Who's this man that caused y'all such trepidation?"

The clerk retorted, "Ain't ya never heard of Jones Gill?"

I responded, "I'm new to tha region and I've never heard of Jones Gill."

The clerk joyously proceeded to disclose all the gruesome particulars he knew about this notorious character.

"Gill is tha meanest hombre in tha region. He and his brother, Seaborne, weren't born. They's hatched by some demon southwest of Harpers' Ferry back in tha Allegheny Mountains. Tha Gills made their presence known in tha area from Harpers Ferry up to Hagerstown, Maryland back in 1848. Tha brothers rampaged over a nine-year period during which they's charged with train robbery, assault, murder and attempted murder not necessarily in that order. However, they finally got convicted in 1857 of train robbery, which got 'em both a term in tha penitentiary for five years. Tha region has enjoyed five years of peace and quiet, but evidently that's come to an end. Tha brothers musta got outta of prison."

The hotel clerk further elucidated, "Jones Gill's distinguishing trademark is a white streak in his beard, which led to his undoing. As a matter of pride he refused to shave his beard or dye tha distinctive white streak to match tha rest of his beard. During a train robbery he pulled up his bandana to force a kiss on a lady passenger and tha white streak was witnessed by tha lady and her companion. Later, he was caught by a posse and at trial tha lady described his unique beard. That's why he was convicted and sentenced to five years in prison along with his brother, Seaborne, who is his long-time accomplice."

The town marshal was apprised of the confrontation by the Gills from the man in the lobby. The marshal summoned his deputy and together they converged on me at the hotel. I was asked many questions about the incident and I felt they were really buying time to allow the perpetrators to possibly leave town so they wouldn't have to confront them. Eventually I was asked, "Where did tha assault take place and how did ya get out of their clutches?" I had to explain the move I had put on the person that headlocked me, but I don't think either of the lawmen understood what leverage can do to an assailant.

Finally, the lawmen, which incidentally were armed to the teeth with shotguns, pistols and knives, went on a search of the town for the culprits. This was no mean feat because it was a very steep walk from Shenandoah Street up to the top of Bolivar Heights.

I left them to their duty, registered in the hotel and, due to my notoriety in escaping the Gill Brothers, was only charged fifty cents for the night. I informed the desk clerk

I would be leaving in the morning for Shepherdstown. I also was given a private room and was soon sound asleep.

ଓ

The Dark Mage's Log: Earth 3' Date: 18620917

Jargunn had returned to Harpers Ferry in the early night. Since he couldn't use the cloaking device and the scent tracker at the same time, he turned off the scent tracker, implemented his cloaking device and stole around town without being seen.

He kept his distance from all Earth animals to preclude any radical behavior on their part. At full dark, Jargunn turned off his cloaking device, and keeping to the shadows, switched on his scent tracker. After working the town by grids, he readily picked up the imposter's scent.

Jargunn tracked the scent to a building on a road near the river. He then activated his cloaking device and took up a vigil across the street.

Jargunn saw the charlatan emerge from the building and followed him. He was getting ready to apprehend him when two men accosted the imposter.

Jargunn decided to let fate rule the day. Hopefully they would kill this pesky Earthling. He retreated across the street to watch the show.

He was surprised. He had to give the imposter credit in employing really good tactics in extricating himself from their clutches.

Jargunn hung around in cloaking mode to hear all the conversations that took place. This phony was imbedding himself more and more into the fabric of this society.

Jargunn left the area, walked to a grove of trees near the river and called Lord Dendaras. He related what had transpired.

Lord Dendaras told him to leave the area tonight. Since during the many conversations the imposter had

indicated that he would be traveling back to Shepherdstown tomorrow, Jargunn was to capture him tomorrow during the day in a secluded area of the road. Jargunn respectfully asked, "Sire, you wish me to make the apprehension during daylight?"

"Yes," Lord Dendaras irritably replied.

"I understand, Sire," Jargunn responded.

Lord Dendaras abruptly cut communication. Jargunn thought, "This must truly be a problem of the highest order. To risk being seen during the day by a local is tantamount to creating a historical paradigm. But I have a direct order so I'll not be at risk. "

☙

I awoke the next morning to the singing of birds outside my hotel room window. The sun was just breaking over the horizon. This prompted me to get up. I went to the wash basin and poured water from a pitcher to the top of the basin, which was situated on the lone desk in the room. I washed the upper part of my body and face with a cloth that was also on the desk.

Once I had finished and dried off with the hotel's miniscule idea of a hand towel, I looked out the window at the town as it began to come alive. Town folk were walking to and fro and an occasional carriage went by. I have to admit this type of slow life style was rather appealing. I felt refreshed and ready to head back to Shepherdstown. I dressed and went looking for a decent breakfast.

Downstairs I found a small breakfast area in a room adjacent to the lobby and ordered coffee. After I ate some decent biscuits and gravy, two eggs over easy and a small ham steak, I paid the waitress and went out on the front porch of the hotel to relax.

I sat in a rocking chair and looked out at Shenandoah Street. Farmers' wagons were now adding to the traffic. Man, this was sure different from the traffic jams I experienced each morning going to work. I began to think about my situation and experienced the depression that accompanied the feeling of helplessness. An idea of how futile this thinking was surged through my mind and I immediately said, "No more. I will not be sorry for myself and whine anymore." Anger flared to the core of my being. Through gritted teeth I vowed, "If I ever find out who made me go through this, I will make them pay for it."

It took me a long time to bring my breathing under control and get my mind back under the influence of the wisdom mind, as the Taoist call it.

Once I had accomplished this feat, I was able to concentrate on the beautiful fall colors of the trees on the banks of the Potomac River. The red, yellow and orange leaves were brilliant and the trees seemed to pop out at me from their three dimensional forms. By that I mean, each tree just individually stood out and said, "Look at me." I looked at first one and then another. Each had its own shape of foliage and height. Some were like tall slender masts on a sailing ship with just a few limbs and angled toward the river. You just knew they would be blown into the river with the next big wind. Others had thick trunks and balloon-shaped foliage with large leaves that completely obscured the limbs. I don't know why they never appeared that way back in my universe. These trees seemed more alive and worth noticing.

I finally stirred back from my oblivion and went to the hotel clerk's booth. He was busy checking out a few overnight boarders. I waited my turn and asked, "Is there a barbershop in town?"

"Oh, yes sir. Turn right and go to tha end of tha street. Turn right again and it's located on tha right," he directed.

"Thank ya," I responded genteelly.

I traversed the two blocks to the barbershop and entered the abode of the 19th century rumor mongers and information dispensers not unlike our 21st century media talking heads. This was a two-chair establishment and one was empty.

I was directed to the vacant chair. The barber was a tidy person with long sideburns and closely cropped slicked-down hair with enough oil that it probably made his mind slip. The aroma of rose water aftershave generously applied to his person wafted through the establishment.

I took my life in my hands and ordered, "I'll have a shave and a haircut. I don't need any oil for my hair or aftershave."

The barber nodded readily, affixed the proverbial barber's cape to my body and jacked the back of the chair down so I was almost parallel to the floor. Then he applied a hot, and I do mean hot, towel to my face. It felt like a hornet's nest had landed on my face. I braved the scalding cloth and gradually the volcanic heat subsided. Thank goodness my nose was left unfettered so I wouldn't be asphyxiated.

I remained in this position for about a good five minutes, after which, the towel was removed, the chair was jacked back to a perpendicular position and foaming lather was applied to my two-day beard. He definitely was a better performer than I with a straight razor. He had me completely devoid of facial hair in about two minutes without any lacerations.

Being the essence of economic movement, he armed himself with a pair of clippers and began a rapid fire snipping around my head hardly touching the hair. He finished and the barber's cape was removed. I was given a mirror to inspect his handiwork. I nodded my affirmation of his work, smiled and asked, "What do I owe ya?"

"Fifty cents," was the reply.

I paid the man and asked, "Where's tha nearest outhouse?" He gave me directions.

After utilizing my handy newspaper in the aforementioned abode, I slung my bags over my shoulder and went to retrieve Beau for the back-breaking return trip to Shepherdstown.

Beau was contentedly munching on hay when I arrived at the livery stable. I swear, when he saw me, he turned and walked farther back in his stall. I know he was hoping I didn't see him and that he didn't have to put up with me again so soon.

I had decided to take the River Road straight north from Harpers Ferry rather than going west to Halltown and then north on the Shepherdstown Pike. I understood that it wasn't as good a road, but it cut off about two miles from the trip and any less time riding Beau was appreciated.

I didn't owe any additional money for his upkeep, since I paid up front and only had to leave him at the livery one night. The livery owner saddled Beau and I got directions where to enter the River Road. I mounted a very truculent excuse for a horse and began the sacroiliac-destroying ride back home.

I had learned from the livery owner that the River Road to Shepherdstown was mostly used by the local farmers, while the main road from Harpers Ferry to Halltown and then to Shepherdstown was mostly used by the traveling public.

I stopped on the way out of town at a local mercantile store and purchased some bread and cheese for lunch along the way.

We, meaning Beau and I, had proceeded about four miles and were about one and a half hours into the ride when I saw a troop of cavalry riding toward me. They were covered in dust and from a distance it was hard to ascertain if they were Confederate or Union.

The leader halted the troop of about thirty men in front of me and asked where I was going. I answered that I was going to Shepherdstown. He wanted to know if there were any cavalry in Harpers Ferry and I answered truthfully that I hadn't seen any.

I kept looking into his eyes, but in the periphery of my vision, I saw that he didn't have any insignia on his collar. Instead there were two insignia stripes on his shoulders. This was a Yankee Captain with a detachment bent on some mischief in or near Harpers Ferry. He bid me good day and I touched the brim of my hat to him. They rode off in a hurry and I sat there wondering how to alert the Confederate garrison in Harpers Ferry.

The fastest way would be by telegraph, but there were no cities on this road that had a telegraph. Also, there were no nearby Chesapeake & Ohio Canal locks on the other side of the Potomac that I could contact to send a messenger. Lastly, there was no railroad in the vicinity that I could flag down to send a message. Even if I was able to contact a boat on the Potomac River, which ran close to the River Road, and give them a message, it would take too long to arrive at Harpers Ferry for any Confederate response.

So I finally decided that the only way to quickly get word to the Confederates was to ride to Harpers Ferry myself. I would have to ride like the wind and somehow get past the Union troops. However, I surely wasn't going to accomplish this on Beau.

I looked around for the nearest farm house, but none was in site. I kicked Beau like the dickens and got him into a fast trot headed north. As we came around a bend in the road, a two story house loomed in the distance so I kept Beau moving hurriedly until I entered the front yard of the house.

A lady in a homespun dress came out on the porch to see who I was and asked, "What cha doing, stranger?"

I hurriedly answered, "I gotta get word to tha Confederate command in Harpers Ferry. There's a Union Cavalry patrol headed thata way. I just met 'em a few minutes ago and something should be done to get 'em out of this area." Abruptly, I asked, "Do ya have a fast horse I could ride back to alert Harpers Ferry command?"

The lady eyeballed Beau and saw my dilemma. Then she looked me up and down and let out a huff. I reassured her, "I give ya my word I am telling tha truth and I promise to return yar horse as soon as I have alerted tha Confederates." As further proof of my good character, I added," I am tha new school teacher in Shepherdstown and Mr. Throckmorton, tha local banker, will vouch for me."

I guess the latter statement sort of swayed her in my favor because she said, "Thar's a black stallion in tha barn, but ya gonna have to saddle him yaself."

I thanked her and kicked Beau into another fast trot to the barn. I didn't have as much trouble with the stallion as I thought I would. He was in a stall and, although we weren't on a first name basis, allowed me to put a horse blanket and saddle on his back and cinch it up tight. Thank heavens I remembered how to thread and tighten all the straps from my horse riding days as a youth.

I tied up Beau and mounted the stallion. I headed back to the house and the lady came out on the porch. I queried, "What's tha name of yar horse?"

"Sampson," she called out. Then she asked," Ya gotst any firearms?"

When I shook my head no, she motioned me to come near the porch and handed me a six-shot Colt pistol. She explained, "If'n ya wanta get past tha Yanks, ya need to skirt to tha west or right side of tha road. The east or left side of tha road is too steep and drops off toward tha river."

I yelled, "Thanks for tha help and wish me luck."

Sampson was a very appropriate name for the stallion. I headed him toward Harpers Ferry and, when I kicked him, he took off like a rocket. I was almost thrown backwards out of the saddle. However, I was able to catch hold of the front of the saddle and pull myself back to a controlled seated position. The stamina and strength emanating from this black galloping machine made me feel like one of the Pony Express riders of long ago running from a band of Comanche Indians. It was all I could do to hold him from running straight out, which would tire him too quickly. I pulled back on the reins to slow him to a gentle gallop.

I had decided to keep on the road until I approached the end of the Union Cavalry column and then veer off the road to the right. I would circle around the Yanks and back to the River Road and then hightail it for Harpers Ferry. All of this was with the hope that the Yank column wouldn't catch sight of me during all my maneuvering.

After a few minutes of travel, I reined in Sampson to a steady lope to further contain his strength. I figured the Yanks were about one mile ahead of me and I hoped they had slowed down to do some reconnoitering.

It seemed like forever, but it must have been only about twenty minutes when I spied the backs of the last two troopers of the Yank column disappear around a bend in the road up ahead.

I tugged on Sampson's reins to bring him to a halt, but he still wanted to run. I was forced to stand in the stirrups and pull for all I was worth to get him under control. Luckily we didn't raise enough of a ruckus to alert the Yanks so we didn't get a sudden visit by any of the band of raiders.

Keeping a firm hand on Sampson, I walked him to the edge of the bend in the road, dismounted and tied this son of Pegasus to a tree. I stroked his forehead for a few seconds to calm him down. Then I approached the bend and peered through some underbrush to see what was ahead.

The Yank column had slowed to a walk on the River Road. I returned to where I had left Sampson. He was breathing hard, but the wild look in his eyes told me he hadn't had a chance to run like this in a long time and he was really enjoying it.

I mounted and walked Sampson up the road from whence we had traveled to get well out of site of the Yanks. Then I directed Sampson off the road to the west. We preceded about one hundred yards through dense woods which harbored not much undergrowth. This was good because Sampson wasn't cut by any bushes or low tree branches. I thanked heaven for that. I went west another fifty yards or so and then turned south toward Harpers Ferry to parallel the Yank column.

Sampson had about gotten his wind back so I kicked him into a trot. The leaves in the woods were apparently damp from a rain because Sampson's hooves left only a muffled sound.

We had traveled about fifteen minutes dodging trees and skirting a few thickets when I heard a horse whinny up ahead. I reined Sampson to an abrupt stop, dismounted and put my hand over his nose. I had seen it done a hundred times in the cowboy movies and hoped it would keep him from answering the phantom horse up ahead.

Squinting to look through the thick woods, I could barely make out a horse and rider about fifty yards ahead. Abruptly, two horsemen rode toward the unknown rider. There ensued a conversation and the three riders rode back to the River Road. I had a hard time holding Sampson's reins with my hand over his nose. He was really acting up because he must have felt an insatiable desire to call to the three horses. I was able to walk him around and settle him down, but it was a hard job. I did get one good look at the riders as they headed to the road. Two were Yanks and the third was a woman. One of the Yanks had her reins and was leading her horse toward the main body of cavalry.

The first thing that entered my mind was: Kidnapped. I mounted Sampson and we continued skirting the Yankee column for a few hundred yards. I figured that the Yanks had their hands full with the woman. Her capture had bought me some time.

I started angling Sampson toward the River Road. After what seemed like an eternity, we entered the aforementioned byway, and I kicked Sampson hard. This time I was ready for his burst of speed when we took off like a shot. I ran him at full gallop for about twenty minutes, but it seemed like an hour. I started to see more houses the closer we got to Harpers Ferry.

Suddenly, the road turned southwest. I wanted to go south so I left the road and angled cross-country toward Bolivar Heights. I reasoned that, if there were any Confederates in the area, they would have a lookout post on the highest point this side of the two rivers.

Sampson was starting to fade so I slowed him to a lope. When we hit the road that ran along the top of the heights, we began to encounter people walking along the road. I reined Sampson to a halt next to a well-dressed gentleman walking along the road and asked, "Where's the closest Confederate contingent located?" He pointed straight ahead and informed me, "'Bout two more blocks that a way." I thanked him and kicked Sampson hard. We rode off in a cloud of dust that hopefully didn't soil the gentleman's suit.

We covered the two blocks to the Confederate outpost in nothing flat. I jumped down off Sampson and tied his reins to a column of the outpost porch. As I ran toward the front door of the small command center, an armed soldier at the door brought his musket from the Order Arms position with the butt of the weapon on the wood porch to a menacing Port Arms position with the musket held diagonally across his body. He also moved in front of the door to prevent me from entering the building and demanded, "What cha want herah?"

I blurted out, "Thar's Yankee cavalry down tha River Road about four miles and they's headed thissa way."

That brought a captain out of the building. He looked me up and down and asked, "Well sir, did ya actually see this herah Yankee cavalry?"

I responded, "Yes, I saw 'em and their captain asked me if therah were any Confederates in Harpers Ferry. I told him I didn't know. It looks like they captured a woman rider also."

He rebutted with a dubious tone, "Would ya be willing to lead us to tha place ya last saw this herah cavalry?"

I assured him, "I would most gladly do so."

Taking me at my word, he immediately called out the guard and told the adjutant to have his horse saddled and to telegraph the garrison's cavalry contingent down in Harpers Ferry to meet us on the River Road in twenty minutes.

With the orders given, the Captain turned back to me and asked, "Would ya like something to drink?"

I replied, "Let me see to my horse first." He acquiesced and I took Sampson to a water trough next to the garrison outpost. I didn't let him drink too much. He was still breathing hard and was frothy. I asked the soldier at the door if there was something that I could use to wipe down my horse. He nodded yes and returned quickly with an old blanket. I rubbed almost all the froth off Sampson. He must have enjoyed the rubdown because he stood contentedly as I administered to him. I let him have one more quick drink of water before our return trip.

The adjutant returned with the Captain's saddled horse, a beautiful roan mare. Sampson whinnied his approval and the Captain and I had a good laugh. We mounted and the captain inquired, "Are ya armed."

I affirmed, "Yes Sir, I was given a colt revolver by a lady from whom I was loaned this noble steed." He raised his eyebrows, nodded and we set off toward the River Road.

We loped our horses cross country and arrived at the River Road in just a few minutes. Sampson had very quick recuperative powers. He did not seem to be tired at all from our previous hurried travel.

However, the Confederate cavalry contingent hadn't arrived.

While waiting on them to appear, I asked him, "If I may be so bold, what's yar name, Sir."

He replied, "Captain John Mosby." I nearly fell out of my saddle.

Chapter 7

Captain Mosby gave me a curious glance due to the reaction to his name. He ventured, "Is something wrong?"

I quickly answered, "No, not at all." I looked more closely at the Captain's face. He was clean shaven, which had confused me, because I had always remembered a picture of him sitting amongst his men and having a beard. But focusing more closely on his features, I recognized him.

Due to my forwardness, he asked, "Have we met before?"

I simply answered, "Yes, in another lifetime."

He was surprised by my reply, but he didn't ask for further explanation because his contingent of Confederate cavalry came galloping down the road.

There were about sixteen troopers in a column of twos. As they came to a halt, a second sergeant, who was apparently in charge, saluted smartly and reported for duty. Captain Mosby asked if any more troopers were on the way. The sergeant replied twenty more were coming, but it would be about forty-five minutes before they would be able to rendezvous with us. Captain Mosby indicated that we couldn't wait. We had to move now. So, we headed north on the River Road to find the Yanks. Captain Mosby was in the lead with me by his side as the guide.

We thundered down the road for about three miles without seeing any Yanks. I could feel the Captain's eyes on me and I knew he was thinking I had brought him on a wild goose chase or possibly even into an ambush.

However, as we rounded a bend in the road, a civilian flagged us down. He introduced himself as Jonathan Shumaker and said that a bunch of Yanks had passed his place about thirty minutes ago and took off cross country to the west, probably to hit the Shepherdstown Pike. Captain Mosby touched his hand to the brim of his hat, thanked the man profusely and promised, "We a-gonna give those Yanks wat fur." I looked at him skeptically since our unit was only about half as big as theirs.

All of a sudden I understood the danger that I had gotten myself into. I could get permanently and truly dead from this little adventure.

We exited the River Road to the west and quickly picked up the Yankees' trail. It wasn't easy going due to the thickness of the woods, but we were able to proceed at a fast trot. After about twenty-five minutes, Captain Mosby held up his hand and we all stopped immediately. He motioned for the sergeant to come forward. Once his sergeant had come abreast, he pointed ahead and said in a whisper, "Yankee cavalry."

In a low voice Captain Mosby ordered the sergeant, "Have the men maneuver as quietly as possible into a single line facing tha Yanks."

The message was relayed to the troopers and they deftly walked their horses into a battle line behind us. I turned around and saw they were centered on the Captain and me, which put us out front and subject to being shot first.

I sort of gulped and looked at Mosby. He grinned and winked at me. He slowly pulled his revolver from his holster with his right hand and held his horse's reins in his left hand. I mimicked him by pulling my revolver from my belt with my right hand and gripped Sampson's reins with my left.

Our unit was hidden from view in very thick dark woods. The Yanks had already been through this area and had broken out into a field of two foot high wheat. They were about seventy-five yards from us walking their horses in a column of twos heading west with their backs to us. They had no flankers or rear guard probably due to their rapid movement and no enemy contact had lulled them into a false sense of confidence.

Captain Mosby looked to his left and right to make sure the troopers were looking at him. When he had made sure that all eyes were on him, he lifted his right hand and holding it above his head began to walk his horse forward. I kept pace with him and our cavalry contingent followed close on our heels.

To say that I was scared is an understatement. Adrenalin must have been flowing in my body like Niagara Falls because my heart was beating ninety to nothing. I was sweating profusely. My palms were so wet that it was hard to hold my revolver and Sampson's reins. But, I kept to the right and abreast of the Captain.

Sampson must have felt my anxiety because I was having a hard time holding him back. I don't know if he sensed what was about to occur and wanted to either fight or take to flight. In my case it was flight. I was just hoping that Sampson would not let go with one of his famous whinnies. I guess the pressure of the bit on his mouth applied by my frequent pulling back on the reins kept his mind off making any sound.

Just as we reached the edge of the wheat field, Captain Mosby brought his right arm down and yelled, “Charge.”

I kicked Sampson and he shot forward like a lightning bolt. I was ready for it and bent forward so I wouldn’t be thrown out of the saddle. Our line of troops broke from the woods in an almost perfect line, which quickly disintegrated into an uneven gaggle as everyone focused on the Yanks. Captain Mosby let loose with a “rebel yell” and fired his revolver. We all echoed the famous battle cry and most of the men fired their first rounds at the Yanks. I didn’t because I had only one revolver. Our troopers had at least two and a few had three.

The Yanks were taken completely by surprise.

The Union Captain, who I saw peel out from the head of the column to look at us, yelled some orders to his troops. They tried to maneuver into a line of battle to face us plus unsheathe their sabers, but we were upon them in a jiffy.

Our unit began to rapid fire as we closed with their confused numbers and our boys unseated about six of them. They were still in one big bunch and our troopers were smart enough to avoid close contact and getting sliced with a sword. We broke off to the left and right and rode around them like a band of Indians circling a wagon train firing at the bewildered melee. I saw some more Yanks fall off their horses during our encirclement.

I had gone to the right of the Yankee contingent. As I neared the front of the column, I saw the Yank captain about thirty yards ahead hightailing for a tree line. He had the horse's reins of the woman, who I had witnessed being taken by the Yanks back near the River Road, and was pulling her along behind him. Captain Mosby saw them at the same time as he came around the left side of the Yankee jumble. We both urged our horses forward with renewed vigor. Sampson was by far the fastest mount and I was about ten yards ahead of Captain Mosby gaining on the escaping Yankee captain and his female prisoner.

The Yank captain looked back, saw the futility of keeping ahead of us with the woman in tow and let go the reins of her horse. The woman's horse now became a runaway. It just kept galloping after the Yank, but the female rider had no control of her mount because her horse's reins were dragging the ground.

I shoved the borrowed Colt into my belt. I gave Sampson a kick and pointed him toward the beleaguered female rider. Sampson quickly came abreast of the woman's horse, which allowed me to reached down and grab the side of the bridle that ran along the right side of the horse's head and jaw. I slowly started to rein Sampson to a stop. This allowed the woman's horse to slow down and come to a complete stop without turning abruptly and throwing her from her side saddle. As I caught up with the woman, Captain Mosby flew past us after the Yankee captain. I heard a few shots and looked up to see Mosby enter a stand of trees at the west end of the wheat field.

I turned to look at the woman and my heart went up into my throat. She was the most gorgeous example of womanhood I had ever seen. She had brown eyes that you could drown in. Her ebony hair was in long tresses and pulled back and captured under a blue riding hat with a short brim. Her face was egg-shaped with a nose that wasn't too long or too short and a mouth that turned up at the corners, giving her a perpetual smile. Her complexion was as white as confectionery sugar. But the single most striking factor about her countenance was that she was the spitting image of my wife when she was about sixteen years of age back in my old universe. I looked at this woman as if I had been hit by a bolt from out of the blue.

At this moment, I realized here was the love of my life and how much I missed her double in my universe. I know I probably had the most ludicrous slack-jawed expression on my face. My heart was racing as I just sat there on Sampson holding the woman's horse and looking into her lovely face. All the recent hellacious trials and tribulations just welled up in me and tears came to my eyes.

I was shocked when the lady, who had started to cry, said in the most beautiful Virginia southern drawl, "Oh thank ya sah! From tha bottom of my heart, thank ya!"

I was a little choked up myself, but was able to croak out, "Please don't cry. I can't stand it when ya cry."

I said the words as if I knew her, because she looked bewildered and asked, "Do I know ya, sah?"

"Yes," I answered, "I have known ya all my life."

Our strange repartee was interrupted when Captain Mosby galloped up and declared, "That Yankee officer had tha fastest horse I've ever seen."

His sudden presence jolted me back to the present. It took all the self-control I could muster to gather my emotions, which I had been wearing on my sleeve, and shove them back into my heart. It hurt me to the core of my being, but I was able to do it.

Captain Mosby solicitously asked the lady, "Are ya alright, Daphne?"

She looked at me and, dabbing her eyes with a handkerchief that had suddenly appeared in her hand, answered, "Yes, thanks to tha actions of this gentleman."

She smiled at us and said, "I owe y'all tha greatest debt. Will ya both please join our family for dinnah tonight?"

The Captain and I both looked at each other and answered almost in unison, "I would be delighted."

I got down off Sampson, retrieved the reins of the lady's horse and handed them to her. She smiled graciously and accepted them.

Further observation of the damsel allowed me to take note of her wardrobe and riding equipment. She was riding side saddle, which was the only respectable mode of horseback riding allowed a lady in the 19th century. She was wearing a blue frilly blouse with white lace that acted as a collar around her throat. The blouse was the same light blue that matched her hat. Her riding skirt was a darker blue and reached the top of her black boots. Her hands were covered in white gloves with lace around the wrists. She had a brown riding crop that was looped around her left wrist.

Her horse was still spooked from the confrontation. So I took time to rub the troubled mount's forehead and nose and speak gently to it. After the short massage, the wild eyes and laid back ears of fright were replaced with a sense of calm.

I looked at the lady and said, "Yar horse is okay to travel now."

She looked at me with a solemn expression and declared, "Again, I must thank ya for yar endeavors on my behalf." She then smiled broadly, revealing the cutest dimples imaginable, extended her hand and said, "Lula Belle and I thank ya for yar gallantry."

I accepted her hand in both of mine and stammered, "It was my pleasure." I hoped my utterances weren't being too forward, but she didn't act offended. So I guess what I said was respectful. I realized I had held her hand too long because she sort of tilted her head and looked at me with an inquiring expression. I quickly let go of her hand and uttered, "I don't even know yar name."

She voiced a delightful little peal of laughter and answered, "I'm Daphne Jane Newcomer and may I ask who is addressing me?"

I smiled from ear to ear and found myself responding, "James Edward Hager, at yar service."

She returned, "Well James Edward Hager, we need to be on our way. I have a lot of things to arrange for our dinnah."

She then looked at Captain Mosby, who had been patiently witnessing the tete-a-tete with a smile, extended her hand and exclaimed, "We meet again Captain. Yar quick action has saved our city and me, personally.

Harpers Ferry and my family owe ya a great debt of gratitude."

He rode his horse close to Ms. Newcomer, accepted her hand and bowed from the waist while removing his hat. It was a sheer act of chivalry and nicely done. It also caused more than a tinge of jealousy to rear its ugly head in my heart. I might have a rival for Ms. Newcomer's affections. What was I thinking? I shouldn't even be considering such thoughts. I was a happily married man already. But I had to ask myself, "How can she look just like my wife, but at a younger age?"

The three of us headed back to the site of the skirmish. The Captain and I were walking our horses to give them a breather, while Ms. Newcomer followed us on Lula Belle.

Sampson must have been in the prime of life because he kept looking back at Lula Belle. When he let out one of his boisterous whinnies, I jerked his reins so that his head was brought close to mine and I said in a stage whisper, "Behave yourself."

I glanced back at Ms. Newcomer, who suddenly averted her gaze, but couldn't conceal the smile on her face. I turned beet red and continued walking my noble but randy steed toward the gaggle of soldiers.

ଓ

The Dark Mage's Log: 'Earth 3' Date: 18620918

Jargunn had set up his ambush north of the farm where the imposter had procured a large four-legged creature of great strength. When the imposter didn't arrive, he sensed something amiss.

He willed his ACV to appear and in stealth mode traversed the road back to Harpers Ferry. It was then that he spied a small armed unit of men all in like-colored clothing on four-legged animals common to this era deploying in a long line at the edge of some foliage. It appeared that they had surreptitiously moved to a point at the rear of a larger armed group.

This larger group also had common colored clothing, but it was a different hue from the group to their rear. The large group moving across the open area

was also on animals of the same four-legged species as the smaller group.

It seemed that the small stealthy group was about to attack the larger group, which was ludicrous.

Watching from his panoramic vantage point, Jargunn witnessed the whole brutal, but brief, encounter. Jargunn relished the sound of their battle and envied the exaltation of triumph the victors must have felt. It reminded him of his service on the planet of Golgoron in the Solar System of Margon in the Galaxy of Esteron decades ago.

He reviewed the total scenario of what had transpired. The two groups utilized primitive weapons on each other. A few of the Earthlings were now in the Great Void awaiting their resettlement into Infinity due to the piercing of their bodies by the small projectiles emanating from the armaments. It was amazing that the small group attained the triumph. They had used a tactic with which he was unfamiliar. He must remember it for possible further implementation.

In addition to the engagement, Jargunn also observed the rescue of an Earthling female from the large group by the imposter. Via the use of an amplifying device, he heard that her name was Miss Newcomer. He also heard the dinner invitation, whatever that was, given to the imposter and the commander of the stealth force and their prompt acceptance.

Lastly, he also beheld the unnecessary display by the female when one of the Earthlings went to the Great Void.

☙

As I looked ahead, I caught sight of the aftermath of battle. With the rescue of Ms. Newcomer, I had completely forgotten about the Yanks we had attacked.

We approached the battle site and I could see that our boys had captured about fifteen Yanks. Apparently they had been ordered to dismount and lay their weapons in a heap because there were numerous sabers, pistols and carbines piled on a blanket. Six Yanks were lying on the ground. Three were dead because they had shrouds over them. Two were alive and had minor leg wounds. The last Yank had been hit in the shoulder. The wounded Yanks were being attended to by one of their corporals and one of our boys was lending a hand in bandaging. It appeared the Yankee captain and eight of his troopers had escaped.

Three of our boys were on the ground and being tended to by some of our troopers. One of them was wounded in the arm and one in the leg. The third appeared to be badly wounded in the chest. Eight of our troopers were holding the horses of the Yanks plus the horses of our troopers who had dismounted to oversee the disarming of the enemy and tend to the wounded.

I was about to suggest to Ms. Newcomer to ride around the group so she wouldn't be shocked by the carnage, when she deftly jumped down from Lula Belle and strode to where our badly wounded trooper was lying. She knelt down, and taking her lace handkerchief from the cuff of her dress, she wiped the blood from around the soldier's mouth, took his dirty hand in hers and looked intently into his eyes. He coughed up some blood, which she immediately dabbed away. Then she took his hand in both of hers again. The trooper smiled, closed his eyes and slowly relaxed as death took him to The Other Side. Daphne suddenly realized that the boy had died. She brought his hand to her check and started to weep.

All the men, both Rebs and Yanks, had stopped moving when she had approached the dying man. We were mesmerized as the gripping tableau played out. These men believed only hospital nurses could overlook blood and carnage to provide comfort to a dying man. So it was incredible for them to see a wealthy young woman give such caring treatment to a poor bloody dying private in the ranks. Tears came to my eyes and I had to blink rapidly and bite my lip to keep the stoic composure, which was required of a 19th century gentleman.

I approached Daphne and gently said, "He's gone Miss. We should let his comrades take care of him." She gradually stopped crying. Then taking one final consideration of the dead youth, she delicately laid the trooper's hand on his chest. Looking up at me, she nodded her acceptance and stood up. She almost lost her balance when she took her first step, but I quickly grasped her right elbow to keep her from falling. She swiftly recovered and said," I'm fine." I let go of her elbow and she continued toward her horse.

Captain Mosby had been holding Lula Belle's reins. When Ms. Newcomer approached the Captain, he draped the reins over the horse's neck and gave Miss Newcomer a leg up to mount. Then he said," Ya need to proceed to yar home. We will join ya later tonight."

She nodded to him and I interpreted it as a thank you for his helping her to mount and that she acquiesced to his suggestion. She looked at him and rasped, "He was so young."

The Captain just bowed his head and replied, "Yes, he was."

As she turned to go, the Captain motioned to one of the troopers and ordered him to accompany her home.

The Captain turned to me and declared, "Please forgive my manners, but I didn't even get your name."

"I'm Jim Hager," I replied.

"Well Mr. Hager, I want to thank ya on behalf of tha Confederacy for yar help and heroism this day. If I may ask, what do ya plan to do now?"

"Why, I plan on attending tha dinnah that Miss Newcomer invited us to. By the way, where does Miss Newcomer's family reside?" I inquired.

He indicated, "Ya can't miss tha Newcomer house. It's tha big two-story house right by tha road about a mile west of Harper's Ferry on School House Ridge. I'll see ya therah." He turned to go, but turned back and added, "You're in for a treat. I wouldn't miss a meal at tha Newcomer's for all tha money in tha world. I just wish my wife had been invited. She would have considered it tha event of tha year." I smiled at the description of the supposed feast we would be enjoying and the information that he was already married.

Looking at the site of the brief skirmish, I surveyed all the weapons, equipment, wounded and dead strewn over the wheat field. I asked in a deflated voice, "What cha gonna do now?"

Mosby replied, "I'll have tha prisoners and their equipment handed overah to tha other part of our unit, which I am hoping will arrive momentarily. They will in turn transfer tha Yanks and their weapons to the Provost Marshal in Harper's Ferry. Tha wounded will need to be turned over to tha Army surgeon. Tha bodies will be given to tha local mortuary for burial or transported to tha Union and Confederate families."

Abruptly, he solicited, "Will ya be riding to tha Newcomer's now?"

"No," I responded, "I have to return my steed to tha owner from whom I borrowed it and procure tha noble horse that I was originally riding."

This seemed to momentarily baffle the Captain, but he finally laughed and said, "I must see this noble steed ya've referred to. He must be something if he's any bettah than tha horse ya are riding now. See ya at tha Newcomer's."

We shook hands. I mounted Sampson and rode back to the River Road.

ଓ

The Dark Mage's Log: 'Earth 3' Date: 18620918

Jargunn contacted Lord Dendaras immediately and related the happenings. Lord Dendaras questioned, "You are absolutely certain he had an exchange with the Newcomer female?"

"Yes, Sire, he did," Jargunn answered.

"Then leave the imposter alone until further ordered. Don't apprehend him. Don't interfere with his movements. Monitor him only and report his activities. Do you understand?" examined Lord Dendaras.

"Yes, Sire," responded Jargunn. As the Watcher disconnected his transmission

he thought, "This is getting more bizarre by the moment."

☙

Once we intercepted the River Road, I turned Sampson north. He must have sensed that we were going home because he was restless and wanted to gallop. I let him feel his oats, but kept him in a gentle lope from which he never seemed to tire.

We ate up the ground quickly. When we rounded the bend in the road that revealed his farm, he whinnied loudly. The lady of the house must have been waiting anxiously for us near the front door because she came out on the front porch followed by two younger men.

She had her hands on her hips and the two men had grim looks on their faces. Once I had ridden into the yard, she said," Well, at least ya brought him back in one piece."

I dismounted and said, "Yes Ma'am, and he was instrumental in tha capture of about twenty Yankees and tha rescue of Miss Daphne Newcomer."

She and the men acted as if they had been hit by a ton of bricks.

I took off my hat, gave a short bow and said, "Ma'am, I apologize that I don't even know yar name, but yar spirit of patriotism in allowing me to utilize Sampson has been a great benefit to our country." Pointing at the two men that stood on either side of her, I asked, "And who might these fine gentlemen be?"

The lady was flabbergasted and quickly closed her mouth that had gaped open due to the news of the enemy encounter, the rescue of Daphne and, if I may say so, the eloquence of my apology.

Gaining her composure again, she uttered, “I am Sarah Throckmorton and these herah are my sons Caleb and Joshua. Tha only reason I allowed ya to take Sampson was that Elias Throckmorton, tha banker ya referred to, is my brother-in-law. I mean was my brother-in-law. His brother Caleb, Senior was my husband. He died last fall of consumption.”

“I’m sorry to hear that Mrs. Throckmorton. Ya have my condolences,” I commiserated. With my hat in my hand, I walked toward Mrs. Throckmorton bowed in front of her and shook hands with her sons, who were still taken aback by my news.

All of a sudden Joshua said, “Well don’t keep us in tha dark. What happened?”

I said, “Could we take Sampson to tha barn and I will relate tha happenings on tha way?”

They all agreed. So we meandered to the barn as I gave them a recap of the day’s adventures. They were interested in all the happenings, but were especially excited at the news of how well Mosby’s cavalry contingent performed.

As we reached the barn, I said, “Oh, yes! Mrs. Throckmorton, I wanted to thank ya for tha use of tha pistol. I didn’t have a chance to use it, but it was an encouragement to know I had it.” I pulled the weapon from my belt and handed her the Colt six-shooter she had loaned me.

The sons really raised their eyebrows at the return of the pistol. I thought that she would have a lot of explaining to do once I had left. Mrs. Throckmorton flushed a bright crimson and took the weapon. "Glad it was a support to ya," she said.

I told them I had to return to Harpers Ferry for a dinner with the Newcomers and wondered if I owed them anything for the use of Sampson. They were very solicitous and said it was their privilege to have helped The Cause. So the sons took Sampson into the barn for a rubdown and I mounted Beau, who seemed very annoyed that he had to continue traveling this day.

Before I left, I touched the brim of my hat and said to Mrs. Throckmorton, "Sampson really was tha difference in what happened today. I really appreciate yar trusting what I said and allowing me to ride 'im."

She actually blushed, gave a little curtsey and stated, "t'was tha least I could do."

When Daphne arrived home, she immediately said thank you to her cavalry escort, dismounted in one swift move, gave Lula Belle to the attendant at the front stairs to the family house and rushed inside.

"Where have ya been child? Ya weren't supposed to leave tha property," chided her mother, who was sitting in the parlor being fanned by a servant girl.

"Oh Mama, ya won't believe tha young man I met on my ride. He is tha most dashing and bravest person I've ever seen."

Mrs. Newcomer stood up and came to her daughter holding up her hands as if to thwart off an avalanche of unsolicited information and commanded, "Where have ya been?"

Daphne let out a sigh and informed, "I went riding down tha River Road."

"Ya what?!" bellowed her mother.

"Yes, I got captured by Yankees and this man and Captain Mosby rescued me."

"Oh, saints preserve us," said Mrs. Newcomer and collapsed in a chair that one of the servants rushed to get under her before she hit the floor.

Mr. Newcomer entered the room to find out what all the folderol was about.

Mrs. Newcomer came to after the servant had applied smelling salts under Ole Miss' nose. "Horus," she said in a determined voice, "I can't abide this child's disobedience any more. Ya will have to deal with her."

Mr. Newcomer looked at Daphne, who was beaming from ear to ear, and asked, "What have ya done now?"

Daphne described her latest adventure to the horror of her parents. The servant had to avert her face to hide a smile at what the whelp had gotten herself into this time.

Finally, finishing her description of the affair and with a starry gaze in her eyes, Daphne proclaimed she was so moved by the experience that she had invited her hero and Captain Mosby to dine with them tonight.

This immediately brought on another round of smelling salts for Mrs. Newcomer and a loud roar of, “Ya did what?” from Mr. Newcomer.

Daphne just stood there unruffled, smiled and said, “Yes, I invited ‘em to dinnah.”

Mr. Newcomer erupted, “From now on, ya will be accompanied by Ahab wherever ya go and ya will not invite anyone into my house again without my consent. Do ya understand young lady?”

“Yes Papa,” Daphne answered reassuringly, but without any semblance of regret.

Mr. Newcomer bawled, “Wake up tha cooks.”

After kicking Beau profusely, we bounced out of the Throckmorton’s front yard and into the River Road heading south to see the beautiful Daphne Jane Newcomer. It took about two hours of kicking and cajoling Beau to travel at his infamous spine crushing trot to where the River Road met the main road out of Harpers Ferry heading west. We then turned toward where the Newcomer House was supposed to be situated.

After a few minutes we topped a rise and saw what had to be my destination. The Newcomer’s abode sat on top of a small knoll to the right of the main road. As was the custom in this part of the country, the house wasn’t set that far off the road. It was a two story home with a dark red brick façade, which must have cost a pretty penny in the 1800s. I speculated that it measured in a range of about three thousand to thirty-five hundred square feet. There were two giant oak trees on either side of the twenty-five foot wide front porch providing shade from the sun. The front porch, which ran across the entire front of the home, was covered with comfortable furniture.

Small trees were situated in rows along both sides of the house, which radiated out giving the appearance that the abode was built in the middle of an orchard. Some of the trees were fruit trees, possibly apple and pear, but interspersed were some sugar maples whose foliage had started to turn the bright golden yellow for which they were famous.

As I rode up into the front yard, Miss Daphne, Captain Mosby and, I believe, additional members of the Newcomer family came out on the front porch to greet me.

Chapter 8

Captain Mosby began to laugh and pointing at Beau said, "I see ya were jesting when ya mentioned tha great steed that ya had to recover for tha trip here tonight."

I laughed and then with a smile said, "Now Captain, I can't believe ya would mock tha noblest steed that Shepherdstown had to offer for this journey."

We all had a good chuckle as I dismounted. I tied Beau to a low limb on one of the oak trees and walked to the bottom of the front porch stairs. I caught Miss Daphne's eyes. She was newly attired in a green dress that accented her dark hair, beautiful white complexion and made her dark brown eyes glisten like deep pools of ebony. It was all I could do to keep from ogling her. What was happening to me? Somehow, I kept my ardor in check. Taking in the crowd on the porch, I bowed and stated, "My name is James Hager and I really appreciate tha invitation of dining at your wonderful home plus tha privilege of meeting all of ya."

This sort of woke Miss Daphne, who seemed lost in thought, because she became quite flustered and uttered,

"Please excuse me. Where are my manners? Please come in."

When I reached the top of the steps, Miss Daphne introduced me to her father, who was about five feet seven inches tall, weighed about one hundred forty pounds, had a thick head of white hair and was impeccably dressed in a white ruffled shirt with black trousers and a green top coat. He took my hand in both of his and said, "I can't thank ya enough for saving Daphne."

I was taken aback by his statement and stammered, "I, ah, well, if it hadn't been for Captain Mosby's quick command of tha situation and lightning speed attack, tha Yanks would still have Miss Newcomer hostage. I really can't be considered tha one that saved her. I was just accompanying tha Captain in this venture."

Mr. Newcomer just said, "Sir, ya are too modest."

I was really shocked by the outpouring of thanks for the small amount of help I had been. I cast a narrow glance at Daphne. She just unfolded her fan and held it in front of her face so that only her eyes were showing, but I could tell she was smiling from ear to ear and thoroughly enjoying my discomposure.

Mrs. Newcomer was the next person to be introduced. She was a dainty woman. She stood about five feet two inches tall, and if she weighed ninety pounds, it would be a miracle. She wore a blue satin dress with a white lace collar that had an ivory cameo pinned at her throat. Her hair was a combination of white and black and she had the most pleasant smile. She offered her hand. I took it and bowed. After a brief moment Mrs. Newcomer said, "Daphne told us ya were most kind in yar rescue of her runaway horse, yar thoughtfulness in calming Lula Belle and yar solicitous attention at tha death of our brave cavalry man. I want to add my 'thank ya' also, Mr. Hager."

I could feel my face turn bright crimson again. I was at a loss for words, but I bent over Mrs. Newcomer's hand again and uttered, "Yes ma'am, I was privileged that I could help." I was wondering what Miss Daphne had told all these people. Captain Mosby was the hero here, not me. I glanced at the Captain and he was smiling broadly. I guessed that he had become a party to this charade that apparently Daphne Jane Newcomer had concocted.

The next in line for introductions were Daphne's two brothers. They were tall lads for 19th century men. The first one introduced was Tom Newcomer. He was about five feet ten inches tall and weighed about one hundred fifty-five pounds. He had a shock of dark brown hair. I estimated his age at seventeen.

His brother, Jonah, was five feet eleven inches tall but was slimmer than his brother. He must have weighed about one hundred thirty pounds, but sported sandy blonde hair. Where his older brother had a solid handshake, Jonah had the handshake of a teenager. Jonah had to be about fifteen years of age.

I quickly reasoned that Daphne must be the oldest child and probably was about eighteen years of age. A thought suddenly hit me. I had married my wife when she was nineteen. Imperceptibly, I shook my head at the thought.

I inspected the boys' clothing. Both of the brothers were dressed in black trousers, unadorned white shirts and dark blue top coats.

The crowd was ushered into the house, and for the first time since I had been in this century, I saw black servants. A short and smiling black woman kindly took my hat.

Mr. Newcomer told Ahab, one of the male servants, to show me to the kitchen to clean up and refresh myself. I dutifully followed him out the back of the house and was glad for the time to recuperate from the onslaught of importance bestowed on my efforts.

Ahab took me to a table in the back yard on which sat a large white ceramic bowl and an adjoining pitcher, which I reasoned was full of water. I also espied a bar of soap along with a hand towel.

I asked, "Is therah a bathroom in tha vicinity?" Ahab tilted his head and looked at me in the most uncomprehending way. I reiterated, "I mean is therah an outhouse on tha property?" He grinned and gestured to a small building about seventy feet further back. I smiled and said, "I would rather utilize those facilities before I wash up." He again smiled with all the patience of Job and bowed. I knew he must have thought that here is another of these idiot people that aren't from around here extolling their weird ways.

Anyhow, I proceeded to the outhouse, relieved myself and returned to the table to wash up. Ahab watched me closely on my round trip journey without a sign of embarrassment. I believe he was the self-appointed guardian of the Newcomer family, and he had decided that I needed to be meticulously guarded.

I removed my coat and rolled up my sleeves to wash my hands and forearms. It was then that for the first time I really got a whiff of how badly I smelled. So after washing up and running my fingers through my hair, I flapped my coat about five times to get the sweaty odor out as much as possible. Abruptly, Ahab handed me a small bottle with a stopper. I accepted the proffered container and uncorked the top. I took a sniff and smelled the distinct scent of lilacs. I profusely thanked him and dabbed the stopper numerous times under my armpits, once on my chest and a few time on the seat of my trousers. This must have been another faux pas in Ahab's eyes because he raised both his eyebrows to their full height.

I grinned at him, donned my coat and said, "Shall we return to tha big house?"

He responded mockingly, "Yes Sir, Marse Hager."

I smiled knowingly and retorted, "No need to call me that. I'm just Jim."

Ahab looked embarrassed and didn't reply. He just extended his arm toward the mansion indicating he wanted me to precede him. I guessed he didn't want this weird white man at his back. I might infect him with a disease or attack him.

I could feel Ahab's eyes boring into the back of my head as we walked back to the house, but we traversed the distance without any mishap. I definitely felt refreshed and I know I smelled better although the odor was probably what you would normally expect from a dance hall girl.

Anyway, I was brought to the assembled guests who were chatting in the parlor of the mansion. I use those descriptive words of the home loosely. It was considered a mansion in the 19th century. In the 21st century it would be a high-end residence with a market value of about $550,000, if it had running water, air conditioning, plumbing and electrical fixtures. The ladies were fanning themselves to try and keep cool. The elongated windows on both sides of the house were opened creating a cross ventilation, which helped somewhat with the cooling. But, it was still humid and the early fall weather hadn't broken yet so the temperature was in the high 80's.

Upon entering the room, I was directed to a chair by Mr. Newcomer and he proceeded to ask me about the rescue of his daughter. I related all that had happened from meeting the Yankee cavalry contingent until Captain Mosby assigned a trooper to escort Miss Daphne home. I played down what I had done and really gave all the credit to Captain Mosby. At the end of my account Mr. Newcomer turned to the Captain and profusely thanked him for the rescue of his daughter and for the service performed to our country. Captain Mosby bowed his head toward Mr. Newcomer in acceptance of the compliment and honor.

Mr. Newcomer then glanced at me and said, "I appreciate tha candid description of tha rescue. Tha way Daphne told it, ya were tha only one therah and did all tha saving yarself."

I abruptly turned to Daphne. She instantly shifted her fan to the front of her face, but I could tell that she was blushing. I turned back to Mr. Newcomer and uttered, "I felt it a privilege to have been allowed by Captain Mosby to accompany tha troop in their daring assault on tha invaders. I was both scared to death and excited beyond all description at tha same time."

This brought a chuckle from Mr. Newcomer and Captain Mosby and giggles from Mrs. Newcomer and Daphne. The brothers tried to look bored with the whole affair, but I could tell they were wishing they had been in on the rescue. It was the same old story no matter what century in which you abide. A boy's transcendence from puberty to manhood was usually proven by successfully surviving participation in a war. I could tell the boys were chomping at the bit to join some branch of the service and I bet it was their mother who had vetoed that action from the get go.

It was at this juncture that the black woman servant announced that dinner was ready. So we all stood to be sorted by couples for the grand march to the dining room.

Mr. Newcomer accompanied Mrs. Newcomer to the dining room, while Captain Mosby was paired with Miss Daphne. Tom and Jonah Newcomer and I brought up the rear.

☙

The Dark Mage's Log: 'Earth 3' Date: 18620918

Jargunn dared not enter the house, but watched from outside at a dining room window utilizing his cloaking device. His directional microphone recorded the conversation and teleported it to Axeylon 5.

ᗢ

Once we arrived at the dining room, I took a moment to look around. The room was exquisite. The crown molding around the top of the fourteen foot ceiling was at least eight inches wide with a dark brown stain. There was a wainscot molding about four feet off the floor that was about six inches wide with the same stain as the ceiling crown molding. Below the wainscot the wall was painted a bright white. Above the wainscot the walls were painted a light yellowish white.

In the middle of the room was a long dark brown wooden table, probably made of oak, with two huge curved and fluted legs at both ends of the table that curved down and turned into cleverly carved lion paws as the finishing pieces that touched the floor. I could just make out that there were also two such massive legs located midway of the table. However these legs faced the ends of the table and ran parallel with the table length giving it sturdiness and keeping it from sagging in the middle.

There were two portraits on the wall behind presumably the patriarch's head of the table. One was of a man that had a striking resemblance to Mr. Newcomer and the other was of a stunning woman with raven black hair and green eyes that held my attention for a moment longer than was really proper. However, since I was flanked by the Newcomer boys, who were paying no attention to me, and the other people ahead of me could not see where my attention was directed, I hadn't committed a faux pas.

A very large oak buffet at the other end of the room was of the same style as the dining table. It stood about four feet high and had to be seven feet long. I could see that there were numerous covered serving dishes and platters distributed across its top. Above some of the dishes, small clouds of steam were rising.

On the wall behind the buffet was a large mirror that must have been four feet wide and five feet tall. The last piece of furniture in the room was located against the inside wall. It was an ornate ebony-stained wine cabinet with numerous crystal decanters that held an abundance of colored liquids.

We were asked to find our seats, which were designated by cards with our names formally written in calligraphy in the dinner plates. Mr. Newcomer was seated, as I expected, at the patriarch's end of the table with the portraits to his back. Mrs. Newcomer was seated at the opposite end of the table. Tom Newcomer, the eldest boy, was to Mr. Newcomer's left. I was to Tom's left and Jonah, the youngest boy, was to my left. Captain Mosby was seated to the right of Mr. Newcomer and to the Captain's right was Daphne.

I peered across the table at her and she smiled coquettishly at me. I returned her smile with a befuddled look. I was purely out of my depth with this formal celebratory gathering of Miss Daphne's return to the bosom of her family and community without any harm to her person.

In the twinkling of an eye, it dawned on me that not only was I out of my depth at this table, but I was out of my depth in this 19th century universe. However, it seemed that I was being enticed into believing I could and should function in this universe and forget about returning to my own 21st century. I had almost begun to buy into the concept. The beautiful creature, sitting across from me with such appealing eyes and body language and who resembled my wife and the woman of my dreams, could be the final inducement to lure me into a renunciation of my former life.

But, for some reason, call it my lack of confidence, the knowledge that I never possessed the looks to garner this type of attention or my normal paranoid attitude, I just knew what was happening wasn't real. Let me amend that last thought. What was happening was real, but it wasn't plausible. It didn't make sense. The comprehension of the series of events that resulted in me being here scared me. I felt weak and was glad I hadn't been standing when these revelations hit me. If I had been standing, I would have reeled and probably would have had to find a chair to sit down.

As it was, I had been leaning forward looking at Miss Daphne, but the sudden impact of the realizations made me settle back into my chair. I must have had the most anguished expression on my face because Daphne abruptly paled and asked, "Mr. Hager, are ya feeling alright?"

I stared at her for a few seconds and then answered, "Yes, I am quite alright, now." The conversation at the table had stopped and everyone was looking at me. Daphne concentrated her gaze on me. It was as if she could read my thoughts. It was very uncanny and I blushed crimson again. I quickly added, "I just had a premonition and it sort of shook me. No harm done. I'm sorry to cause such a stir. Please forgive me."

To get the scrutiny of everyone off me, I quickly turned to Mr. Newcomer and asked, "Sir, I have been admiring tha portraits on tha wall behind you. Can ya enlighten me as to who they might be?"

He answered, "Don't tell me that ya had a premonition about them?"

I smiled broadly and responded, "No, not at all. However, not to be disrespectful, they are an intriguing couple, wouldn't you say?"

This brought a smile from Mr. Newcomer that literally animated his whole being. I could tell the likenesses in the portraits were his favorite people and I was about to hear quite a family story.

Mrs. Newcomer immediately chided, "Horus, if we are going to hear this tale again, at least let us start tha dinner."

He considerately answered, "Of course, my dear. Ahab, please serve tha guests."

Mrs. Newcomer turned to me and stated, "Mr. Hager, ya don't know what ya have let yaself in forah."

I was glad the object of conversation and observation had shifted from me to Mr. Newcomer. At least I hoped it had. I took a quick glance around the table and everyone was now looking at Mr. Newcomer, except for Daphne Jane. She was still staring at me as if she would bore a hole through me. I quickly turned and focused on Mr. Newcomer.

Ahab and the black woman servant began to ladle steamy soup into bowls and put them in front of the dinner participants. I made a surreptitious peek around the table to see which of the two spoons on the right side of my plate to utilize. I observed Captain Mosby take the spoon that was farthest from the plate and I followed suit.

In the meantime, Mr. Newcomer, warming to his tale, leaned back in his chair. Then with a wistful look began, "Well, tha man in tha painting is my father and tha lady is my mother. Nobody knows how they got herah, but tha story goes that they arrived in this area around 1798 from New York. They sort of appeared out of tha blue. One minute they weren't here and tha next they were."

"My father was a genius when it came to making money. At first he hired himself out to a local farmer and helped clear trees from land for a crop of corn and wheat. He talked his employer into cutting tha oak trees as close to tha ground as possible so therah were just a minimum of stumps and then cutting tha harvested wood in eight foot lengths. Father then got in touch with several government officials in Washington who were in charge of constructing tha armory herah in Harpers Ferry in 1799. He was able to get a contract for his employer to provide tha wood for tha building. Father also was able to sell wood from tha clearing of other woodlots owned by his employer in tha local area. This was a very enterprising approach at tha time."

"Father's employer was so amazed at tha success of tha wood trade that he put father in charge of tha enterprise and increased his pay. Consequently, Father was placed in charge of overseeing tha clearing of all his employer's woodlands and tha selling of any wood products garnered.

Therah always seemed to be a demand for wood down rivah."

"Not to be outdone, my mother bought a bolt of cloth and visited tha local merchant in Harper's Ferry. She contracted to make a dress to be displayed in tha merchant's store and, if it sold, she was to get one third of tha price. Well, her dress sold within two days and tha merchant contracted for more. She ultimately was providing a dress every two weeks for tha merchant. Hiring a local seamstress, she expanded to providing dresses for a Hagerstown merchant. She always contracted with only one merchant in any town to sell her dresses."

"That's how they got their start in this area. Tha portraits were painted around 1814. I was born in 1810. My older brother and sister live in Martinsburg, Virginia and my younger sister lives near Shepherdstown, Virginia. Tha family mystery is that around 1835 my parents just disappeared. Whatever happened to them is unknown."

My head snapped up and I looked intently at him after his last statement. He had sort of a reminiscing look on his face. For some reason I felt Daphne's eyes on me. She had witnessed my reaction. I looked in her direction and she was regarding me with a knowing smile on her face.

I was glad the object of conversation and observation remained on Mr. Newcomer. At least I hoped it had. I took a quick glance around the table to see if anyone else had observed my reaction, but, thank heaven, no one had. I slowly turned my head back to consider Daphne Jane Newcomer. She was still staring at me as if she would bore a hole right through me. I blushed and quickly turned to refocus on Mr. Newcomer.

Mrs. Newcomer chided Mr. Newcomer, "Horus, you need to eat yar soup lest it gets cold." So he stopped his family chronicle to grab a few spoonfuls.

All the dinner participants were concentrating on their soup bowls, while again I was drawn to look across the table into what I considered the most alluring brown eyes of this century.

Daphne now was smiling at me ever so slyly. I didn't understand her continued exploratory stares. So I returned her gaze intently for a few moments, searching for some readable facial expression that would explain her knowing grin. This ultimately made her feel uncomfortable, so she shifted her gaze to her father.

Mr. Newcomer looked up with the intent of continuing his saga, but Mrs. Newcomer decreed, "Horus, I think ya have given a quite adequate description of tha family history to our guests. Then turning to me, she asked, "Why don't we discuss what Mr. Hager was doing on tha River Road that led to tha rescue of our daughter?"

All eyes at the table abruptly were turned toward me. Ahab, as well as the black woman servant, stopped their serving functions and were looking at me with great interest. I had told the extent of the cavalry escapade when I had arrived, but this was a more personal in-depth question. I didn't think this was the type of query that was usually asked of dinner guests, so I knew something was going on that I didn't understand. Since I was taken completely by surprise, I didn't have time to compose a good fabrication, so I told the truth.

"Well, Mrs. Newcomer, I have just been employed to be tha day school teacher in Shepherdstown this fall and I was at tha newspaper office researching tha battles and campaigns that have taken place so far during tha War herah in tha east. I thought some of tha students might want to discuss what has happened in regard to tha history of our new country."

Mrs. Newcomer nodded approvingly and then inquired, "I understand that ya are originally from Arkansas. Is yar family originally from therah?" I could see that this was going to get down to the nitty gritty before long. I was either being interrogated about my lineage to determine whether I was good enough to be considered a friend of the family or a fit husband for Miss Daphne Jane Newcomer. I was sure it wasn't the latter. For some reason, I looked at Mosby. He was biting his lip and trying not to laugh out loud. Apparently he had been through this interrogation before. I smiled broadly and thinking fast began my family saga.

I stated, better make that lied, "My family is originally from Alabama (which was a half-truth). They migrated to a small river port in southern Arkansas on tha Washita River called Champagnolle (pronounced Shamp an knoll) in tha 1820's. My father started a mercantile store therah and also became an agent for tha sale of any of tha local wood, vegetables or cotton down river into Looziana."

I saw Mrs. Newcomer grin at my pronunciation of Louisiana. I continued, "I grew up working in my father's store and learned cyphering from him at an early age. A friend in town had some books and taught me to read at night and by age twelve I'd learned to read pretty well. By age sixteen I'd become very good at my father's business, but longed to see some of tha places mentioned in tha books I'd read."

“At seventeen, much to tha chagrin of my father, I left Champagnolle and headed to Little Rock. In 1856 tha town was rowdy and full of unwholesome characters, as was true for most river towns. I approached some of tha well-to-do families and proposed to teach their children reading, arithmetic, and penmanship. About ten of the families liked tha idea of having a private school and decided to hire me to teach their children. One of tha families even provided a building for tha school. Tha teaching job allowed me to meet some of tha prominent citizens of tha Arkansas Legislature and Government. In 1860 I decided to go east and see a little more of tha world. I made my way by railroad, stagecoach and riverboat to Baltimore, Maryland and again was able to procure a job as tutor to some of tha children of Baltimore’s mercantile families. I came west when tha War broke out. I didn’t want to be under Yankee rule.”

I had been looking at Mrs. Newcomer during this whole time. At the end of my little performance, I glanced around the table. Mr. Newcomer had ceased slurping his soup and I could tell he had been weighing each of my words. Captain Mosby gave me a nod and smile that conveyed his acceptance of a well-told story. I don’t know if he believed me, but I could tell he thought it was well presented. The Newcomer brothers had finished their soup and looked bored. Ahab had settled with his back against the buffet table. The expression on his face and the crossed arms across his chest gave the impression that he didn’t believe a word I had said. Lastly, Miss Daphne Jane Newcomer had pursed her lips and gave her head a nod just before she hid behind her fan. I think she was giving her acceptance of my fable, but it was hard to tell, since she fixed her gaze on Mr. Newcomer.

Mrs. Newcomer shifted her gaze from me to Mr. Newcomer, who seemed to come to a decision. As Ahab retrieved his empty soup bowl and adroitly replaced it with a dinner plate, Mr. Newcomer looked at me and stated, "Mr. Hager our family would again like to extend our thanks to ya and Captain Mosby. If therah is anything we can ever do for either of ya, please don't hesitate to ask."

Captain Mosby beamed from ear to ear and bowed his head toward Mr. Newcomer and then Mrs. Newcomer. Then he declared, "I know that I speak for Mr. Hager and myself, when I say we were just doing our duty. However, we are so glad that it resulted in tha return of yar daughter without injury. We appreciate yar friendship and commendations. If y'all ever need our assistance, please feel free to call on us."

I was flabbergasted at Captain Mosby's acceptance of Mr. Newcomer's appreciation and avowals of our continued service in the future, but who was I to go against tradition. So I chimed in, "Herah, herah." And raising my glass of water, I really laid it on thick when I toasted, "May God eternally hold this family in his protective hand."

I think I caught Captain Mosby by surprise with that utterance. But, he gamely picked up his glass and we both looked in turn at Mrs. Newcomer, Mr. Newcomer, Daphne and then the boys before drinking to their familial security.

In response to our toast Mrs. Newcomer had tears in her eyes. Mr. Newcomer simply nodded his appreciation. Daphne blushed and the boys rolled their eyes. I happened to glance at Ahab. He had been deftly exchanging everyone's soup bowls for dinner plates. He felt my fixed stare alight on him and, looking up, gave me a swift conspiratorial grin as if to say, "Ya really know how to spread it on thick, don't cha?" Then, he continued to distribute the dinner plates.

At that moment Mrs. Newcomer said, "Ahab, ya and Bessie can serve tha vegetables and beef and pour tha wine." Everyone except the Newcomer brothers was suddenly released from the rapturous presentations of the Captain's and my promise of future fealty and my entreaty of a heavenly blessing of protection. The two youths were bored out of their minds and like ravenous wolves ready to pounce on any food put in front of them.

Roast beef, creamed corn, melted cheese over cut up cooked potatoes, some kind of cabbage dish, green beans and bacon bits, fresh baked biscuits and gravy were individually presented by Ahab and Bessie, the black servant woman. We shoveled food onto our plates with large silver spoons or forks. Needless to say the Newcomer boys lit into the victuals with the gusto of hound dogs. There was plenty of food and wine for all of us. I didn't partake of too much wine, since it always hits me pretty hard. I didn't want it to loosen my tongue and spoil the Newcomer family's present image of me.

In my estimation, the meal's piece de resistance was the dessert of blackberry cobbler. I hadn't tasted anything as delicious since eating my grandfather's blackberry cobbler back in Alabama, when I was a boy. Which opened up another question for me, since my grandmother was here, was my grandfather in this time period also? There was enough to deal with at the present time. I saved the question of my grandfather for another day.

Once the dinner was completed, the men and boys all gravitated to the parlor, while Mrs. Newcomer and

Daphne went out on the porch. Captain Mosby, Mr. Newcomer and I were offered cigars and brandy by Ahab. The Newcomer brothers were denied the cigars, but offered a smidgen of brandy. In years passed I had smoked cigars and a pipe, but had gotten to where the tobacco made me sick to my stomach. So I graciously turned down the cigar, but accepted the brandy. I sipped it judiciously while listening to Captain Mosby's opinion of how the War was progressing. The Newcomer boys were hanging on his every word. They couldn't get enough of this supposed insider's information.

I couldn't help but steal a glance at Ahab during this recitation. He seemed to be taking it all in as he performed his duties of supplying us with the after dinner niceties.

The sun was just above the horizon, when Mr. Newcomer suddenly asked, "Mr. Hager have ya made any provision for where to stay tonight?"

I uttered, "I am going to proceed back to Harpers Ferry for tonight and then resume my trip back to Shepherdstown tomorrow."

He said, "Nonsense. Ya will stay with us tonight and resume yar trip from here tomorrow." Too tired to argue, I inclined my head to him and thanked him graciously for his friendly offer, which I readily accepted. Mr. Newcomer then proposed that we join the ladies on the porch.

When we went out on the porch, Captain Mosby bowed and asked to be excused, "Mr. and Mrs. Newcomer, I want to thank ya for tha elegant dinner and tha gracious cordiality of yar home. However, I must take my leave. I have a lengthy report to write plus I need to check on my troops." He in turn shook Mr. Newcomer's hand, bowed over Mrs. Newcomer's proffered hand and shook the hands of the brothers, who were excited to be considered good enough by their idol for this manly display of respect.

Lastly, Mosby went to Daphne and tilting his head to one side gazed fondly into her eyes. Daphne stretched her right hand to the captain. He took her hand in his and bending over her extended appendage declared gallantly, "Always a pleasure Miss Daphne." She smiled broadly as any damsel to a brave cavalier. Then she demurely extracted her hand from his. Mosby smiled and turned to look out in the yard.

Ahab, who seemed to be able to read minds, had already given the order for the Captain's horse to be brought around to the front of the house.

When the Captain turned to me, I said, "I would appreciate it if I may walk down the lane a ways with ya."

He smiled and said, "Gladly."

The Captain and I proceeded down the steps of the house. At the bottom of the stairs the Captain gathered his horse's reins from a young black servant and we walked out toward the road together. I looked straight ahead as we wandered along. I finally got up enough nerve to say, "Thank ya for allowing me to accompany ya on tha track down of the Yanks. I am not a brave man, but yar presence made me brave and it did tha same for tha men that followed ya."

He looked at me and said, "As I recall, I didn't give ya much choice."

I chuckled and retorted, "I guess yar right. But ya will never know how scared I was."

He smiled and stated, "We don't really know what we can do until tha time comes and then we react bravely or we don't. You reacted bravely. I was glad ya were along and I know Ms. Daphne Jane Newcomer was also. Now, ya need to go back up therah and claim that woman's hand because I believe she is yars for tha asking."

We stopped and faced each other. He stuck out his hand and I shook it vigorously. He then mounted, turned his steed toward the Newcomer family, did the most graceful bow and sweeping movement with his hat and rode off into the night. It seems that some people are knights errant no matter what universe they are situated in.

I took a deep breath, turned, went back up the steps and joined the Newcomer family. They were all still standing and looking at the dust left in the wake of Captain Mosby's departure. Mr. Newcomer commented, "Therah goes a great leader. We'll hear momentous things from him."

Mrs. Newcomer added, "I just hope tha Good Lord will protect him for I feel he's brave but too bold."

Daphne looked at me and asked, "What did ya discuss with Captain Mosby?"

Mr. Newcomer gasped, "Daphne Jane that was a private conversation and is none of yar business. Now ya apologize to Mr. Hager this instant."

I broke in, "It is alright Mr. Newcomer." I turned to the beet red beautiful face of Daphne Newcomer and said, "I thanked him for allowing me to accompany him on his bold enterprise against tha Yanks."

Daphne demurely looked down as she rasped, "I apologize for asking such an impertinent question." Then she looked up and as her eyes locked on to mine she added, "But I appreciate yar answering it."

I smiled broadly and, turning to her father, requested, "Mr. Newcomer, may I escort yar daughter into tha parlor?" He reluctantly nodded his head in consent. I offered my arm to Daphne. She coyly entwined her arm in mine and, turning toward the front door, we strode into the house.

Once in the parlor I parked Miss Newcomer in a high back wing chair and took a seat on a small two-person sofa opposite her. The rest of the family followed us into the room. Jonah sat next to me. Mr. Newcomer sat in the largest wing back chair, which I assumed was the patriarch's parlor chair. Mrs. Newcomer sat in a chair that was a smaller version of her husband's. Tom sat in a small wooden chair next to Daphne.

We all looked at each other awkwardly for a few seconds. Then, Tom asked me, "What's Arkansas like?"

I responded, "Well, I was raised in what could be called a semi-settled area. Tha state is vastly different from east to west and nawth to sowth."

He seemed interested and asked, "How so?" I wondered if he had itchy feet and wanted to follow Horace Greeley's admonition of "Go West Young Man, Go West." He seemed mature beyond his years.

I continued, "Well, tha eastern third of tha state is flat delta from nawth to sowth and planted in cotton. The central and western part of tha state is mountainous in tha nawrth and rolling hills in tha sowth with tha industries being tha raising of cattle and farming."

After my monologue about Arkansas, Mrs. Newcomer queried, "Are ya ever going back to Arkansas?" I knew where this was leading and I wanted to put everyone's mind at rest.

I responded, "I doubt it. Even though I've lived in Arkansas most of my life, I really prefer this part of tha country. It is so much more civilized. Ya don't have to worry about being attacked by a panter or a wild hog when you go out into tha woods. Also, even though ya might have colder winters herah, ya definitely don't have scorching hot summers like we do in tha Deep South."

Mrs. Newcomer's countenance showed relief. Tom quickly asked me, "What's a panter?"

I glanced at him and apologized, "Tom, please forgive me for using an Arkansas colloquialism. A panter is what we call a panther."

He swiftly asked, "What's a panther?"

Mrs. Newcomer admonished, "Tom quit bothering Mr. Hager!"

I held up my hand to Mrs. Newcomer and said, "It's no bother, Mrs. Newcomer. Turning to Tom, I answered, "A panther is a large cat, just a little smaller than a mountain lion."

He looked astonished and quizzed me further. "Have ya ever seen one?"

I answered, "No, but I have heard one. It is one of tha eeriest sounds you can imagine. Their cry is like tha squall of a new born baby. It will send shivers up and down yar spine"

The boy's eyes were so wide you could see the whites around his irises. Then, he realized how I had captured his imagination. Not to be thought an uneducated youth, he crossed his arms and said, "Truly Mr. Hager, ya must be having fun at my expense."

I looked at him with a serious expression and vowed, "I would never do that to ya Tom. Panters have scared me ever since I heard one when I was twelve years old. They're not to be trifled with."

We looked at each other for a few seconds. Then he nodded his head in my direction. He knew I was not lying to him or trying to make him the butt of a joke. I hoped he understood that I would treat him as an adult in the future, and if I could keep from it, not lie to him.

After a few more moments of small talk, I asked Mr. Newcomer, "May I take a walk around yar delightful yard to help the digestion of the wonderful food of which I had the privilege of partaking and may Daphne accompany me with a chaperon?"

Daphne looked expectantly at her father, who in turn looked at Mrs. Newcomer with questioning raised eyebrows. Mrs. Newcomer gave Mr. Newcomer a resigned nod of her head. Mr. Newcomer nodded his acquiescence and, turning to Ahab, directed, "Ya will accompany Mr. Hager and Daphne."

Ahab looked at me at once with a stern expression that indicated he would tear me limb from limb if I so much as breathed in her direction.

I thought, "Oh Great. Now I'll have this ebony Hercules as an accompanying party pooper."

I let out a sigh that made Mr. Newcomer grin and got to my feet. Daphne followed suit and I asked her, "Where's tha best place to stroll?" She pointed toward the back of the house with her fan so we traipsed out the back door with the ever vigilant Ahab a few feet behind us.

The sun had gone down and twilight had ensued. We walked leisurely keeping a small distance between us as we strolled toward the kitchen.

The Dark Mage's Log: Earth 3 Date: 18620918

Jargunn enjoyed the repartee of the various members of the dinner party. He wondered how much of the story of Mr. Hager, the nom de plume assumed by the imposter, was true. This Captain Mosby was a brave earthling. He had led the small stealth force earlier in the day and achieved the triumph. He could be quite helpful in the future.

Jargunn left the area for a moment and communicating with Lord Dendaras, asked what further information he should procure before transporting back to the Mother Ship. While receiving further instructions, something of importance occurred.

To be sociable I asked Daphne, "Are Jonah or Tom gonna join up with Mosby's Cavalry?"

She smugly answered, "Tom has already tried, but Momma forbade it. So, Daddy hired a substitute for $200 to take his place."

I thought it best not to follow that line of questioning any further, so, I asked, "Have ya attended a school herah in Harpers Ferry?"

She replied, "No, but I have had a few tutors. One taught me music and how to play tha piano, which I have studied since a little girl. Another taught me how to read and some arithmetic. I also spent two years in finishing school in Baltimore."

I raised my eyebrows and said, "Oh that explains it."

She immediately turned toward me and demanded in a truculent voice, "Explains what?"

Ahab was immediately behind me and no doubt ready to carry out the coup de grace at this young girl's command.

As we say in the South, "her color was up" and she was definitely ready to defend her person from a smart mouth hooligan from Arkansas. I instantly put my hands up in front of me as if to ward off an attacker, smiled and uttered, "It explains tha grace and charm that emanates from yar person when ya enter tha room."

She suddenly smiled, looked at me coyly and returned, "Well Mr. Hager, don't ya have a gentlemanly way with words."

I breathed a sigh of relief. I decided she was not one to trifle with. I smiled and, not wanting to make any more social gaffes, said, "I believe we should return to tha house now."

Why I made the next moves I don't know. I guess I just finally gave into the beauty of Daphne Jane Newcomer and her fetching ways plus I wanted to put one over on Ahab.

I turned abruptly and positioned myself directly in front of Ahab. Daphne followed my lead. Ahab was flabbergasted that we had out maneuvered him. He shifted as best he could to get behind us again. When he turned to go around me, I reached down and took Daphne's hand and squeezed it. I expected her to reject my sudden romantic and courtship flouting act. But, when I glanced at her, even in the semi-darkness, I could see that she smiled. For some reason it raised love's budding desire in me. I let go of her hand, but I looked deeply into her eyes, and she saw the passion and the promise of romance that she had awakened in me. Her smile suddenly melted and in an instant she returned an answering look of acceptance, hope and fervor. I felt my legs almost turn to jelly. That this beautiful woman child responded to me in such a way filled me with astonishment and a little fear.

The union had taken just a second, but the fervency of passions it awakened was overwhelming. My heart was beating like a drum and the adrenaline that surged through me was a perpetual fountain of youth. I felt like I was twenty-five again.

We both tried quickly to recover which wasn't easy to do. I coughed loudly and Daphne began to fan herself rather swiftly. I stole another quick peek at her countenance. Her face and neck were flushed. Her breathing was rather ragged as was mine. We dutifully started our return trip to the house although we walked a little closer together.

Ahab trooped along behind us, but, if he were any judge of human nature, he sensed there was a definite change in the atmosphere. I wondered if he knew something out-of-sorts had occurred during our confrontational turn back toward the house.

Daphne's fanning motion created a rather furious current of air that she was applying to her face and neck. My heart was finally slowing down to some semblance of normalcy.

To cover for the awkwardness, I cleared my throat and asked, "Do ya have an occasion to visit Shepherdstown?"

She turned to me and smiled. "Yes, as a matter of fact I do. My aunt lives there and our family has visited her a few times during tha last few years. Although she is younger than my father, she has a breathing problem and we periodically drop in to see if we can help her. She is attended by her widowed daughter and a few servants."

"If I may inquire, what are their names? I responded.

"Mrs. Mumma is my aunt's name and Mrs. Douglas, her daughter, is my cousin's name" she replied. The latter name piqued my interest.

"Was yar cousin's husband kin to Henry Kyd Douglas?" I gently solicited.

"Why, yes. Her husband was a younger brother of Henry. His name was William and he died a year ago in a boating accident near Hagerstown," she returned.

"I'm sorry to hear that. I know it must have been a shock to tha family," I rejoined.

"Yes, it was a tragedy and was a sorrow especially felt by my brother Tom. He was quite close to William," she added.

We had reached the back door of the house. As I gallantly put my right hand under her left elbow to guide her up the stairs to the back door, I suddenly felt a hand of iron grip my right shoulder and Ahab in a booming baritone voice stated, "Ya don't touch Miss Daphne."

Chapter 9

I don't know what came over me. It could have been years of pent up aggression, the frustration and confusion of my transference, the fact that my person had been violated or that I had been wrongly assaulted for such a gentlemanly act. In reality, it must have been a combination of all these factors because I let loose with a primal scream and simply reacted out of habit.

Daphne had already stepped up to the threshold of the back door and was out of harm's way. So I let go of her elbow with my right hand and clamped down on Ahab's hand with my left. This held Ahab's hand in place as I turned quickly to my right to face him. It was fortunate that Ahab had grabbed me with his right hand. My turning to the right had crimped his right wrist. He conveniently moved in a circle to his right to relieve the pressure on his wrist. In response, I continued to move to my right in a tighter circle so that I ended up behind his right elbow. Once in that position I just looped my left elbow over his extended right arm, rotated his right arm until I could see his palm, and went to my knees.

I heard a crack and a cry of pain. I knew that I had either broken his right wrist or right arm. I let go of his hand and arm, but quickly shifted both of my hands to the back of his right elbow and pushed his arm down to the ground while putting all my weight on his extended right appendage. In a jiffy he was face down on the ground and yelling bloody murder.

We were quickly joined by the Newcomer household. One of them had a lantern and everyone was asking what all the uproar was about.

ଓ

The Dark Mage's Log: Earth 3 Date: 18620918

Jargunn suddenly heard all the commotion. He informed Lord Dendaras that something significant had transpired and he needed to see what it was and report back. Ending the conversation and reinstituting his cloaking device, he advanced as close as possible to the uproar in the back of the Newcomer home.

ଓ

I had reacted so quickly I didn't know what had happened to Daphne. I searched the scene for her and saw her at the edge of the lantern light. Looking from the backdoor threshold, she was white as a sheet with one hand clenched in a fist over her mouth and the other hand on her chest as if she was experiencing a heart attack. Her eyes were wide with terror while looking at me kneeling on Ahab's arm and hearing his yells. She seemed to be regarding me like a horror from some deep dark dungeon meting out torture to her family body guard.

Ahab was yelling that his wrist was broken and to let him up. Mr. Newcomer put his hand on my shoulder and said, "Let him go."

I released Ahab's arm and stood up. I backed away five paces and went up on the balls of my feet ready for his attack, which I expected to happen immediately. Ahab got to his feet holding his wrist and stared at me with a hate that could have burned a cauldron of demons. I knew I had just made an enemy that would find any way he could to kill me in recompense.

Mr. Newcomer said for Bessie to attend to Ahab and told the rest of us to go into the house. Bessie and Ahab retired toward the kitchen, but I made sure that Ahab was moving away from me before I followed the Newcomers into the house.

We all retired to the parlor and settled down in the sofas and chairs. I noted that Daphne had taken a seat in a chair on the far side of the parlor from me and was dabbing her eyes with a handkerchief. Mrs. Newcomer was sitting next to Daphne and trying to comfort her. The boys were planted on a sofa and staring at me with a kind of curiosity. I could just almost hear their thoughts, "How did this small man get tha best of Ahab."

Mr. Newcomer went to the spirits cabinet and poured a glass of wine for Daphne and glasses of brandy for him and me. This time the boys were left out of getting their smidgen of booze. He took the wine to Daphne, who took a few quick sips. Daphne began to get some color back in her cheeks and rein in her fear. Mr. Newcomer then handed me the freshly poured elixir without looking me in the eye. He turned back to stare at Daphne a moment and then asked, "What in tha name of all that's holy happened out there?"

She quickly dabbed at her eyes with a handkerchief and bawled, "I don't know. We were just fixin to enter tha house, when Mr. Hager let out a bloodcurdling yell and abruptly turned like a whirlwind. Tha next thing I know, therah was a crack and Ahab was on tha ground yelling that his arm or wrist or something was broke."

Everyone turned to look at me. I had been wondering how Daphne would describe the altercation. After her less than full description, I resigned myself to being thrown out of the Newcomer's house, out of their favor and out of Daphne's heart which, against all my self-sabotaging negative thoughts, I had finally decided to pursue.

Mr. Newcomer raised his eyebrows, turned to me and growled, "Is this true?"

I sat up straight and rejoined, "Yes sir, but that's not tha whole story."

Mr. Newcomer retorted sarcastically, "Well, what's tha whole story?"

"As Miss Daphne and I were fixin to enter tha door to tha house, I put my right hand under her left elbow to help her up tha steps into tha house. Ahab clapped his hand down on my right shoulder and gruffly said I wasn't to put my hands on Miss Daphne. I was just trying to help her up tha steps. When he grabbed me as if I was violating Miss

Daphne's person rather than acting as a gentlemen, I guess I lost my temper and reacted crudely," I explained.

"Crudely?" Mr. Newcomer yelled. "Ya just broke tha arm of tha best and most trusted servant of this household. His prowess in fighting and his brute strength has protected our family for twenty years and ya come here and break his arm in a matter of minutes," he roared.

I came out of my seat at the speed of light and stood with one fist clenched and the other with a strangle-hold on the glass of brandy. I saw the Newcomer boys stand also. I didn't move toward Mr. Newcomer, but Tom took one step toward me. The malevolent stare I directed toward him stopped him in his tracks.

I turned my attention to Mr. Newcomer and uttered through gritted teeth, "I did it in a matter of seconds, not minutes." Turning my attention back to Tom, I continued, "And, if anyone ever again unjustifiably lays hands on me, it won't just be a broken wrist they'll receive."

I turned back to Mr. Newcomer, handed him the brandy glass, bowed and declared, "I 'spect I'll be leaving now." I turned to Mrs. Newcomer and Miss Daphne, bowed and uttered, "Ladies." Then I walked out of their house with the most satisfied feeling I have ever had in my life.

In my old 21st century, if I had reacted to an unjustified attack on my person, I would probably be talking to the police right now or, worst, be in handcuffs. I guess there were some perks in this version of the 19th century.

ℭℨ

The Dark Mage's Log: Earth 3 Date: 18620918

Jargunn was able to hear the conversations of all the participants in the altercation, except Ahab. He immediately reconnected with Lord Dendaras and informed him of what had transpired.

Lord Dendaras rubbed his chin with his right forefinger and mused, "So, the imposter broke Ahab's wrist. How astounding!"

Jargunn gently asked, "Sire, do you know this family and their servants?"

Lord Dendaras abruptly replied, "Never you mind. Where has the imposter gone?"

"Back to the town of Harpers Ferry", answered Jargunn.

Lord Dendaras quickly added, "Well, make sure he is okay for the night. He is getting more interesting by the minute."

"Yes, Sire", responded Jargunn. He then waited for Dendaras to cut communications, which was almost instantaneous. Jargunn then prepared to follow the imposter.

Jargunn began to evaluate the whole 'Earth 3' situation. Absently, he mused the following questions out loud to himself, "What does Lord Dendaras know that he isn't relating to me? How am I going to accomplish my mission if I don't have all the information about the participants?"

Making a fateful decision Jargunn made the following promise to himself, "I need to contact the Eternal Oracle when I get back to Axeylon 5 and find out any previous missions with all the people the imposter has contacted on 'Earth 3'."

Once I marched down the front steps, I walked over to Beau, who had been fast asleep on his feet, and untied him from the tree. He aroused himself as I mounted and I pointed him back to Harpers Ferry. I didn't prod him into his famous back-breaking trot, but just let him mosey along. I took a few deep breaths and began to ponder why I had responded to the events tonight in such a way to cause injury.

I had just reacted without any thought for my safety, which normally would predicate any actions I took. I didn't even worry if I died or not. Also, the feelings I had experienced for Daphne Newcomer were well off the charts from my normal subdued sentiments. In that regard, I guess my altercation with Ahab had quelled any further communication with Ms. Newcomer. I had to admit I really would miss her. However, overall, I don't believe I had ever enjoyed such freedom, such an unfettered attitude toward life. It was as if a great weight had been lifted off my shoulders. It was the closest I had ever allowed myself to just live life as it comes and not try to control it.

Finally coming back to the present moment, I realized it was dark, but there was a full moon with no clouds. Thus, I could see the road well enough to keep Beau moving in the right direction. Finally, I came to where the road branches off to the north and passes the Confederate outpost on Bolivar Heights, where I first met Captain Mosby.

Getting over my narcissistic feelings of justice, reality set in. I had made an enemy of the most prominent man in the area. All of a sudden the great weight that had been lifted returned with a vengeance. My name will be notorious in a matter of days and I will probably be kicked out of the day school job in Shepherdstown within the week. I had to tell someone what had happened. On a whim I turned Beau in the direction of the Confederate outpost, hoping that the Captain hadn't finished his report and gone to his lodgings in Harpers Ferry.

Kicking Beau furiously got him into his famous vertebra-jolting trot. In just a few minutes I arrived at the Confederate outpost. I dismounted Beau, who let out a long sigh, and immediately went to sleep. I really didn't believe it until I walked around to tie his reins to the hitching post and saw that his eyes were closed and heard his wheezing breath. I just shook my head and turned to go up the outpost stairs to the porch.

There was a new soldier on guard at the door, who immediately positioned his musket to guard the door and asked, "Whatcha want?"

I snapped, "I need to see Captain Mosby if he is still on tha premises."

The soldier curtly replied, "He's busy writtin his report to tha Colonel and dudn't wanna be disturbed."

I retorted, "Well, could I see him for just a moment? I promise I won't take much of his time."

He smirked and declared, "That ain't possible."

I immediately took a position as if I was at attention and commanded, "Listen Private, I am the person that reported the Yank cavalry in tha area today and accompanied tha Captain on tha skirmish. I need to see tha Captain without further delay. Do I make myself clear?"

This really got the soldier's attention and to my delight wiped the smirk off his face. He hesitantly mumbled, "Wait herah on tha porch." Then he left his post to seek Mosby.

I fidgeted around walking back and forth on the porch for a few moments. Finally, Captain Mosby walked out and without any preliminaries asked, "What are ya doing here? I figured ya would be wooing Ms. Newcomer as we speak."

I blurted out, "I broke Ahab's arm."

Mosby bellowed, "Ya did what? This is not tha time for a joke of this nature."

"It's true," I admitted.

Mosby looked at me in disbelief for a moment and then announced, "Well ya better come inside and let's talk."

The Captain took me into his quarters, dismissed the sentry and offered me a seat and a glass of bourbon, both of which I readily accepted. Almost immediately we were both startled by fearful noises from the stable in the rear of the outpost, which abruptly stopped. The Captain shrugged it off and brought his chair from behind his desk so that we were sitting face to face and only about three feet apart. In a belligerent voice he demanded, "Well, what happened?" I related the whole occurrence including my crude response at the conclusion of the fracas and hasty departure.

At the end of my tale, Mosby leaned back in his chair and contemplated me with a confused expression. It seemed like hours that I was under his close scrutiny, but it was probably only about sixty seconds. Abruptly he appeared to have deduced an answer to a perplexing question.

He leaned toward me and declared, "Hager, undeniably ya are tha most bewildering person I have ever met. Ya are just full of surprises. Tha town barber was telling me all tha local gossip this afternoon when I was getting a haircut. This was before ya arrived with tha news about tha Yank cavalry. He vowed and declared that a person had gotten away from being robbed by Jones Gill last night. Tha barber mentioned that tha victim, who had been jumped by Gill and his brother, had just come from tha newspaper office. When we were at the Newcomer's tonight, ya had shared that ya had been at tha newspaper office yesterday. I nevah believed in my wildest dreams that tha person who got away from tha Gills was you, but it was you, wasn't it?"

I just nodded my head.

Mosby added, "I just now made tha connection about tha Gills. Well my friend, ya really know how to make an impression. First, ya get away from tha two worst characters in tha region. Then ya best tha meanest bare-hands fighter in western Virginia. And best of all, ya threaten tha richest and most influential man in the region. Good Lord! Just for starters, yar gonna have everybody in tha area try to pick a fight with ya just to see if they can whip tha man that bested Ahab Dugan. Plus, Ahab will be after ya in tha foreseeable future. Ya can bet on that."

I just stared at him in stunned silence. Then I blurted, "What do ya mean tha meanest bare-hands fighter in western Virginia?"

Warming to the subject, Mosby informed me, "About thirty years ago Ahab was a field slave for tha employer of our dinner host's father, Mr. Newcomer Senior, who had seen Ahab fight for his employer against all comers. Ovah tha years Ahab earned a lot of fight money for his master."

"Well, tha story goes that Mr. Newcomer Senior somehow procured Ahab his freedom and he's been tha guardian angel, if ya want to call him that, for tha Newcomers ever since. And tha rumor is that any antagonist of tha Newcomers visited by yar new found nemesis never lived to tell about it."

"Man, when ya step into a bed of snakes ya do it in style. Jones Gill and brother Seaborne aren't going to take kindly to being outdone by a school teacher either. They have a reputation to uphold. But, tha danger from Mr. Newcomer is by far yar most serious problem. After he gets to spreading around what ya did, ya are gonna be shunned by every person of any standing in the community."

The impact of what I had done and who I had done it to literally took my breath away.

I stared at Captain Mosby and finally said, "Cap'n, what am I to do?"

He replied, "Well, I don't envy ya tha enemies ya have made in tha last forty-eight hours, but tha first thing I'd do is start carrying a revolver. If ya aren't proficient in shooting, the second thing I'd do is get that'a way as soon as possible."

I asked, "Do ya have a pistol that I can borrow?"

"Unfortunately, I personally don't," he answered, "but our northern brethren did supply us with a cache of arms, and I can give ya two pistols before they're entered into our inventory. I am gonna give ya two Navy Colts and some ammunition. They're our favorites, as well as tha Yankee cavalry's. I will show ya how to load 'em, but yar gonna have to learn how to shoot 'em."

"Captain, I don't know how I will ever be able to repay ya for yar help in this matter. I really appreciate it," I acknowledged.

"Jim, yar alerting us to tha presence of tha Yankees today helped to put a crimp in their operations and, if I may say so, advanced my career immeasurably. I am obliged to ya."

I responded, "Well, it was tha least I could do for tha country."

We stood and shook hands not as just friends, but as comrades in a cause for the first time.

Mosby then shook his head and said, "The only thing I can think of in regard to Mr. Newcomer is to get to Shepherdstown as soon as possible. Word of yar run-in with him might not get there for a while. If'n I was ya, I would try quickly to engrain myself in the community in some way that would keep ya from being ostracized."

I dejectedly nodded in agreement.

Captain Mosby quickly perked up and directed, "Come let me show you about the Colt pistols." His instruction lasted about half an hour and included the intricate loading of the Navy Colts. He also gave me a few extra cylinders that I loaded under his tutelage. Then he showed me how to quickly change out spent cylinders with loaded ones. This could mean the difference between life and death in a fire fight.

Finally, he asked me, "Where ya gonna sleep tonight?"

I thought for a minute, scratched my head and uttered, "I don't have a place to stay."

He informed me, "Well, there's a bunk in tha back room of tha outpost that I normally use when on night duty. Yar welcome to it. Tonight I have a meeting with my commander in Harpers Ferry at 10:30 pm to go over my report. So, as soon as it's ovah, I'll be staying in town."

"In that case, I'll take ya up on tha offer," I said.

The Captain had his orderly unsaddle Beau and bed him down for the night with the two other horses in the outpost stable.

I bade the Captain goodnight, thanked him profusely and went to the back room. I undressed except for my underwear and hung up my clothes on wall pegs. Then lying down in the proffered bunk, I was so exhausted that I fell into a beleaguered stupor.

The Dark Mage's Log: Earth 3 Date: 18620919

Using his cloaking device, Jargunn had approached the back of the Confederate outpost to listen to the dialogue of the

imposter and the soldier, but horses in a nearby stable raised such a ruckus that he had to leave and couldn't record any conversation. He subsequently reported his findings to Lord Dendaras who bade him to leave 'Earth 3' for the night.

Lord Dendaras immediately went to the Imaging Room, ordered the staff to leave, engaged the Imaging Instrument for 'Earth 3' Date: 18620918 and walked into the projecting ray. He was immediately in Daphne Jane Newcomer's room as a three dimensional hologram.

Daphne was in her night clothes and lying on the bed crying. She rose with a start and was about to scream, when Lord Dendaras raised a hand and whispered, "It is only me, child."

Daphne put her hands together in a pleading gesture and extended them to Lord Dendaras. Her heart was palpitating so hard Dendaras swore he could hear it roaring in his ears.

Lord Dendaras cooed, "Calm down child. Everything is alright."

Daphne took a deep breath and choked out, "Each time you appear, it is so sudden that it frightens me." Then tearfully she stammered, "You promised that my husband would be a very learned man, loving and not like all tha violent people that surround me daily. It was such a shock to see such brutal violence erupt from Jim Hager. I just knew he was tha person ya had informed me to be on tha alert for, but when he broke Ahab's arm, I knew I must have made a mistake." Weeping uncontrollably, she croaked out, "I so wanted Jim to be tha man of my dreams." She then buried her head in a pillow.

Lord Dardanus could hear her muffled sobbing. He took pity on her and confessed, "Child, he is the man I promised, but he has a very dangerous mission to perform that will require him to be a man of action. We have spoken of this before. He will need your help in its execution."

Daphne abruptly stopped crying and looked up. "Really?" she exclaimed.

"Yes, child," Dendaras answered. "Tomorrow you need to find him and let him know you are still interested in him. You are still interested in him, aren't you?" Lord Dendaras examined with a questioning tone of voice.

"Oh, yes, Guiding Spirit. I will do what ya ask," she promised.

"Good. Now go to sleep. You will need rest for your quest," murmured Lord Dendaras. He moved his hand in a clockwise and then a counterclockwise circular motion, while mouthing an ancient mantra. Daphne was instantaneously put in a restful trance. Hurriedly Lord Dendaras shut down the holograph on Axeylon 5.

Jargunn arrived back on Axeylon 5 and found that Lord Dendaras had ejected the crew from the Imaging Room and taken it over for his own purposes.

Jargunn perceived, "It is time for me to find out what is going on." He approached the abode of the Eternal Oracle, a grizzled old man in a hooded

cloak, who perpetually sat behind a desk rocking and humming to himself in a room the size of a closet.

The Oracle looked up and questioned, "What may I do for you my son?"

Jargunn requested, "I need to see any files for 'Earth 3' on a Newcomer family during the 19th century in western Virginia."

The Oracle's eyes glazed over as he looked at Jargunn. Then he uttered, "Those files are for the eyes of Lord Dendaras only." Immediately he went back to his incessant rocking and humming.

Jargunn understood he had been dismissed. As he retraced his steps to Lord Dendaras's throne room he thought, "Interesting."

ꟹ

I really didn't know how tired I had been until I was aroused out of my coma at about 7:00 a.m. by the Captain's Adjutant. He asked me, "Ya want some coffee?" I readily accepted.

I covered up my pistols, which I had put under the flimsy pillow on the bunk, before following him in a catatonic shuffle to the campfire at the back of the outpost. The Adjutant poured me some of a black brew into a tin cup from a pot suspended over the fire. It scalded my tongue, which brought me wide awake, and the taste was somewhere between cod liver oil and blackstrap molasses. It was excellent for getting the morning ablutions started.

Once I had gotten all my gear together, tucked the pistols into my belt under my coat and procured Beau from the stable, I began my trip back to Shepherdstown using the River Road.

Beau and I wandered the byway stopping once by a small stream that meandered to the Potomac. I let Beau eat some of the grass that had sprung up alongside the roadway, while I ate some stale bread the Captain's Adjutant had so kindly supplied.

About two hours into the easy ride, I came to the farm house of the Widow Throckmorton. I didn't see her or either of her sons near the house or in the fields out back. But I did hear a woman's muffled scream and men cursing from their barn.

I quickly dismounted Beau, walked him over and tied his reins to a tree in front of the house out of sight of the barn. Carefully, I took out my pistols, cocked the hammers and skirted the right side of the house. Coming to the back of the house, I saw there were about eight apple trees in a row from the house to the right side of the barn. I jumped to the first tree and then progressed from tree to tree until I was within ten feet of the barn's front entrance. The barn door was almost shut, but I clearly heard a gruff voice yell,

"Tell us whar tha family cash and silver's buried or I'll hit one of yar boys agin."

The lady pled, "Please don't hurt my boys anymore."

A groggy voice rasped, "Don't tell him Ma."

I heard a smack and then the woman screamed.

All the years of being bullied in grade school, of being unable to fight back except in football practice, of being the butt of jokes because of social ineptness, of being in this weird time travel situation and now men hitting a defenseless woman welled up in me to the point that all reason was thrown to the winds. I cared not for my safety or survival. All my angst was focused on avenging myself and the injustice the people in that barn were experiencing.

I suddenly rushed forward to the barn door, slid through the small opening, brought both pistols up in front of me and yelled, "What's going on in here?" Regrettably, I couldn't see very well in the dark gloom of the barn.

Two figures in black turned toward me. I had taken them totally by surprise. As my vision became accustomed to the darkness, I could see the Throckmortons tied up to the fencing of a horse stall. One of the boys was sagging forward as if he were unconscious. I felt overpowering hatred for these terrorists, for these oppressors, for these cowards. Hot anger like I had never known flashed through me like white hot lava.

The two men initially looked at me with mouths agape, but quickly recovered and began to draw their pistols.

All I wanted to do was to hurt them. No! What I wanted to do was kill them. In a fit of rage I pulled the triggers of the Navy Colts I had pointed at them. There were tremendous simultaneous explosions and my hearing was temporarily muted due to the loud reports. In addition, the recoils from the weapons almost wrenched them from my grip, but I was able to hold on to the smoking revolvers.

In almost slow motion, I witnessed one of the men hurled backwards and the other spun around. The gunman who was spun around faced me with a useless right arm, which was hanging down to his side. He screamed in rage, "Ya agin. Ya ain't getting away this time." He pulled one of his pistols from his belt with his left hand, pointed it at me and fired.

I was still in shock from firing my artillery and was amazed the wounded man reacted so quickly. I felt the bullet barely nick my right ear. The pain jolted me out of my stupor. Pure fear and the survival instinct took over now. I cocked both my Colts and again pulled the triggers simultaneously. The man was lifted off his feet and thrown backwards. He came to rest on his back and didn't move. The other man I had hit never stirred.

The widow Throckmorton began crying and repeating over and over, "Praise God for our deliverance. Praise God for our deliverance."

Caleb in a quaking voice asked, "Could ya untie me and help tend ta Joshua?"

I nodded, stuck my smoking revolvers in my belt and began to release the terrorized family. Somewhere in the process I heard Sampson's familiar whinny from his stall in the recesses of the barn. He seemed to be adding his 'thank you' for the rescue of his owners.

Once all three of the family members were untied, we examined Joshua. He was hurt pretty bad. It took all three of us to transport him to the house. We put Joshua in his bed and the widow Throckmorton began tending to his injuries. His face was so puffy that both his eyes were closed. His nose was broken and still bleeding. He was unconscious, but after a few moments of his mother's labors, he stirred and moaned.

Caleb said, "Thank God for that." He looked at me and solemnly declared, "Thank ya for saving us. I believed they'd a killed us if ya hadn't showed up. By tha way, yar ableeding," he added as he pointed to my right ear.

I felt of my ear and winced. When I pulled my hand away and looked at it, there was a small amount of blood on my thumb. That had been a close call. The spike in adrenaline was wearing off and I was starting to shake. I just looked at Caleb and nodded. I didn't trust myself to try and speak.

Caleb looked at the barn, shivered, sighed and in a low voice said, "Well, I 'speck I bettah go see who those blackhearts are."

I stammered, "I'll go with ya."

Caleb looked at his mother and asked, "Will ya be okay staying with Joshua?"

With tears running down her checks, she replied, "Yes, I'll be alright, but I think we need to get Joshua to tha Doc in Harpers Ferry."

Caleb reassured her, "We won't take long."

We rapidly retraced our steps and opened the barn doors wide, allowing as much daylight as possible to illuminate the crime scene. Then we surveyed my handy work. The two men were quite dead. The first man to go down had been hit square in the heart and must have died instantly. The second man had been hit in the right shoulder and there were also two bullets in his chest from my second volley. After the brief examination, I was surprised that I felt nothing for these men I had killed. It was as if I had exterminated rabid dogs. I began to wonder if I had really been a closet sociopath all my life, but was too afraid to react violently to any injustice for fear of legal reprisal. For some reason, I knew that these killings wouldn't precipitate much of an official inquiry in this 19th century.

Although the dead men's hats had come off their heads in the melee, they still wore neckerchiefs employed to hide their faces. To try and identify the first man I had killed I pulled his neckerchief off, but I didn't recognize him. However, when I pulled down the neckerchief of the last man I shot, I actually jumped back, gasped in amazement and uttered, "Oh, my lord." The dead man had a white streak in his facial hair.

I startled Caleb when I jumped back, which made him lurch back too. He stammered, "What?"

I pointed at the dead man with the white streak in his beard and asked, "Don't ya know who that is?"

He just shook his head and said, "No."

"It's Jones Gill," I replied.

He shifted his gaze to the dead man, and then with a skeptical look at me, interrogated, "Are ya sure?"

"Yes," I rebutted. "He and his brother tried to jump me in Harpers Ferry night before last."

"How ya knowd it's him?" He rejoined.

"Cause of tha white streak in his beard," I answered. "And I bet tha other man is his brother, Seaborne, but I can't be for sure cause he was behind me when they grabbed me," I explained.

"Well, don't that beat all? Ya done kilt Jones Gill and his brother. Getting rid of them will make a whole lots of people feel safer. I wonder if they's a reward. I bet ya gonna to be a rich man," he expressed with a bit of glee in his voice.

I just shook my head and muttered, "Two down and one to go." Caleb looked at me quizzically, but he didn't ask the reason for my utterance.

We got Sampson hooked up to a wagon to transport Joshua and the bodies of the Gills to Harpers Ferry. I thought this was definitely a dreadful way to utilize such gallant horseflesh, but Beau was too light to pull the wagon and the Throckmorton's other horses and mules were in a pasture. It would take too long to round them up.

We had constructed a pallet for Caleb and his mother on one side of the wagon. After Caleb and I put Joshua in the bed of the wagon with his head in his mother's lap, we stacked the Gill's bodies on the other side, covered them with a blanket and began our trek to the doctor's office in Harpers Ferry.

ଔ

The Dark Mage's Log: Earth 3 Date: 18620919

Jargunn had been following the imposter utilizing the ACV in the stealth mode since he left Harpers Ferry. It had, once again, turned into a most boring assignment since the imposter rode that slow-moving, putrid-looking, four-legged Earth animal. However, Jargunn looked forward to hopefully an uneventful and uninterrupted journey.

Jargunn had to admit that this imposter had been full of surprises. He had gotten into a few dangerous situations both socially and confrontationally, but had extricated himself quite admirably. So it didn't take Jargunn completely by surprise when he saw the imposter respond to noises coming from behind an isolated rural structure by dismounting, tying his worthless little

animal to a tree, covertly approaching the subject building and quickly slipping inside.

When multiple explosions erupted from the outbuilding, Jargunn quickly landed his ACV, sent it into orbit, implemented his cloaking mode and rushed toward the building to investigate what had happened. He stayed just outside the building's door, but could hear all the conversations. He moved back behind a stand of trees and watched as a human threesome carried an unconscious male to the main house.

Momentarily, the imposter and the unhurt male returned to the barn. From their dialogue and the previous conversations, Jargunn was able to ascertain who the dead antagonists were and what had actually occurred. Jargunn quietly muttered, "This imposter has more escapades than our Outlander Shengs at the galaxy core. Whether he can stay out of harm's way in the future is anyone's guess."

Once the imposter and the other male had entered the main living building

again, Jargunn immediately retreated to his ACV and reported the particulars of the confrontation in the earth structure to Lord Dendaras.

His Sire was quite excited by the news. He thanked Jargunn and told him, "Protect the imposter at all costs. Do not let him be harmed in any way."

"Yes, Sire, I will." Jargunn answered.

Jargunn was shocked by the Lord's response to the imposter's actions. Jargunn perceived that somehow the imposter had clearly acquired more importance. He thought, "Could the Lord be considering the imposter for utilization in this time period? But how could that be if he hadn't been recruited? Plus he has no restraints on his actions in this time period and he can't be tracked, since his body has no tracking device installed. And who had Lord Dendaras contacted in the transporter room?"

These questions welled up in Jargunn's mind and he was determined to find the answers. Because, if he followed the

orders of Lord Dendaras and they violated the Prime Meridian, he still could be sentenced to a slow death over a thousand kronos.

☙

It took about three hours to make it to the Doc's office, but, by the time we got to the outskirts of town, people who saw Joshua's predicament and the stacked bodies were asking what had happened. I let Caleb tell all the particulars of his family's incarceration and rescue. People began asking me what my name was and where I was from. I finally just pulled my hat down low over my face and said I needed to talk with the marshal before giving out any information. Word quickly spread and, by the time we got to the Doc's office, we had a crowd following us with the town marshal and his deputy joining the caravan.

The doctor got some of the townsfolk from the crowd to take Joshua into his office. Mrs. Throckmorton followed in close attendance.

As the town marshal and his deputy began purveying the bodies, the marshal actually gasped when he recognized one of the bodies was Jones Gill. He had members from the crowd carry the bodies of the Gill brothers to the undertaker's parlor. The deputy was left in charge of coordinating the body identifications and burials with the mortician.

The marshal looked shaken as he stared at the bodies being carried away. He finally turned and stared at me and

Caleb for a long moment. Then he savagely beckoned us to follow him. Caleb and I got into the buckboard like two sheep being led to the slaughter and slowly walked Sampson behind the marshal as he strode toward his office.

Caleb whispered, "Let me do all tha talking. Ya know that tha marshal and tha Gill family err distantly related, don't cha?"

I looked at him in shock and then murmured, "No I didn't, but it would explain why he took such a long time to try to find my assailants a few nights ago."

We arrived at the marshal's office and entered what was a one room building with two cells in the back of the room. Each cell had one cot and I bet every bedbug in the county had taken up residence there. Once you entered the office, there was a desk to the left of the door and a cot in a corner to the right of the door for the law officer assigned to night duty. Two chairs faced the desk and the marshal indicated for us to sit down.

Leaning back with his elbows propped on his chair arms and his fingers making a church and steeple over his chest, he snapped, "Okay, tell me what happened?"

Caleb began describing what had occurred prior to my appearance and then gave a harrowing account of the shootout. Several times the marshal glanced at me with incredulous looks.

Once Caleb recounted the story and the weaponry I utilized, the marshal finally spied the bulges made by the twin colts stuck in my belt underneath my coat and sat forward warily. I thought it was quite humorous. He went from being a Type A personality to an attitude of fearfulness. I was able to keep from smiling because I wanted this meeting to end without a hitch and I wasn't about to give the marshal a reason to hold me.

Finally, in a reasonable voice the marshal asked Caleb, "Will yar brother and mother back up your story?"

Caleb replied, "I know my mother will, but Joshua was unconscious when tha shootout went down."

The marshal looked at me and curtly asked, "Is that what happened?" I nodded in the affirmative. He suddenly spoke in a belligerent voice, "What were ya doing therah?"

I replied kindly, "I was on my way back to Shepherdstown and thought I'd stop again to pay my respects to tha Throckmorton's for tha use of their horse in tha capture of tha Yankee Cavalry."

The marshal's face turned pale. The fight with the Yank cavalry must have reached his ears. He suddenly realized I must have been the civilian described as the guide for Mosby and a participant in the engagement. I believe he also recognized the political and perilous consequence if he didn't tread lightly in dealing with my part in the Throckmorton farm shootout. All of these significant factors were evident by his sudden change in demeanor and his approach to a possible solution to his dilemma of me being armed and dangerous when he said, "Okay, I understand all tha circumstances, but I'll need to confiscate yar pistols."

It took me a minute to see his ploy of disarming me, which would make it easier for him to arrest me. I blushed and a look of fear crossed my face. The marshal smiled at my discomfort. I thought quickly for a solution and it came to me like an arrow hitting a bullseye. I bucked up and, looking the marshal straight in the eye, stated, "That will be impossible Marshal. These pistols were given to me by Captain Mosby for my protection and only he can confiscate them."

When I mentioned Captain Mosby's name, the marshal's jaw dropped, his face turned red and a look of sheer terror spread across his face. The shoe was now on the other foot. I knew I had somehow struck a nerve. I didn't want to lose a chance of thwarting this possibly corrupt official, so I pressed my luck by adding, "I'll be glad to send for Captain Mosby to corroborate my statement."

The marshal quickly back peddled, "No, if Captain Mosby gave 'em to ya for yar personal protection, then they's yars."

I looked the marshal squarely in the eye, trying to ascertain why he had relented in my disarmament so quickly, but he looked away. I didn't know what was going on. Ultimately, I needed to get to the bottom of his fear of Mosby, but that was something that would have to wait.

The marshal's deputy suddenly burst into the room and practically shouted, "Jones Gill twas one of tha bodies, but Seaborne t'wern't tha other man kilt. It t'was one of Gill's old gang, Lemuel Ellis."

Caleb and I turned around to face the deputy and he realized that he had said too much without knowing who was in the office with his boss. I turned around quickly to face the Marshal and he gave the deputy a withering glance. The deputy lamely uttered in a low voice, "I just thought ya'd like to know."

I suddenly realized that I had eradicated only one of the threats to my life instead of two. It must have shown on my face because the marshal grinned. He knew Seaborne Gill would retaliate quickly.

I looked at him and tried to muster the most evil leer I could. It must have worked because the marshal suddenly said, "Well, I guess that's all I needed ta know. Y'all can leave now."

Caleb and I nodded, got up, walked past the red-faced deputy and headed out the door. The townspeople had scattered, but there were enough of them left to point at Caleb and me and whisper back and forth as we walked toward the doctor's office. I felt like a bull facing a matador in a corrida and everyone was taking bets on how long I was going to last.

We made it to the doctor's office to meet with Mrs. Throckmorton and get the doctor's diagnosis. The doctor had dressed Joshua's wounds. Then he elaborated on Joshua's condition, "He's pretty well beat up. I don't know if'n tha head injuries will addle his brain so I'd like to keep him for a day or two and see what happens." He turned to Caleb and continued, "Your Mom wants to stay herah and look after him, which is mighty fine with me. I 'spect you boys need to get a room at tha hotel for tha time being."

Caleb embraced Mrs. Throckmorton and reassured her, "He's gonna be alright Ma."

She broke down and sobbed, "I ain't never seen such evil as those men." Caleb hugged her and she cried for a few moments. Then she abruptly straightened up, stepped back from him and said, "Y'all go on and go ta tha hotel. I'll be alright." Caleb pledged, "If'n ya need us for anything, come get us."

She looked at me and I nodded that I was included in this promise. Then she suddenly hugged me and sobbed, "Oh thank ya! I prayed for help and ya showed up. Ya saved us and I ain't even thanked ya."

I wrapped my arms around her and didn't know what to say. So I just held her until she quit crying. She got it out of her system and released her hold on me. She stepped back and, dabbing her eyes with the apron she still wore, reiterated, "Y'all go on ta tha hotel. We'll be alright."

We again gave our promises to help and then took our leave. Caleb and I were silent as we headed to the local hotel to procure a room for the night. We both were in our own private worlds of woe. I was thinking about what Seaborne Gill was going to do to me and I expect Caleb was concerned over the sudden setback to his family.

We arrived at the hotel and the same clerk that was on duty the night I was assaulted by the Gills was manning the desk. He gladly checked us in amidst a multitude of questions about the shootout. I finally cut off all interrogation by lying, "The Marshal is still investigating and doesn't want us blabbing about it."

The clerk sullenly gave us our keys. We quickly vacated the lobby and ascended the stairs to our second floor room. I know I needed to eat some food, but was too exhausted by the shootout, the interrogation by the town marshal and learning I still had Seaborne Gill to deal with. Caleb was tuckered out too. I propped a chair against the bedroom's door knob and we both flopped in our respective beds and went immediately to sleep.

☙

The Dark Mage's Log: 'Earth 3' Date: 18620919

Employing the stealth mode for his ACV, Jargunn had followed the rescued humans and the imposter in the slow-moving earth vehicle. It seemed it would take all day to get to the 'Earth 3' town of Harpers Ferry.

Jargunn landed his ACV, put it in stealth mode, sent it into orbit, implemented his personal cloaking device and stayed in town long enough to see the procession through town.

Dodging Earth animals to prevent any wild demonstration, he positioned himself to listen and record from afar the interesting exchange between one of the rescued males, the imposter and the local authority, who was called a town marshal. Once the meeting had concluded, Jargunn journeyed back to Axeylon 5.

Jargunn dutifully stood in the Imperial Throne room and reported to Lord Dendaras what transpired at the confinement office.

"So, he challenged the town marshal, did he?" said Lord Dendaras in a barely audible voice while rubbing his chin with his right forefinger.

"Yes, Sire," replied Jargunn.

"Well, this Mr. Hager, our imposter, is looking more interesting by the moment. Do we have any information on him?" queried Lord Dendaras.

"Yes, Sire," answered Jargunn. "From the clothes he buried, which I recovered, our hospitable Laboratory recovered his DNA and traced his existence. His Name is Shelton Owen Woods, a simple mid-level salesman in a small agricultural state in a 21st century 'Earth 9' country called The United States. I believe Jardean is working on an assignment there now."

Lord Dendaras snapped, "Never you mind about that. Continue."

"Yes, my Lord," Jargunn responded. "This Shelton Owen Woods has never accumulated a great fortune or been a courageous being. His only admirable quality is that he did train in a fighting art for twelve years. He never was an exceptional student, but he did learn a few moves."

"That would explain his escape from the men who accosted him at night in that 'Earth 3' town," Lord Dendaras observed.

"Yes, Sire," Jargunn dared to utter with a patronizing tone.

Lord Dendaras jerked forward and pointing at Jargunn declared, "Jargunn, for a human to learn a fighting art is one thing. It is quite another for them to utilize it to the degree our imposter did on the servant of the Newcomers."

Jargunn had snapped to attention at the onslaught of the Lord's rebuke. Fearing he had gone too far, Jargunn replied in a conciliatory voice, "Yes, my Liege."

Lord Dendaras scrutinized Jargunn very closely for almost a minute. Jargunn felt the small rivulets of blood begin to run down his back and stain his uniform.

Lord Dendaras slowly drew back into the sanctity of his throne and commanded, "Back to your mission Watcher."

Jargunn wheezed in relief, "Yes, my Master." He abruptly bowed, clicked his heels, about faced and marched from the throne room.

Lord Dendaras smiled when he saw the back of the Watcher's stained uniform.

☙

Caleb and I awoke almost simultaneously about 6:00 a.m. the next morning. Sluggishly we washed our faces and ran our fingers through our hair. "I really needed to get a comb," I thought. Then we staggered down the hotel stairs and ambled to the doctor's office.

We banged on the door and were shushed by the doctor. Mrs. Throckmorton had tended to Joshua during the night and had been relieved of her monitoring by the doctor around 5:00 a.m. She was asleep on a couch in the doctor's office and he wanted her to get some rest.

We retired to the doctor's examination room, and he informed us, "Joshua rested well during the night. He hasn't regained consciousness, but as soon as he does, I'm a-gonna evaluate his condition and I'll let ya know what I find out. Ya might as well get some breakfast and come back later."

We both thanked him and returned to the hotel. On entering the dining room, I spied Captain Mosby seated in one corner by himself. Once he saw us, he motioned us over. I introduced him to Caleb, but, before we sat down at his table, the horses outside at the rail went berserk. We went to the window and looked out. There didn't seem to be any reason for the sudden display of terror, but horses at the hotel hitching rail were being calmed by the local citizenry. Then, all of a sudden, the horses quit behaving in such a disconcerting way and resumed their normal placid existence.

I looked at the Major and he just shrugged his shoulders. We went back to our table.

The Dark Mage's Log: Earth 3 Date: 18620920

Jargunn arrived back on 'Earth 3' and followed the imposter and his friend to the hotel in stealth mode. He caused quite a stir when he forgot about the

effect he had on Earth animals and walked by the rail in front of the hotel where the horses were tied. They went loco. One pulled its reins away from the rail and galloped down the street. Two others reared up, whinnying to the top of their lungs. A few passersby lent a hand in calming them down, but they didn't quit their rants until Jargunn went into the hotel.

Jargunn took up a station at the end of the dining room, an area rarely, if ever, occupied. He had a front row seat to the conversation between the rescued male, the imposter and Captain Mosby, the hero of the brief battle previously witnessed two 'Earth 3'days ago.

ଔ

When we were seated again at the table, a waitress brought coffee, a big dish of hominy grits, a plate of biscuits, bowls of gravy, a platter of eggs sunny side up, and a stack of ham steaks on a tray. Caleb and I lit into the food like a pride of lions. Captain Mosby joined us but didn't display quite the same frenzy. He let us settle down from our ravaging of the victuals. Then he eyeballed us for a moment and in a low voice said, "What's this I hear about a shootout at a farm on tha River Road?"

I shrugged my shoulders and looked at the Captain with an "I don't know" look on my face. Caleb quickly came to my rescue and related the essence of the story. When he got to where we were interrogated by the marshal, Captain Mosby suddenly sat up in his seat. I stopped Caleb and supplied the context of the marshal's interrogation. When I had finished, I asked, "Once I mentioned yar name to deny his order to turn over my pistols, ya should have seen his face. Why is he so scared of ya?"

Captain Mosby grinned and responded, "It is a good thing that ya did use my name. Ya don't know who tha marshal is, do ya?"

"Not really," I answered.

Captain Mosby leaned closer and began, "Tha marshal's name is Owen Gill. He is kin to Jones Gill or should I say he was kin to Jones Gill, who ya eliminated so extremely well. I believe tha marshal is a Unionist and tha reason tha Yankee cavalry unit we intercepted was down in this area was to rendezvous with Owen Gill and get information about our Confederate outposts."

"Tha marshal and I had a confrontation a while back when he bamboozled some of my troopers into jail for some loud drinking at one of tha local saloons. I put tha fear of God in him when I entered his jail and poked him a few times with my saber to make him let my men out of his hoosegow. That was tha last time he rode rough-shod over my troopers. He knows I'll kill him if he does it again."

Mosby continued, "I also believe he was in cahoots with Jones Gill and got a cut of every robbery that Jones Gill instigated. According to tha local residents, tha marshal was living high on tha hog when Gill was running wild in this region. Brand new boots, expensive cigars, a new saddle and two new horses were just a few things he was able to afford supposedly on a town marshal's salary. The marshal musta thought, since Jones Gill and his brother got out of jail, that things would be like old times. But I guess ya sort of brought that to an abrupt halt. I can promise ya that as long as our cavalry troop is billeted in Harpers Ferry, what's left of tha Gill gang won't try anything around here. But, if I were ya, I'd be very careful once I got back to Shepherdstown."

I stared at the Captain for a moment and let his information soak in.

The Captain turned to Caleb and, leaning toward him, said in a conspiratorial voice, "Caleb, I've heard good things 'bout yar family. I believe ya are a patriot and can be trusted, but we are still keeping an eye on tha Marshal and I wanna catch him red-handed passing information to tha Yankees. So I would appreciate it if ya would keep all this information to yarself. I would love to hang Gill for treason along with his whole clan."

Caleb nodded his agreement and stated, "Ya can rely on me, Captain." Mosby smiled and, clamping Caleb on the shoulder, declared, "I know I can."

I finally came to my senses after contemplating what Captain Mosby said. I leaned forward and requested, "What can I do to help?"

The Captain grinned and rejoined, "Be on tha lookout for anything out of tha ordinary; anyone acting differently; or anyone that's new in town. Shepherdstown has a lock on tha C&O Canal, a shallow ford on tha Potomac River and even an old rickety bridge over tha Potomac. It is an important place and well worth tha effort of a Yankee raid. So, keep vigilant. If'n ya think something is out of kilter, have tha local telegraph office contact me, or else send a rider to our outpost."

I nodded my concurrence. We all stood and shook hands. Then Caleb and I left for the doctor's office.

Once we got to the doctor's office, he informed us, "Joshua has regained consciousness. Some of tha puffiness of his face has gone down and now he can see out of his right eye. He has some blurred vision, but he doesn't have any nausea. He needs to be looked after for at least another day. Let's keep him until tomorrow morning and see how he fares."

We both expressed our gratitude that Joshua was recovering and agreed to the doctor's plan of further medical care. Mrs. Throckmorton was still sleeping so Caleb and I retired back to the hotel and occupied porch chairs to wait until she woke up.

Chapter 10

The Dark Mage's Log: Earth 3 Date: 18620920

Jargunn trailed the Earthlings, but he was getting tired of just following the humans around as ordered, witnessing their foibles and listening to their primitive conservations. This was boring work. So, he slipped back into the hotel dining room and watched the pair from a hotel window. It was expedient that he did, because he got a front row seat to a rather unexpected and quite different exchange.

ɞ

Sitting peacefully in the rocking chairs, I was able to sort of let myself unwind. I nodded off for a few minutes, but jerked awake when I heard, "Well, Mr. Hager, is this any way for a local hero to spend his time?"

Standing on the porch at the entrance to the hotel was Miss Daphne Jane Newcomer in all her radiant glory. And guess who was standing behind her. Yep, you guessed it, Ahab with his arm in a splint and resting in a sling.

I came out of my chair like a shot and unbuttoned my coat, all in one movement.

It startled them both. Ahab's reaction was to step in front of Ms. Newcomer.

I put my hands on my pistols, which were tucked down in my belt with the handles facing forward. I didn't draw them out but looked to see what Ahab was going to do. His eyes widened when he saw the pistols and he went very still. It was like looking at a weaving cobra which is both dangerous and unpredictable.

Daphne regained her composure and stepped to Ahab's side. "Gentlemen," she pleadingly said, "There's no reason for any animosity herah."

Ahab and I just kept looking at each other. Neither of us was backing down. I knew he would kill me in a heartbeat if I let down my guard.

Daphne finally suggested, "Ahab, why don't ya pick up tha things we ordered at tha bakery and tha hardware store. I'll be along. I need to talk with Mr. Hager in private." Ahab nodded his consent and backed away a few steps before turning and walking away.

Daphne uttered, "My, my. Ya've turned into quite a shootist in tha span of one day."

I slowly relaxed and buttoned my coat. "Ya can't be too careful in this day and time, especially when ya've made enemies of one of tha most feared men in this area, a clan of robbers and killers and yar daddy to boot," I intoned.

She looked at me so intensely that I felt as if she stared deep into my soul and performed a total reappraisal of my character in a matter of seconds. I was totally mesmerized by her gaze. When suddenly she took my arm and declared, "Well, why don't cha tell me all about it?" I was so completely surprised by her friendliness that without another thought, I went with her willingly as she directed me toward the hotel dining room.

As we left the porch, I looked back at Caleb over my shoulder with an 'I don't know what is going on' look. He just grinned.

Daphne ushered me to a back table in the dining room. The place was empty except for us. The waitress came and asked if we wanted to order food. We settled for coffee. The waitress left and I looked long and hard at this vision of loveliness. Then I asserted, "Why so friendly? This is an abject reversal from two nights ago."

Daphne's face turned red and she said, "I must apologize for tha way I acted, but Ahab was under strict orders from Father to keep us from becoming, how shall I say this, more involved."

I stared back at her and said, "Why did he do that?"

She shifted in her chair and I realized this was a delicate family subject. She came to a decision and in a ferocious voice quickly stated, "Father and Mother have been trying to get me to marry tha son of a local banker down in

Charles Town, but I can't stand him." After her truthful outburst, she looked down at the table and added in a low slow voice, "When I started to talk about yar help in rescuing me and how nice ya had treated me, I guess it scared 'em."

I nodded and replied with a bit of sarcasm, "So, tha primitive from Arkansas was too much of a wild man to suit their tastes?"

She kept her eyes averted and whispered, "Something like that."

I came to a sudden heartfelt decision. I finally gave up all hope that I could return to my universe and to my time. I thought, "I don't really believe there is a way I can make it happen. What did I know about time and space travel? I'm just a lowly insurance salesman. I know nothing about quantum physics and all that scientific garbage. I'm never going to get out of here. So if there is any happiness to be had in this universe, it is sitting across the table from me, right now."

Leaning forward, I demanded, "Look at me Daphne." Her head snapped up and she stared at me with trembling lips. "Do you believe in love at first sight? Well, I do. Ya are tha woman of my dreams. I know ya have been told that before and I know ya must have had a multitude of suitors, but I mean it from tha bottom of my heart." I couldn't believe I had uttered those words, but I meant them. I guess there are times when you just say what is truly in your heart. My face had taken on a fierce expression and I continued to look at her in that manner.

She just stared back at me and then a tear escaped her left eye and slowly coursed its way down her cheek. "Oh, Jim," she cried. And pulling out a handkerchief, she buried her face in it and began to weep.

I was so ashamed of myself. I truly believed she wouldn't have heard me out if I hadn't forcefully expressed how I felt. I only wanted to get the truth off my chest, but I hadn't meant to be so bold and such a bully. So I stammered, "Daphne, please don't cry. I didn't mean to make ya cry. It was heartless of me."

She ceased sobbing and looked at me. Choking a bit, she said, "No, no Jim. Don't apologize. I feel tha same way too."

I felt like I had heard a crash of thunder and been hit by a lightning bolt at the same time. In all my wildest dreams I never thought I would hear those words from her. My lower jaw must have dropped to the point I looked ridiculous because Daphne sort of half chuckled which, thank heavens, brought her sobbing to an end.

Her crying aroused Caleb because he stuck his head in the dining room and asked, "Is anything wrong?"

I smiled at him and said, "Everything's just fine." He just shook his head in bewilderment and went back out on the hotel porch.

Daphne dabbed at her eyes with her handkerchief and removed all the tear stains from her cheeks, but her eyes were red from crying.

I continued to look at her in disbelief. Finally, I stuttered, "Daphne, what are we gonna do? Yar family doesn't like me. I broke Ahab's arm and he's likely to kill me tha first chance he gets. Is our love doomed from tha start?"

Daphne suddenly gathered herself together, sat up straight and proclaimed, "I don't believe tha man that just expressed tha most beautiful and truthful passion of his love for me would ever quit until we were together."

I took a deep gulp of air and made another momentous decision. Looking her in the eye, I said ferociously, "I will never stop loving ya and I won't rest until we are together in holy matrimony."

Well, I had taken another enormous step of breaking all ties to my past life in another universe. I felt a release as if the weight of a herd of elephants had been taken off my shoulders. I now fully accepted my previous reasoning and my new mantra was, "I won't be able to go back and why shouldn't I enjoy love in this universe."

Daphne's eyes widened. I reached across the table and took her hands in mine. She looked as if she would start crying again. So I quickly added, "Please don't cry again. If Ahab sees ya like that, I know I'll have to kill him on tha spot."

This also must have seemed ludicrous to her because she started to laugh. "Ya don't have to worry about Ahab," she avowed. "His pride was hurt, but I think he respects ya in his own way. I can keep him in check because of something I know. So don't think about him as a threat. As far as daddy's concerned, let me handle him."

I looked at her for a long moment and then nodded my head. I was about to ask her what she knew about Ahab, when speaking of the devil, he made his appearance in the dining room.

Just to make sure of my safety. I let go of Daphne's hands, immediately unbuttoned my coat and pulled one pistol from my belt. I held it under the table and out of sight. He took one look at Daphne and then looked at me with the blood lust of a lion and began moving in for the kill.

Daphne saw the look on Ahab's face and yelled, "Stop." The loud utterance must have jolted Ahab because, just as he had started his move toward me, he suddenly faltered and had to regain his balance to keep from stumbling.

Daphne had come to her feet and swiftly moved between Ahab and me. She faced him and put her hands on his chest and said in a low voice, "I'm alright, Ahab. Mr. Hager has not hurt me."

During Ahab's faulting move toward me, I had moved in a crouch to my left and out of the line of his attack as per my Aikido training. I also had a pistol in my right hand, cocked and pointed at Ahab's head.

With his eyes glued to mine Ahab stammered, "But yar eyes are red Missy and he's made ya cry."

Daphne confessed, "I have been crying, but tha tears are tears of joy. We will talk on tha way home."

Ahab turned his head to look at Daphne and his face suddenly took on the protective look of a father. Then he acquiesced, "Yes, Miss Daphne, if ya say so."

At that moment Caleb came into the room and beheld all of us standing in an awkward silence. He asked again, "Is everything alright?"

When Caleb asked his question, I lowered the pistol to my side, but Caleb waited for me to indicate what to do. I couldn't help but see a very long knife held in his left hand, which he held covertly next to his left leg. I raised my eyebrows at the weapon because, during our time together, I thought he was totally unarmed.

I nodded to him that everything was okay. He nodded back and left the room.

Ahab looked away from Daphne. His facial features went from one of endearment to a hard stare as his vision fixated on me. Then he asked, "Is it true ya killed Jones Gill?"

"Yes," I answered in a cold voice.

Again he queried, "Is it true ya saved tha Throckmorton's by doing this?" Daphne turned toward me to see my response.

I just nodded in affirmation to his second question.

Daphne smiled at me and said, "I didn't know ya saved a family when ya shot Jones Gill."

"He and one of his gang were hurting my friends. It made me mad. I had to help," I mumbled.

Daphne's smile widened and her face took on a heavenly light. The pistol suddenly seemed to weigh a ton and I felt weak in the knees.

The look of respect, admiration and love that emanated from her face melted my heart. I must have had the look of a love-sick puppy, but I couldn't help it. I didn't even mind that Ahab was within five feet of me and could kill me barehanded at any moment, even with a broken wrist.

Ahab looked from Daphne to me and back again. Finally, he just shook his head.

Daphne turned toward me and said to Ahab, "Please wait on tha porch for me."

Ahab continued to shake his head and responded, "Yes 'um." Then he left the room.

With a shaking hand I gently uncocked my pistol and put it back in my belt. I turned to this dream of a girl, and said, "Come to me." She rushed forward into my arms and we kissed like two frenzied star-crossed lovers. With all the obstacles in our way, I didn't know if we would ever be permitted to have a life together, but I was going to give it one heck of a try.

After we exchanged more kisses, I looked deep into her eyes and said, "How have I been so lucky to have ya love me. Ya are tha most beautiful woman in tha world." Tears came to my eyes and I hugged her close to keep her from seeing a grown man with tear-stained cheeks. I was barely able to keep the crocodile tears from flowing.

She let out a few sobs and then we released each other. Miraculously a handkerchief had appeared in her hand and she was dabbing her eyes.

I smiled and said, "Well, I guess we have devastated the norms of acceptable courtship for one day."

She smiled and rejoined, "I hope ya don't think me a wanton woman."

"Not in tha least," I responded. "I don't think I could have lived another moment without taking ya in my arms." This brought a sly smile to her face which made me love her even more.

She entwined her arm in mine and asked, "What will ya be doing now?"

I responded, "I need to help Caleb and his mother get Joshua back home. Then I'll be gettin back to Shepherdstown and get tha children, and I use that term lightly, signed up for school."

I suddenly had a brain storm and answered, "Can ya make up an excuse to visit yar relative in Shepherdstown?"

"I'll find a way," she assured me.

I kissed her one last time. She gripped my arm tightly as we walked out on the hotel porch and presented ourselves to Caleb and Ahab.

ଓ

The Dark Mage's Log: 'Earth 3' Date: 18620920

Jargunn didn't turn on his directional microphone when the two lovers entered the dining room. He wanted to observe Lord Dendaras' response, when he

personally reported this newest exchange between the imposter and Daphne Newcomer.

Jargunn smiled, and when the humans left, he slinked out the back entrance of the hotel to make his report.

☙

We both looked like the proverbial cats that ate the canary. Daphne was smiling broadly and I had a sheepish grin on my face. Some passersby saw us and turned to look at the odd couple: Daphne Jane Newcomer, the daughter of the local power mogul and James Hager, shootist and killer of the local terrorist, Jones Gill.

Ahab just stared at Daphne and shook his head. Daphne grinned back at him.

Caleb was smiling from ear to ear.

I gave Daphne up to Ahab, who gave me a look of pity. Apparently he knew something that I didn't.

Daphne said, "Goodbye Jim." It was all I could do to keep from taking her in my arms again. Then, she and Ahab boarded a carriage and drove away. It felt as if a part of me was leaving with her as she waved and disappeared around the corner, specifically that part of me was my heart.

Caleb started laughing and slapped me on the shoulder, which brought me out of my reverie. He said, "Well, Jim, ya sure know how to pick em. Daphne Newcomer is tha prettiest girl in tha county and also tha richest."

I just scoffed at his declarations and said, "We better get back to the doctor's office."

☙

The Dark Mage's Log: 'Earth 3' Date: 18620920

Jargunn reported via his ACV to Lord Dendaras all that had happened between Daphne Newcomer and the imposter. The Ruler of the Eastern Third of the Fourth Galaxy turned away from the reflection of Jargunn in the monitor screen on Axeylon 5 and took a moment to assimilate this new information. He smiled, while running his right index finger over his chin, and murmured, "Very good."

Turning back to the screen, Lord Dendaras issued his commands, "You will continue to stay close to the imposter and protect him. When he

finally leaves for Shepherdstown and is alone, capture him and bring him to me."

Jargunn was so startled that he dropped his guard and said, "A human? On board Axeylon 5?"

However, observing the mask of anger this outburst produced on Lord Dendarus' face, Jargunn bowed deeply and spoke in a mollifying voice, "Yes, Sire. It will be done."

Lord Dendaras broke communication with the Watcher and thought, "Jargunn will have to be eliminated when this mission is completed as well as all personnel affiliated with it."

☙

At the doctor's office, we found Mrs. Throckmorton had rested and was again attending to Joshua. The doctor said Joshua needed to stay one more night and, if he continued to improve, we could transport him home tomorrow morning.

Mrs. Throckmorton wanted to freshen up and get a bite to eat so she and Caleb went to the hotel while I stayed with Joshua. He was still hurting from the facial injuries so the doctor had administered some laudanum to make him sleep and ease the pain. I basically just sat near an opened window with a view onto a side street and listened to Joshua snore. That was when I first spied two horsemen slowly ride by the Doc's office and toward the hotel. For some reason, I just didn't like the way they looked. Their hats were pulled down so that their faces were in shadow. And I had glimpsed, when they passed, that each of them had two pistols in holsters at their sides and a third pistol tucked in a holster attached to their saddle horns.

I went in the back of the office and told the doctor to take over because we possibly had trouble brewing. Then I burst from the office at a dead run for the hotel.

ꞷ

The Dark Mage's Log: 'Earth 3' Date: 18620920

Jargunn, petulantly following his Lord's command and anticipating a boring night, powered his ACV back to 'Earth 3' in the stealth mode. He arrived just in time to see the imposter tearing wildly down the street. He thought, "What is this exasperating human doing now?" Hurriedly he landed his invisible ship in an alley behind the hotel and willed it into orbit. Then, implementing his

individual stealth device, he entered the hotel backdoor in his cloaking mode.

☙

I don't know why I had such an ominous feeling about the riders. But they just seemed to have a deadly aura about them.

They had already turned onto Shenandoah Street and were headed for the hotel, when I finally reached the corner. I could see them in the distance tying up their horses at the rail in front of the hotel. I was about fifty yards from them and running like a scared jack rabbit in their direction, but their focus was on the hotel. They ascended the steps and I could see them pull their pistols as they went in.

I was breathing like I had just run a marathon when I got to the hotel. I bounded up the porch stairs, pulling my pistols as I entered the front door of the building. No one was in the lobby. I peeked in the dining room, but no one was there either. Approaching the sign-in desk, I saw the clerk lying on the floor with a bloody gash across his forehead. I reasoned that the intruders had gotten our room number from him and were now stalking Caleb and Mrs. Throckmorton. I laid my pistols on the desk and quickly removed my boots. Then I picked up my pistols and tried to control my breathing. I cocked both Colts, and like a jungle cat inching toward its prey, I slowly stalked up the stairs toward the second floor landing but in a stooped position.

The stairs were old and creaked a few times during my climb.

As I reached the last few steps to the second floor landing, a figure suddenly came around the corner and fired his pistols in my direction, but he had not reckoned that I would be nearly supine to the stairs. His shots went over my head. Before he could cock his pistols for another barrage, I rose up and pulled the triggers on my pistols. The figure screamed and was lifted off his feet and thrown backwards. He dropped his pistols and grabbed for his legs. I could see blood spouting from between his fingers as he pressed down on wounds on both his upper thighs. He began to shriek and yell for help at the top of his lungs.

I climbed the last few steps to the landing, summarily kicked his pistols down the stairs and demanded, "Where's your partner?"

Before he could answer, I heard a deep voice declare, "Here I am." I turned to look down the hall toward our room and saw Mrs. Throckmorton and Caleb facing me. A dark complexioned man stood behind them with a pistol pointed at each of my friends' backs.

The gunman had a tobacco-stained black beard that reached his chest. His ominous dark brown eyes peered out from under a large-brimmed brown hat that had seen better days. His clothing was covered by a very long riding duster that was faded from trail grime. It was so long you could barely see the mud-caked black boots that stuck out from the bottom of the coat. He had two large revolvers, probably 45 or 44 caliber Dragoon pistols. He raised the pistol in his left hand and pointed it at the back of Mrs. Throckmorton's head. The pistol in his right hand was still pointed at Caleb's back. The gunman had made one mistake. He had positioned his hostages so there was a gap between them probably so he could see me clearly.

"Drop your guns!" he commanded. "Or I'll shoot this herah woman."

"Who are ya?" I countered.

Caught off guard by the sudden question, he answered, "Seaborne Gill."

"Well," I said. "Ain't this my lucky day. I get to kill me another Gill in just twenty-four hours."

My retort got the response I had hoped for. His eyes suddenly widened and a gleam of pure hatred radiated his face. He swung both his pistols toward me.

Caleb reacted about a half second later. In one motion he grabbed his mother and pulled her down. Both of them hit the floor in a kneeling position.

When jawing with Seaborne Gill, my pistols were pointed toward the floor. Caleb's quick movement had destroyed my focus and I had failed to raise my Colts. Concentrating on Gill again, I looked down the huge barrels of the two cannons he had at arm's length and saw his eyes gleam as he pulled the triggers. The only thing I could do was turn to the right and face the wall. This movement made my body the smallest target possible.

I felt one of the gunman's bullets crease my chest leaving what felt like a trough an inch deep. Another bullet hit the flesh at the back of my left shoulder. It spun me to my left, made me drop the pistol in my left hand, and brought me face to face with my assailant. He grinned unmercifully as he cocked his pistols for a second round that would no doubt result in my demise.

He had me dead to rights. So, I cocked the pistol in my right hand, turned my body to the left and faced the wall. This presented him again with the slenderest of targets. I quickly turned my head to face this malignant creature and raised the pistol in my right hand to fire.

Caleb, in a lightning quick movement, pulled a double-edged knife from his left boot and from his position on the floor stabbed Seaborne Gill in his right thigh. Gill screamed in agony. He fixated on the knife sticking out of his leg and forgot all about shooting me.

I jumped at the sound of his shriek, but calmly pulled the trigger of my Colt. My aim wasn't too good due to the pain from my wounds, but my bullet hit him in the abdomen. It must have gone straight through him because he didn't fall, but just looked at me with a bewildered stare. I cocked my Colt and fired again. This time I got more of a reaction as he was lifted off his feet and crashed backwards onto the plank floor of the hallway. He didn't move. I lowered my pistol and just stared at the crumpled dead man.

Caleb got his mother to her feet and held her as she sobbed into his shoulder. "It's okay Ma. He's done for and we're safe," Caleb reassured her.

I felt kind of woozy and abruptly sat down with my back against the hallway wall. I finally dared to look at my left shoulder. There was very little blood trickling down from a tear in the shoulder of my coat. It must not have been too bad a wound if the blood flow was this small. Next I laid my pistol on the floor and unbuttoned my coat with my right hand and looked at my chest. There was a red stain on my shirt from just above my left pectoral muscle to just above my right pectoral muscle. The wound began to ache like the dickens. I laid my head back against the wall and just sighed.

Caleb turned to me and said, “Thanks again for saving our lives.”

I smiled and retorted, “If ya hadn’t of used that big pig sticker of yars, we’d all be dead now. I believe I need to thank ya for saving our lives.” He grinned and nodded toward me.

The shooting had raised such a ruckus that the townspeople were coming up the stairs to see what was going on. Caleb retrieved his knife from Seaborne Gill’s body. Then he picked up my pistols and got me to my feet. With his help I made it down the stairs. Mrs. Throckmorton followed us and began to tell the crowd what had happened.

Marshal Gill suddenly appeared at the bottom of the stairs and registered a surprised look once he saw me in one piece. I grinned and said, “Your cousin’s upstairs.” The marshal’s face turned white as a sheet. He hurried upstairs while Caleb helped me to the lobby of the hotel.

In the lobby the desk clerk’s head wound was being tended to by the doctor. Caleb said, “Doc Morton, I gotsa another ‘un for ya to work on.” The doctor looked at me and replied, “Son, I don’t mind tha added business, but ain’t ya sort of pushing it?” I grinned and sat down to wait my turn with the sawbones. (Yes, I remember the colloquial name for 19th century doctors.)

Presently, Doc Morton helped me take my coat and shirt off. He examined me and said that he had better take me to his office for some medicine, which he didn't have in his kit bag, to treat my wounds. I slipped on my coat and my boots which had mystifyingly appeared at my feet and began to walk to the doc's office with Caleb and Mrs. Throckmorton, who kept telling people that tried to question me, "Can't ya see he's wounded. Leave him be." She even took my right arm to guide me through the crowd. I guess my few days of gun fighting were the most excitement the town had experienced since Stonewall Jackson, please make that General Jackson, ran the Yankees out of this area of the state back in 1861. I also believed that I had a surrogate mama now, whether I wanted one or not.

Once at the doc's office, I asked, "Doc, can ya apply some alcohol to my wounds?"

Doctor Morton asked, "Why's that young fellow?"

I explained, "To stop any infection." He looked at me as if the wounds had affected my mind, but reluctantly he dabbed some brandy to the injuries with some cloth dressing. I let out a holler that would wake the dead. Finally, the sting subsided and was replaced with a resulting ache.

The left shoulder wound was superficial. The bullet wound across my chest had taken some flesh out of my pectoral muscles. The doc had to wrap my chest with a type of 19th century gauze.

Mama Throckmorton, Caleb and I had a confab and decided to take Joshua home the next day. We all decided to stay at the doc's office for the night. We figured it would be safer.

I paid the doctor two dollars for his fix up of my wounds, while Caleb went to the hotel and paid for our room and board, for which I was grateful, since I didn't have a whole lot of travel money left.

☙

The Dark Mage's Log: Earth 3 Date: 18620920

Jargunn had just gotten through the hotel's back door when the imposter had reached the top of the stairs. Jargunn heard the tremendous explosions that reverberated in this small building. In cloaking mode he carefully advanced up the stairs to the second floor landing but did not make a sound nor leave a mark in the pools of the henchman's blood on the landing. He looked at the henchman who slowly bled out his life. He even witnessed the final shoot out. Actually, one of the kidnapper's bullets that grazed the imposter had continued down the hall and been deflected by Jargunn's cloaking device. Although too late to help the imposter, Jargunn saw the

imposter's wounds were merely superficial.

Jargunn activated an anti-gravity facet of his armaments and rose up near the ceiling. He witnessed the imposter being ushered to the doctor's office. Then he propelled himself along the ceiling until he could gently lower himself to the first floor in a remote area away from the crowd. Slipping out the back door, he hurried to his vehicle.

Jargunn immediately reported the results of the gun fight to Lord Dendaras utilizing his ACV's monitor screen. At the end of the recital Dendaras screamed, "Why weren't you there to protect him."

Jargunn stammered, "Sire, I had just landed on "Earth 3" and this human was already pursuing another precarious and possibly lethal situation. It was too late to perform any protective maneuver. I swear by the Prime Meridian that I would have eradicated the imposter's enemy if I had been in time. But, he had already killed his adversary by the time I had followed him to the scene of their deadly contest. Sire, I do have to admit

that this human has indulged in more serendipitous killings and hand-to-hand combat than any I have witnessed in over five hundred years." Blood poured from the pores of Jargunn's back, staining his uniform.

Lord Dendaras stared at Jargunn for a full minute before his anger began to cool. Finally, he choked out, "If this Earthling is harmed in any additional manner, you will be sentenced to one hundred years of slow death by the Shadow Dwellers."

Jargunn was so shocked that he went down on his knees and promised, "My Liege, he will be presented to you on Axeylon 5 in perfect health."

Lord Dendaras uttered, "He'd better be. Now abduct him and bring him to me when he begins his trek back to Shepherdstown. I hope you understand your orders, Watcher, because you are one tick away from the Shadow Dwellers' realm. Do you understand?"

Jargunn began to shake. He bowed forward putting his forehead on the floor of the ACV in front of the monitor screen and cried, "I understand my Master. I understand."

Lord Dendaras disconnected the transmission with a smirk. Then he considered the imposter for a moment and muttered to no one in particular, "Yes, human. You are either one of the bravest, one of the most foolish or one of the luckiest creatures we have encountered in several hundred years. Maybe we should consider you for our ultimate task in the 19th century on 'Earth 3'." The Lord of the Eastern Third of the Fourth Galaxy wandered into the bowels of Axeylon 5 pondering this provocative idea.

Jargunn continued to shake and dared not raise his head for fear of having to look at Lord Dendaras. When there was continued silence, he raised his head to look at his monitor. It was dark. He sighed and cried in relief, "Oh, thank Tantas." Then he pleaded, "Great Benefactor of the Universe, please hear my cry of mercy and protection." Then he cried tears of blood.

Chapter 11

Caleb and I each took two hour shifts during the night staying awake to make sure we didn't get surprised by any more of the Gill gang.

The night passed without incident. Early the next morning, we prepared to move Joshua back to the Throckmorton farm. Caleb went to the livery stable and retrieved Sampson, who was harnessed to the Throckmorton buckboard. I was so overcome with the goings on of the last few days that I had forgotten all about Sampson and the buckboard.

Caleb and I carried Joshua from Doc Morton's office and put him in the back of the buckboard where Mrs. Throckmorton had prepared a pallet of blankets for him. She put his head in her lap and we were getting ready to leave when Marshal Gill suddenly appeared and asserted, "Whar do y'all think yar agoing?" This time the marshal had backup. He was accompanied by his deputy and one other man and they were armed to the teeth.

☙

<u>The Dark Mage's Log: Earth 3 Date: 18620920</u>

Jargunn had lost so much blood that he had to access the ACV's emergency blood supply and implement a transfusion process to replenish his strength. He also cleansed his body and donned a change of clothing devoid of blood stain. Lastly, he kept an all-night protective vigil on the imposter.

☙

Overnight the sharp bite of the gunshot wounds had finally settled down into dull pains, but I was in no mood to parlay with this slippery character. However, he had the drop on us. We were outnumbered three to two. So instead of a confrontation, I answered, "Well Marshal, Joshua has healed enough for travel. So we're gonna transport him back home."

"What do ya have to say for yarself about yestadee?" he questioned.

"Not much," I replied. "I saw Mrs. Throckmorton and Caleb were in trouble and went to thar aid."

"That ain't tha way I heard it," he rejoined.

"Well then, ya heard it wrong," I snapped. I definitely hated this poor excuse for a lawman and would give anything to pistol whip him within an inch of his life. The marshal and his backups definitely had surprised us and I hadn't had a chance to unbutton my coat and get my hands on my pistols. Being at such a disadvantage, I quickly probed, "What did ya hear and from who?"

The marshal grinned and stated, "I heard ya jumped two men in tha hotel and shot 'em in cold blood."

"That's a lie," Mrs. Throckmorton interjected. "If Jim hadn't come to our rescue, there's no telling what those kin folk of yourn wudda done."

The marshal turned beet red and barked, "Ya keep out of this."

Mrs. Throckmorton mouthed right back at him, "I won't keep out of this. And another thing, why haven't ya found tha blackhearts that robbed and beat my husband. They hurt him so much he died of consumption."

This was news to me. I turned and looked at Mrs. Throckmorton. Then I faced the marshal with a quizzical look on my face. We all waited for an answer.

The marshal countered, "We ain't dealing with that right now." Looking at me, he declared, "Ya better come down to tha jail with me."

The Dark Mage's Log: Earth 3 Date: 18620921

Jargunn had already pulled his wand ray, once he comprehended the newest confrontation of the imposter would probably escalate into a firing of weapons. He was just about ready to violate the Prime Meridian, when the imposter reacted.

ଔ

Just at that moment Captain Mosby and about ten of his troopers rounded the corner. I surmised they were probably going out on patrol. I waved and yelled at the top of my voice, "Captain Mosby!"

Captain Mosby heard me over the din created by rattling sabers, creaking saddles, snorting horses, the clop, clop, clop of hooves and the early morning town noises. He halted his patrol and looked to see who had shouted. Seeing me, he grinned, waived and rode over to where the impasse was at hand.

He tipped his hat to Mrs. Throckmorton and said, "Hello folks."

I smiled back and questioned, "Did ya hear about tha shoot out yesterday?" He laughed and said, "Don't tell me ya were in on that too."

I nodded and said, “The marshal wants to take me in for rescuing the Throckmortons, who were held hostage in the hotel by Seaborne Gill and a henchman.”

The Captain’s face darkened as he shifted his gaze to Owen Gill. “Why?” he demanded.

Gill retorted, “Ya don’t have any authority in this. It’s a town matter.”

“Let’s just say, when it comes to a person responsible for thwarting a Yankee foray into our territory, I have a vested interest in what happens to him. Why do ya want to arrest him?” Mosby growled.

“I wasn’t gonna arrest him,” stammered Gill.

“Then why did ya say ya had a witness that said I shot tha men in cold blood?” I countered.

“I have Alton Jones’ statement. He was with Seaborne Gill. He died just after I went upstairs at tha hotel and before he died he said ya shot him and Seaborne in cold blood. That’s a dying man’s declaration and it’ll stand up in court.”

“You might have a dying man’s declaration, but there are three of us that are alive and will testify that Gill and this Jones character held tha Throckmortons hostage at gunpoint. I will also testify that Gill and Jones, his henchman, shot at me without any justification. So, I believe we have a better and more logical story if ya wanna go to court,” I summarized.

The marshal blushed and stuttered, "Well, I also asked some other people that were on tha scene."

"Then, why didn't ya come see us last night instead of waiting until this morning and who were these other people on tha scene?" I interrogated.

"I was getting all the facts together last night and it was late before I got through talking with those people," he declared.

"It would be interesting to know who those people were who said they were on the scene because tha only people who witnessed tha fight were Mrs. Throckmorton, Caleb, Seaborne Gill, his henchman, Jones and me. I didn't shoot anybody in cold blood and I have tha wounds to prove there was a shootout. You can ask Doc Morton," I blurted.

Mosby shifted in his saddle and shouted to his men to countermarch. When the troop was even with us, he commanded them to front (face) toward our little gathering and halt. He then told them to draw carbines. At this last command Gill's eyes widened and he swallowed hard.

Then Mosby pointed at me, looked at Marshal Gill and declared through gritted teeth, "This man has repeatedly risked his life for tha Country and tha people of this region. I don't wanna hear of any trumped up charges against him. He is under tha protection of tha Confederate Cavalry and I better not hear of any sort of retaliation. If I do, I'm gonna come looking for you. Do I make myself clear?"

Gill was too scared to say anything. He just nodded his head, turned and walked away with his men.

Mosby watched the remnant of the Gill gang disappear round the corner. Then he sighed, turned back to me and said, "Looks like yar enemies keep after ya no matter how many ya dispatch."

"Sure looks that way," I added. "Again I have reason to thank ya for yar help. I really appreciate it," I acknowledged.

Mosby smiled, saluted me, tipped his hat to Mrs. Throckmorton and Caleb and rode off with his men.

I turned to Caleb and said, "Let's get outta here while tha getting's good." "Amen," He said.

"One of these days I'm going to shoot Gill myself," Mrs. Throckmorton prophesied.

"Mama!" Caleb scolded.

☙

The Dark Mage's Log: 'Earth 3' Date: 18620921

Jargunn quickly boarded his ACV so he wouldn't be heard by the Earthlings and cried bloody tears of relief.

☙

Caleb and I got on the buckboard's bench seat. I untied the reins from the brake handle and handed them to Caleb. He snapped the reins and we started for the Throckmorton farm. It was not a pleasant trip. Sampson after having been in a stall for almost three days wanted to stretch his legs. Caleb had a hard time keeping him under control. Also, the vehicle didn't have any springs and we all were jolted around something terrible due to the rough road. We even had to stop two times to let Joshua and I rest and recover from all the bouncing.

We reached the Throckmorton farm at about 11:00 a.m. Caleb and I got Joshua into the house and into his bed. I think he was woozy from the trip. Caleb and I unharnessed Sampson from the buckboard, for which I could tell he was eternally grateful, and put him in a stall for which he wasn't very appreciative. Then we stored the buckboard in the barn and retreated to the house.

ൽ

The Dark Mage's Log: 'Earth 3' Date: 18620921

Jargunn followed the imposter and his fellow Earthlings back to the rural building where the gun fight had occurred. He was so glad that the idiots had made it with no impediments that he projected a token of his substance to

the temple of the Almighty Tantus. Then he set up surveillance for hopefully a very tranquil 'Earth 3' night.

☙

Mrs. Throckmorton rustled up some victuals. We all ate as if we hadn't had a bite to eat in a week. After lunch, I asked, "Is there a stream, pond or river near here where I might take a bath?" I got shocked looks from all present, which made me blush. I just shrugged my shoulders and they all laughed. "Thar's a stream on tha back side of tha field behind tha barn," Mrs. Throckmorton acknowledged.

Once Mrs. Throckmorton provided me with a towel and lye soap, I headed to the back forty. I stopped in to see how Beau was doing. He was standing in his stall, completely slumbering. I didn't bother him, but just proceeded on my way.

Reaching the stream, I stripped naked, which is pronounced nay'kid, and has no bad connotation, as opposed to neck'ed, which has a wicked connotation. I put my clothes on some dry rocks by the creek. I really didn't know how bad I smelled until I disrobed.

Gingerly I walked barefooted out into the stream and sat down in the shallow cooling water. I closed my eyes and enjoyed the gentle current of the water as it washed over my body. My thoughts drifted to the Yankee cavalry fight, the confrontation with Ahab, the gun fights with the Gills, the friendship of the famous Captain Mosby and the love of Daphne Newcomer. I believe I must have dozed off because I suddenly felt myself start to fall backwards. I had to quickly put my arms behind me to keep from falling into the water. This jolted me fully awake because it stretched the injuries to my pectoral muscles. I gasped and waited a few moments for the pain to subside. Then I leisurely took a bath being very careful not to get water in my bullet wounds. I scrubbed myself raw from my stomach to the bottom of my feet with the lye soap Mrs. Throckmorton had provided me. I toweled off and then knelt down on all fours at the edge of the stream and washed my hair. Again I took great care not to get water in my wounds. After toweling my hair dry, I dressed in just my trousers, coat and boots. I carried my undergarments, socks, and shirt back toward the house. I let out a laugh and thought, "This 19th century rendition of 'Shall we gather at the River' was a very cleansing experience."

When I got back to the house, Mrs. Throckmorton procured a pair of trousers and a shirt of Joshua's for me. She said she would wash my dirty linen and trousers and brush out my coat. Not only did she brush out the coat, but she repaired the small tear in the left sleeve and the entry and exit holes on the front face of the coat created by Seaborne Gill's bullets. She said I should keep Joshua's shirt since mine was ruined. I thanked her profusely for all she had done for me. Caleb and I settled in chairs on the front porch and listened to the insects buzzing, the cattle lowing and the calls of a multitude of birds.

We were both thinking the same thing, "It is good to be alive."

I slept in the house on the floor in Joshua's and Caleb's room. Believe it or not, I think I passed out. I really got some good sleep for the first time in about a week. I felt great when Mrs. Throckmorton got us all up at about 5:00 a.m.

Joshua felt well enough to get up on his own. He did feel a little woozy at first, but soon got his bearings and was able to get dressed.

Mama Throckmorton had laid out my dried and mended clothes on a table in Caleb and Joshua's room. Once we had donned our apparel, the Throckmorton brothers and I proceeded to the kitchen where we were treated to a great breakfast of eggs sunny-side up, biscuits with honey or gravy and ham steaks. I was so stuffed when I finished that I must have waddled from the table instead of walked.

The Throckmorton's neighbors had really helped take care of the farm, cattle and horses while they were in Harpers Ferry. That included Beau, bless his little back-breaking heart. Sadly, I went to the barn and saddled him. He accepted this degradation in his usual sullen mood when he was forced to travel. I walked him to the front of the house and tied him to a tree in the front yard.

As I was getting all my paraphernalia put on the saddle, the Throckmorton clan trooped out on the porch. Mrs. Throckmorton and Caleb continued down the front stairs to see me off. Joshua just leaned against a porch post and watched me prepare for my journey. Mrs. Throckmorton gave me a letter and asked, "Would ya please deliver this to my brother-in-law Elias Throckmorton at tha Shepherdstown bank?"

"Of course," I graciously assented and asked, "Is therah anything else I could do for ya."

Suddenly, she hugged me, which hurt a lot due to the chest wound, and whispered in my ear, "If it hadn't been for ya help, we would all be dead now. Thank ya, Jim."

I winced from the pain, blushed from the heartfelt thank you and tried to think of something to say. Not being able to think of anything chivalrous, I just nodded and said, "If ya ever need me, ya know where to find me."

She turned and went up the porch stairs dabbing her eyes with her apron. Caleb and I shook hands and just looked deeply in each other's eyes and nodded. We knew if either of us were ever in trouble, we could count on each other. Joshua just waved as I mounted the "Shepherdstown Flash" and rode out of the front yard.

Once on the road I turned back to my audience and tried to do one of those flourishes with my hat like Mosby, but I know it looked ridiculous. After making a fool of myself, I kicked Beau hard and headed him up the River Road toward Hattie's place.

The Dark Mage's Log: 'Earth 3' Date: 18620922

Jargunn submissively made his call to Lord Dendaras.

The Ruler answered the call and croaked in a sullen manner, "Report."

Jargunn hesitantly replied, "Sire, the imposter spent an uneventful night at the abode of the people he helped protect in Harpers Ferry. I will intercept him today at coordinates, 77 47 30/ 39 24 30 and bring him to you."

Lord Dendaras glared at Jargunn for what seemed like eternity then broke the connection.

Jargunn breathed a sigh of relief.

☙

I got to thinking about the last six days. All the fighting, gunplay and loving were enough to last a life time. It seemed like a month since I left for Harpers Ferry. However, I doubt that much had changed back in Shepherdstown due to the slow 19th century pace of life.

About two hours into the ride I came around a bend and there was a hooded figure standing on the side of the road as if he was waiting on me. The figure was in what appeared to be a priest's black cassock. As I drew closer, Beau suddenly picked up his ears and stopped in the middle of the road. I kicked him, but no bullying could get him to move forward.

I was about twenty-five feet from the black specter. I surveyed his clothing and demeanor. His feet were hidden by the cassock. A black wool muffler covered his face under the hood so that only his eyes could be seen. His eyes even at twenty-five feet were hypnotic. I swear they gleamed and seemed to change colors, first robin's egg blue, then jade green and finally black onyx. His eyes began to mesmerize me and bore into my brain at the same time. I felt a shiver run through me and the hairs on the back of my neck stood up. His look became heinous and serpentine. His hands appeared to be clasped behind his back.

Beau began to back up.

I closed my eyes so I didn't have to look into those ever-changing, spellbinding orbs and reached for my pistols. When I opened my eyes to aim my Colts, the figure quickly pointed a long wand-like instrument at me. Without warning there was a crack and a force like a sledge hammer hit me square in the chest. The last thing I remember was Beau rearing and the ground coming up to meet me.

☙

The Dark Mage's Log: 'Earth 3' Date: 18620922

Jargunn watched the imposter slide to the ground. After which, the stupid little

Earth animal let out a shrill sound and stampeded up the road in abject terror, voicing what could only be described as a scream every time it drew breath.

Jargunn laughed at the terror he had generated in the creature. Then he walked over to the prostrate figure and summarily kicked him in the ribs as hard as he could. "That is for all the trouble you have caused me, all the boring tracking I had to endure and the problems you have created for me back on Axeylon 5," he hissed through gritted fanglike canines.

Picking up the imposter, he walked into the woods with his burden under his left arm to his hidden Astral Conveyance Vehicle. Depositing the imposter in the cargo compartment, he got in the pilot's chair and set the destination for Axeylon 5.

Jargunn smiled and mused under his breath, "Well Lord Dendaras, now that this earthling is under our control, how are you going to explain all the chaos he has created? If you try to send me to the Shadow Dwellers, I swear I will deliver

the log of my time here on 'Earth 3' and my belief that you have violated the Prime Meridian to the Temple of Tantas on Golden Mean."

COMING SOON

SHELDON OWEN WOODS,
ALIAS JIM HAGER,
IN HIS NEW ADVENTURE

ASSASSINS OF HISTORY:
CREATORS OF CHAOS

I awoke again, but this time there was no bodily pain. I felt well enough to take stock of my body. I patted my upper chest feeling for the trough across the flesh of my pectorals created by Seaborne Gill's bullet. Amazingly the wound was gone. I couldn't even feel a scar through the garment in which I was dressed.

Subsequently, I felt the lower rib cage. It made me wince a little. It was still tender to the touch, but not as painful as the last time I was conscious. Looking down at my left arm, I saw that there were no longer any hookups of intravenous needles. A quick glance at my right forearm gave assurance that the scar I remembered seeing was gone and the arm showed no other signs of surgery.

Swinging my torso to a sitting position, I experienced some pain in my ribs and slight vertigo, but both hindrances quickly dissipated. My feet were dangling off the pyre so I had to jump down to the floor. A small buzz when off in my head and I swatted at an imaginary bee that made the noise.

Looking around the room, I took an inventory of my surroundings. Other than the pyre there was no other furniture. The only light source was a two-foot sphere attached to the ceiling above the pyre that emitted a greenish illumination for the room. The greenish glow was both restful and mesmerizing. The luminosity seemed to come in waves of both sound and light. The sensory onslaught staggered me and I had to put my hand on the pyre to maintain my balance. I shook my head to keep from lapsing back into a slumber.

Unexpectedly, one whole wall of the room became

transparent and I saw a humanoid observing me. I was so startled by the appearance of the figure that I gasped and took a step backwards.

On the other side of the wall was an entity that was skeletal in appearance. He stood about six feet six inches tall, but couldn't have weighed more than 150 pounds. His head was totally covered with long silver hair that was pulled back and braided in a long queue down his back. His face was elfin in nature with a long jaw and nose. Plus, he had almond shaped eyes, which were subsequently changing color from green to blue to violet. His frame was housed in a form-fitting dark purple robe that periodically seemed to sparkle. The width of his body from shoulder to shoulder was no more than two feet, which gave him the appearance of a super tall and skinny runway model. But what had elicited my fearful reaction was the wicked grin that exposed sharp elongated canine teeth. It gave the being an almost wolfish facial façade. Once I finished my inventory of the creature's physicality, I shivered as a chill ran up my spine.

This made the entity lean back his head and laugh. Apparently, he enjoyed my fear.

I couldn't detect a sound in my prison, but I could almost feel the cruelty emanating from the creature. It made me mad as a wet hen and I bellowed, "Why am I here?"

Seemingly, he could hear me even though I couldn't hear him, which made me even angrier.

I yelled, "Listen, you miserable excuse for a leering

pervert. You better let me out of here."

That got his attention. I guess he wasn't used to being criticized. He suddenly quit laughing and hit a button on the transparent wall that I hadn't noticed. In a sibilant serpentine voice, he said, "You'll pay for those words, human."

I knew I had crossed the line and I wished I hadn't. It must have shown on my face because he cackled like some Halloween witch riding a broom. Usually in dire circumstances, a person doesn't react in an amusing way to threats. However, the cackle was so unexpected and so uncharacteristic that I pointed at him and, in the internet jargon of the 21st century, laughed out loud.

That was the straw that broke the camel's back. He hit another button that I hadn't detected and the wall reverted to a prison wall again.

☙

The Dark Mage's Log: Axeylon 5: Galaxy Date: 16320

A red light began to pulsate on the wall of Dendaras' inner sanctum. He excused himself and, picking up a communications device from his desk, demanded, "What do you want?"

A whimpering voice answered, "Sire, the imposter has escaped."

"What?" roared Dendaras. "I just left him a few moments ago. Can't you track him?" he added.

"Lord, how can we track him? The device that was implanted hasn't been in his system for the forty sectares required to become compatible with a human's chemistry. Therefore, the tracking device won't become operational for another thirty sectares," explained the voice.

"Idiots! Imbecilic morons! Don't you know he couldn't have gotten off Axeylon 5? Organize a search of the area using a scent droid, you fool! Now leave me alone!" snapped Dendaras as he closed the communication line.

ABOUT THE AUTHOR

Vernon Dutton was recognized in 2013 for his first book, *Civil War Reflections*, an anthology of original poetry and prose that honors the battles, soldiers and spirits, as well as contemporary reenactors who recreate historic moments from the American Civil War.

He holds the rank of High Private in the 3rd Arkansas Infantry, an organization dedicated to the preservation of Civil War history. Since his first event at Prairie Grove Battlefield in northwest Arkansas in 1994, Dutton has participated in more than 25 national reenactments at historic battle sites, including Gettysburg, Shiloh, Corinth, Perryville, Pea Ridge, Red River Campaign and Antietam.

Dutton served his country as a decorated United States Marine Corps helicopter pilot in Viet Nam and taught flight training in Pensacola, Florida after his tour of duty.

He is a retired attorney, a retired executive of a large insurance agency and holds a 4th Degree Black Belt in Aikido. Vernon practices Qi Gong for mental clarity and physical longevity. He and his wife Nancy are approaching their Golden Wedding Anniversary.

Vernon's websites:
vdutton.com
vernondutton.com

Social media:
Facebook.com/CivilWarReflections
Facebook.com/AuthorVernonDutton
Twitter.com/VernonDutton

73123297R00190

Made in the USA
Columbia, SC
09 July 2017